MARIE

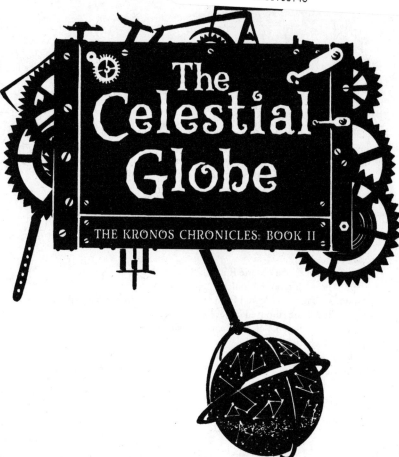

The Celestial Globe

THE KRONOS CHRONICLES: BOOK II

SQUARE
FISH

FARRAR STRAUS GIROUX
NEW YORK

This book is dedicated to my rowsy sibs:
Aimee, Andy, and Jonathon

SQUARE
FISH
An Imprint of Macmillan

THE CELESTIAL GLOBE. Copyright © 2010 by Maria Rutkoski. All rights reserved.
Distributed in Canada by H.B. Fenn and Company Ltd. Printed in February 2011 in the
United States of America by R. R. Donnelley & Sons Company, Harrisonburg, Virginia.
For information, address Square Fish, 175 Fifth Avenue, New York, 10010.

Square Fish and the Square Fish logo are trademarks of Macmillan
and are used by Farrar Straus Giroux under license from Macmillan.

Library of Congress Cataloging-in-Publication Data
Rutkoski, Marie.
    The Celestial Globe / Marie Rutkoski.
        p.   cm. — (Kronos Chronicles ; bk. 2)
    Summary: Thirteen-year-old Petra, her tin spider Astrophil, and their friends
Neel and Tomik are surprised by revelations about Dee, Kit, and Petra's father as
they face Prince Rodolfo of Bohemia, who will do anything to possess a powerful
object, the Celestial Globe.
    ISBN 978-0-312-65919-6
    [1. Magic—Fiction.   2. Princes—Fiction.   3. Romanies—Fiction.   4. Fantasy.]
I. Title.

PZ7.R935Cel 2010
[Fic]—dc22

                                                                                2008035599

Originally published in the United States by Farrar Straus Giroux
First Square Fish Edition: April 2011
Square Fish logo designed by Filomena Tuosto
Book designed by Jay Colvin
www.squarefishbooks.com

10   9   8   7   6   5   4   3   2   1

AR: 4.5 / LEXILE: 640L

Contents

The
Celestial
Globe

1

The Gray Men

SOME DAYS are just born bad. You know the type. The kind you want to sweep into your palm like spilled salt and toss over your left shoulder, hoping that if you don't look back nothing worse will happen.

Petra Kronos snapped awake. Her heart thudded. The bedsheets were damp with sweat.

She turned her head to the left and looked out the window: it was foggy, wintry, dreary.

She turned her head to the right, and there was Astrophil. The tin spider was curled into a tiny, spiky ball. With a squeak, he bunched his shiny legs together, sprang them into the air one by one, and wriggled onto the tips of his legs. "Petra, is something wrong?"

"I had a bad dream." Her pulse was still racing.

"Ah. Was it . . . relevant to the events at Salamander Castle?"

"No." Petra didn't want to think about what had happened more than a month ago. "Anyway, dreams don't mean anything. They're just empty pictures."

"Was it," said the spider gingerly, "related to John Dee?"

"No." Petra huffed with annoyance and got out of bed. Astrophil had the frustrating habit of pointing out exceptions to her rules. She would claim something (dreams did not mean anything) and he would immediately provide a counterexample (John Dee).

"If you dreamed of him," Astrophil persisted, "it might have been real. He could have been sending you a message. Your minds are connected."

"Don't remind me." She shivered as she dressed.

"Do you remember what you dreamed?"

"No," she lied. She pulled a necklace out from under her shirt. A small horseshoe swung from the thin leather cord. She flipped the horseshoe over and looked at the engraving. It was written in a language she didn't understand, but she saw her name, and a friend's. "Where do you think Neel is now? Do you think he's still in Spain?"

There was a reproachful pause. Astrophil wasn't fooled by her attempt to distract him. "I do not know."

"Let's go out to the forest. Before Father wakes up."

"If you wish."

She got down on her hands and knees, and rummaged under the bed. When she stood up, she held nothing. But her hands, though empty, moved oddly. Petra seemed to buckle an invisible object at her waist. She looked like an actor playing a pantomime.

Astrophil crept up her arm, and she smiled at him cheerfully.

But that was an act, too. Petra was troubled. She remembered her dream well enough. She had been angry—more than angry. She had been filled with a rage that was almost panic, almost despair. She had been pounding at a door. The room that trapped her was luxurious, with carved furniture and brocade fabrics. But that didn't change the fact that she was in some sort of prison.

JAREK WAS FLUNG into the corner of his cell. His cheek grazed against the stone wall as he fell to the floor, and the door shrieked shut.

The session had been mercifully short. After all, he had given them the information they wanted.

There was a window in his cell, Jarek reminded himself. Not a window, really, just a square hole. It was big enough for one hand.

Jarek struggled to his feet. As he reached up, pain shot through his arm. He shoved his hand through the hole. Cold rain tingled over his bloody fingers.

Then something besides the rain tickled his palm. A small body nestled into Jarek's cupped hand. He felt warm feathers and a quick heartbeat. *My poor friend,* the sparrow murmured in Jarek's mind.

Jarek imagined what the bird could see: his own wrist growing out of the dungeon wall like a twisted root, the sky blurry with rain, and the red rooftops of Prague.

The idea of the sparrow leaving him alone was perhaps the worst torture of all. Still, he said to the bird, *I need you to bear a message for me.*

THE HOUSE at the Sign of the Compass was filled with echoes. Most of the furniture had been sold, or loaded into the cart Josef and Dita had driven with their son, David, into southern Bohemia. Dita was Petra's older cousin, but she was more than that. Dita and her husband, Josef, were like a second set of parents to Petra, and David was like her little brother.

When Petra's father had first proposed that the entire family leave the village of Okno, everybody began arguing. Petra protested. Josef disagreed by refusing to respond at all. Dita said flatly, "It's a foolish idea, Uncle Mikal."

Mikal Kronos talked about his plan every morning, and every morning a fresh battle erupted over breakfast until one day David dropped his spoon into his porridge, covered his ears, and yelled, "*Shut up! Shut up,* all of you!" He burst into tears. His tin raven swooped anxiously overhead. His parents exchanged a glance.

"Think of the children's safety," Mikal Kronos urged Dita and Josef. "When the prince discovers who is responsible for ransacking his Cabinet of Wonders, he won't be merciful to anyone in this family. The four of you need to move as quickly as possible. I don't want to leave behind anything that he could use, so I'll need some time to dismantle the workshop. I promise I won't be far behind."

Slowly, Dita nodded.

"I won't go," Petra told her father. "You can't make me."

There was a long pause. "No," he finally said, "I don't suppose I can. You will leave with me, Petra, as soon as we're able to join the others."

Petra had won something. But it didn't feel that way now.

"Ahem," Astrophil coughed, startling Petra out of her memory. "Do you plan to stare into space all day, or will we actually do something important and worthy, like, say, attend to the business of breakfast?"

"Sorry, Astro."

Petra opened her nightstand drawer, which clattered with unwashed silver spoons. She fed the spider his daily meal, a spoonful of green brassica oil. When he had drained it, Petra ran a finger over the greasy metal and rubbed the leftover oil on her chapped lips.

She opened the wardrobe, pulled out a leather cloak lined with rabbit fur, and then began searching for the woolen cap Dita had made for her. It itched like mad, but Petra loved it. She rescued it from under a pile of worn books and dirty socks.

"What are *books* doing there?" Astrophil was horrified.

Petra ignored him, tucking the hat and cloak under her arm. She walked downstairs to the kitchen with Astrophil perched on her shoulder, muttering about Petra's shameful treatment of the books.

She took a wizened apple from the kitchen fruit bin and sawed some bread from a stale loaf. She would have liked a mug of warm milk, but starting a fire in the stove would take far too much effort. Petra arranged a slice of cow cheese on the tough bread and bit into it.

"In some societies," Astrophil informed her, "it would never cross anyone's mind to eat cheese. To them it would be nothing but spoiled milk."

"Too bad for them," Petra replied, chewing. The bread tasted like tree bark, but at least the cheese was fresh.

When she finished eating, she tiptoed down the stairs and through the shop.

Petra held the bell on the door frame so that it wouldn't ring as she slipped outside. The cold air hit her. She pulled the hat down over her ears, breathed deeply, and her head seemed to clear. Maybe she would be able to shake off her bad mood. Maybe the day was salvageable after all.

Her boots had crunched over just a few yards of snow when it began to rain. Astrophil ducked under her hair. Petra looked up at the falling drops. "Oh, *perfect*." She thought about going back into the house but then changed her mind. Petra drew the cloak tightly about her and trudged on.

"YOUR HIGHNESS, the prisoner has broken."

"And?" replied the young prince. "What have you learned?"

"He still claims that he doesn't know the name of the Gypsy who participated in the theft in November."

"No matter." Prince Rodolfo tried to control his irritation. "We will find out the boy's name the hard way. Sweep my country clear of this Gypsy trash."

"We've already begun to do this, Your Highness. As you recall, you ordered us last month to begin arresting Prague's Gypsies for questioning."

"I am not forgetful." The prince's voice was even but danger-ous, like thin ice covering a deep pond. "I want you to have *all* of Bohemia searched for Gypsies. You know their ways. They travel everywhere, and quickly, like a disease. Watch our borders. Do not let them leave, and do not block the borders from those who wish to enter. Imprison them as well.

"Now, as for Jarek: I hope you have gleaned *some* useful infor-mation from him?"

"Yes, Your Highness. He has confirmed your suspicions. The girl who stole from the Cabinet of Wonders was not working for your brothers. It was Petra Kronos, the clockmaker's daughter."

The prince remembered the girl: a tall, unlovely thing who had scarcely pretended to be afraid of him.

Well, she would learn.

"I want there to be no mistakes," the prince said. "Send the Gristleki."

The guard flinched.

"Did you hear me?" the prince hissed. "Send the Gray Men."

The guard jerked his head in a nod. "Yes, Your Highness. What should I do with the prisoner?"

"Let them start with him. They are hungry."

2

The Sparrow

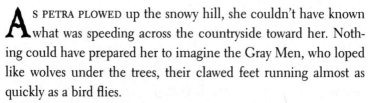

As PETRA PLOWED up the snowy hill, she couldn't have known what was speeding across the countryside toward her. Nothing could have prepared her to imagine the Gray Men, who loped like wolves under the trees, their clawed feet running almost as quickly as a bird flies.

When Petra and Astrophil had reached the forest, the spider said, "Perhaps you could try talking to him."

"Try talking to who?"

"The link John Dee made between your mind and his should be accessible by both of you. Neel said that such links are used between generals and soldiers, and between criminal allies. Surely forging a connection like that is valuable only if each person can mentally reach the other. Instead of waiting for Dee to contact you, you could try contacting him."

"I could try eating rotten goat intestines, but I'm not going to," Petra scoffed. "And let's get one thing straight: I'm not *waiting* for that man to pay a visit to my mind as if it were his summer cottage. My thoughts are my own. Not his."

"A mental link does not allow him to read your mind," Astrophil said. "When you and I speak using our thoughts, I hear only what you say to me, not your inner secrets. A mental link is simply a form of communication. You know this already. Neel explained it to us in Prague. You are just being difficult."

Petra pushed through the pine trees, and green bristles showered her with freezing water. She yelped.

"Petra, we are all worried about what the prince knows of you, and how he will react. It is not as if you lost one of his papers while cleaning his study. You broke into his prized collection of magnificent and magical objects, took your father's eyes—"

"They didn't belong to the prince! Now they are back where they belong, and Father can see."

"You also stole a small fortune of gold and jewels—"

"*Neel* did that. Not me."

"—and managed to destroy a hidden part of the Staro Clock that Master Kronos built, a part that would have allowed the prince to use the clock to control the weather, thereby wielding an enormous amount of power over all of Europe."

"That's right. You'd think someone would thank me for it."

They reached a clearing. The ground was rocky and uneven, and the space wasn't as large as the one she preferred to use, but that spot of woods was a mile ahead. She squinted at the rain. She would stay here. "All right, Astro: tree or ear?"

He clung to her earlobe tightly. "I am quite fine where I am, thank you. I believe it may be useful for me to learn how to be part of a skirmish. I could be an extra set of eyes. I could warn you if an enemy approaches. Plus . . . it is raining."

"Tin doesn't rust, Astro."

"Even so, the brim of your hat makes a nice umbrella."

Petra pulled at something by her left hip. There was a scraping sound, and her closed fist arced in the air. Raindrops plinked and halted in a horizontal line in front of her. Petra's fingers grasped the hilt of something long, thin, and wickedly sharp. It was a sword, and an invisible one at that.

Astrophil cleared his throat. "To return to my point—"

"I wish you wouldn't."

"—the prince is not likely to reward you with sugar plums for your actions. Once he learns who you are and, thus, *where* you are—"

"I *know*, Astrophil. Why do you think Josef, Dita, and David are halfway to Sumava by now?"

"John Dee is a trusted adviser to the queen of England."

"I think his official title is Arrogant Spy," Petra retorted.

"He is also a former ambassador to the prince of Bohemia. I am merely trying to suggest that John Dee may have useful information to share with you. Can you afford to make no effort to gain it? Dee promised to help you one day, if you ask for it. You should try contacting him to learn what the prince knows about you, and what he might do with that knowledge."

"Even if—*if*—I agreed with you, I have no idea how to tap into Dee's head. What am I supposed to do, go to the top of a hill and shout, 'Hey, Dee! Speak to me, you annoying, smirking—'?"

"It is a pity we cannot consult Neel. If his people know as much about mind-magic as he claims, he might be able to ask one of them about this situation."

"Neel is someplace warm and sunny. Not here." Petra tried not to care. Why should you miss someone you will never see again? It wasn't fair. Feelings like guilt and anxiety and missing people should have a certain life span. Like fruit flies.

"But perhaps—" Astrophil continued.

"Astrophil? You know what's so great about books?"

"Why, many things. I am so glad you asked. They possess many wonderful properties. They awaken the imagination, inform one about history—"

"And they *close*. Like this subject. I don't want to talk about John Dee. He threatened my father and me, and made *me* destroy the clock's magical power, all for the sake of his precious English queen."

"You would have done that anyway, once you knew the havoc the clock could wreak."

"Maybe, but John Dee got to sit snug in his little velvet chair, doing nothing to risk his neck while you, Neel, and I could have gotten caught and killed. Dee's always looking out for his best interests, and any help from him would come with so many strings attached I'd be tied up like a trussed pig. I don't want anything more to do with Dee, or to even think about him."

Astrophil's green eyes glowed with frustration. But he knew Petra. It would be easier to coax a stone to grow into a flower than it would be to make her listen to an idea she hated. "Very well. Shall we begin by running through a series of positions? I have consulted several books on sword-fighting. This took me some time because most of them were written in Italian, but I have translated several passages."

"Let's just do what we've been doing for weeks."

"Would that be: I watch while you slash at the air until you are tired?"

"Yes."

Astrophil sighed. "You could at least comment on how well my knowledge of Italian is progressing."

"Bravo," Petra said, and crouched. She felt ridiculous, shuffling back and forth over the snow and swinging the invisible sword. But she did it anyway.

"You can grip that hilt with both hands," said a voice behind her.

Petra spun around.

Mikal Kronos stepped forward. "You're letting your left hand dangle at your side. That's a waste. This sword is thin and light, like a rapier, but not as long as one. I thought a true rapier would be too long to keep unnoticed when sheathed. Of course, even an invisible sword isn't easy to hide. But if you're going to forge one, you obviously have some interest in secrecy, so why not do what you can to maximize that?

"Now, what did I want to tell you? Ah, yes, the left hand. Since the blade is on the short side, your ability to thrust it at your opponent is limited. Your *reach* is limited. So that means that you need to compensate by learning how to use your left hand, too. With that hand you can hold a dagger, and use it to block blows and swipe at your opponent. What happens if your dagger is knocked away? There's room enough for your left hand as well as your right on this hilt. That will give your blows more force. Do you feel the swirls of steel arcing over the hilt? That's to protect your fingers, in case someone tries to make you drop the sword by hacking at them. Remember that a master of fencing should be able to wield a sword just as well with the left hand as with the right. If you let your left arm stick out uselessly like a tree branch, it will get lopped off like one."

Petra stared. She had often wondered what would happen if her father ever caught her with the sword he had made and hidden away. Usually, she imagined a lot of yelling. Not this.

Mikal Kronos noticed her surprise. "I thought carefully about how to craft a sword that would work best for you."

"You really made it for *me*?"

He nodded. "You're a tall girl, Petra, and quick. But slender. The sword had to be light enough for you to wield easily. That"— he tapped the invisible sword and it rang like a bell—"is made with crucible steel. It has a hard spine yet also enough spring to absorb shocks. It won't break. This blade is double-edged, which gives you the freedom to cut from many directions as well as thrust at your opponent with the sword's point. This sword is meant to do damage, Petra, and I mean for you to do damage against anyone who tries to hurt you. *Anyone.*"

These words were so unlike Petra's gentle father, who always shook a log free of beetles before placing it on a fire. "How do you know so much about swords?"

"Now, really, Petra," said Astrophil. "Where do you think I found books on fencing? Where else but Master Kronos's library?"

"But, Father, you never told me you know how to fence."

"I don't. I only know the principles. You have to know the basics of fencing in order to forge a sword." He hesitated, and then said exactly what Petra hoped he wouldn't: "If you were able to go to the Academy, you would be taught how to use a sword properly."

Petra gritted her teeth. This argument wasn't old, but it felt that way. "Well, I can't go to the Academy. And I don't want to. You never even asked me if I wanted to." The Academy was a school for magic that admitted only children of high society, not lowly villagers like her. Petra's father had hoped, however, that an exception would be made in her case, and that is why he had agreed to build the prince's clock.

"Petra, you should have the opportunities I didn't. You've been gifted with a magical ability. If you learned how to use it, you could be better than I am—"

"No, I couldn't!" she burst out. "I can't do anything!"

That is not true, Astrophil spoke silently in her mind.

"Talking with Astro the way you do doesn't count, Father. I don't have your talent. I can't make metal move just by thinking about it. You *know* that. We've been practicing for *weeks*."

"You are still young. It may take some time."

"I'm not *that* young. I'm thirteen. Tomik made his first Marvel when he was my age." Petra pressed her point, even though she hoped to be proven wrong. "In Prague, I thought that maybe . . .

that maybe I was more talented than I am. Astrophil and I could talk without opening our mouths. When I picked up a knife, I thought I could *feel* it inside my mind. But that was my imagination."

"You broke the clock's heart."

"That was dumb luck."

"You *can* communicate with Astrophil."

"But that's all. If I inherited anything from you, it was just some watered-down version of your magic. Nothing to get excited about. Nothing worth sending someone to the Academy for. I probably wouldn't pass the entrance test, even if I were allowed to take it." Saying this somehow stole all of Petra's anger. Now she felt only cold and wet.

"Come here," her father said, and hugged her. "You're shivering. Let's go home, Petra. We'll start a fire and warm some milk over it. You'd like that, wouldn't you?"

WHEN PETRA and her father reached the Sign of the Compass, it had stopped raining and they were laughing at Astrophil as he tried to imitate a human sneeze.

They didn't see the sparrow leap from the roof. Astrophil spotted the bird before the others did and hid in Petra's hair.

The bird dived at them, stopping right in front of Petra's face. It hovered, screeching.

Astrophil, boomed a voice in the spider's head.

Master Kronos? Astrophil jumped in surprise.

Keep still. Don't let Petra know we're having this conversation.

But why?

Do you remember what we discussed?

Astrophil paused. *Yes.*

Good. Then go along with whatever I tell Petra to do. See that she does it.

Surely there is no cause for alarm.

Yes, there is, insisted Mikal Kronos. *The sparrow.*

Nonsense. If the bird poses a threat to anyone, it is to me. It wants to eat me!

No, Astrophil. Something is wrong. It is trying to warn us.

The spider had a sinking feeling in his tin stomach. *You are making far too much of the bizarre flight pattern of one bird.*

Maybe so. But I can't take the risk.

If this is a warning of some kind—and I do not agree that it is— will you not be in danger as well?

Astrophil, you gave me your word. Keep it.

"What's wrong with that sparrow?" Petra stared at the bird as it darted back and forth.

"Nothing," said Astrophil. "Or, hmm, well, I expect it has mad dog disease."

"Mad dog disease affects *dogs*, Astro."

"Petra," her father interrupted, "I need you to deliver something to Tomas Stakan. There's a tin sheet leaning against the wall in the shop. Bring it to the Sign of Fire."

"Sure. I'll just change my clothes first. I'm soaking wet."

"No. Take it to Tomas now."

Petra was puzzled by her father's stern expression. "Can't it wait until later?"

"Can't you just do as I ask?" he snapped. "For once in your life, do as I tell you!"

Petra felt as if she had been slapped. "Fine!" she shouted. She stalked into the shop.

The bird flew after her, but the shop door slammed shut, the bell jangling. The bird flapped outside the closed door, which soon burst open again. Petra gripped the tin sheet under her arm.

"Goodbye, Petra," Mikal Kronos said in a softened voice. Although the sword he had forged was invisible, he could tell that it was still buckled around Petra's waist. He tried not to show his relief. He tried not to show anything that would keep Petra at the Sign of the Compass.

Petra's lips thinned into a line. She whipped around and strode toward the village. Astrophil rode on her shoulder, gazing back at Master Kronos.

The bird landed on the melting snow and watched Petra storm off. Then it hopped toward Mikal. It cocked its head, scrutinizing the man. It couldn't be sure, but it thought that its message had been received, even if the man was behaving very strangely. But then, the bird never understood humans, who saved food rather than eating it right away, and whose nests were closed to the sky.

Mikal Kronos went inside the house, returning with a slice of old bread and a dish filled with water. He set the bowl on the ground, crumbled the bread onto the snow, and then walked around to the back of the house. He took a stool from the smithy. He brought it back to where the bird perched at the edge of the bowl, drinking deeply and flipping back its wings. Master Kronos placed the stool beneath the wooden sign with its many-pointed compass, hoping that if the prince seized him, he might not try to find Petra. Mikal sat down to wait.

3

The Sign of Fire

BEFORE PETRA had reached the edge of the village, she wanted to go back and apologize. Why had she overreacted? If her father was angry with her, could she blame him? They were leaving the village he had lived in all of his life. Who was responsible for that, if not she?

She turned around.

Astrophil pinched her ear.

"Ow! *Astrophil!*"

"Where are you going?"

"Home."

"Why? That is not what your father asked you to do!"

"Master Stakan can't need the tin sheet so badly that he won't be able to wait fifteen minutes more. I just . . . I want to tell Father I'm sorry. I shouldn't have been so . . . sulky."

"But sulking is a great talent of yours. You should practice it. You should continue to sulk."

"Astrophil, are you trying to be funny?"

"I simply do not see what is to be gained by ruining such a dramatic exit as the one you just made. To return to the Sign of the Compass now, well . . . it would not be artistic. A heroine in a novel would never turn back at this point."

"May I point out that her tongue is five times the size of my entire body?"

Tomik poured green brassica oil into a large bowl and set it down in the corner of the workshop. "Come here, you great big hunk of tin."

Atalanta slurped up the oil, green drops scattering around the bowl.

Petra looked at the pile of sand in a pan next to the fire. "What are you making, Tomik?"

"Wineglasses. I'd love to get my hands on some pure white sand. When you heat up white sand you get the clearest glass in the world. Not like that dull tan stuff there. But your father gave me iron oxide to add to that batch, which should turn the glass a decent red. If you can't make glass clear, you might as well make it colored."

"You don't seem too excited about it."

"The glasses will be pretty, but they won't be *special*. Know what I mean?"

Petra leaned forward. "Have you made anything *special* lately?"

Eagerly, he reached into his pocket and pulled out something shaped like an oval pebble. He set the glass object on the table with a small thunk.

Petra picked it up and turned it in the light of the fire. It was almost clear, but held a tint of light blue. It shone more brightly than normal glass. "What is it?"

"Guess."

After swearing Tomik to secrecy, Petra had told him about her ability to speak silently with Astrophil. Sometimes she regretted this, because Tomik was so excited that she had a magical talent that he often pushed her to use it. Like now. Petra looked at Tomik, wishing that he hadn't challenged her on this morning, of all mornings, when it seemed like she wasn't able to do anything right. She rolled the stone between her fingers, conscious that both Tomik and Astrophil were watching her. Closing her eyes, she focused on the slippery glass. She felt something flutter in her mind. "Lead?" Petra opened her eyes. "Is there lead in the glass?"

"Got it in one guess! Watch this." Tomik took the pebble from her and squeezed his hand around it. When he opened his fist, the glass radiated with light. "I call it a Glowstone. All you have to do is squeeze hard, and the warmth of your hand will activate the lead inside the glass. The longer you hold the Glowstone, the stronger its light will be. It'll be great for exploring caves, don't you think? Here." He handed her the Glowstone. "Keep it. I made others."

Petra put it in her pocket.

Atalanta ran back toward Tomik and Petra. When she reached the table, her long, wagging tail knocked against the tin sheet. It clattered to the floor.

Tomik noticed the sheet for the first time. "What's that?"

"Father told me to bring it. He said you needed it."

"For what?" He picked it up and inspected it. "For float glass?"

"I guess."

"But float glass is used for making windows."

"So?"

"Our windows haven't sold well lately. We've got a huge stack of them in the back. We definitely don't need to make any more."

Petra furrowed her brow, confused.

Then, suddenly, she seemed to hear a horrible scream. It came from far away, but pierced through her.

The Gray Men were howling with pleasure. They had easily captured one of their prey, and they were sure the other one was close at hand.

Petra gasped.

"What's wrong?" Tomik asked. Petra's face was pale.

"Don't you hear it?" she cried.

"Hear what?" Tomik said.

"I do not hear anything." Astrophil frowned.

Atalanta whined, bewildered.

Petra stumbled to her feet. The howling stopped. In that first moment of silence, Petra stared at the tin sheet and realized something: her father had lied to her.

She sprang for the door.

As she raced out of the Sign of Fire, a silvery line trailed from her back. Astrophil clung to the end of the web, pulling himself up as quickly as he could, hoping that they would be too late.

EVEN BEFORE Petra reached the edge of town, she saw smoke. She shoved past people on the street. When she burst through the last ring of houses, she saw the Sign of the Compass. It was burning.

She was only a few feet from her home and calling for her father when the first of the Gristleki slipped onto its two feet. Three more Gray Men oozed out of their crouched positions. Petra had seen nothing but the flames and didn't notice the Gristleki until they moved.

She skidded to a stop, and the four creatures slithered toward her, their claws squealing against the cobblestones. They could have seized the girl immediately but moved slowly because they liked it. They savored the fear that would freeze her face as they grew closer.

The Gristleki were the color of ash, and covered in scales. Their skin was dry and cracked, as if something had sucked the fluids out of their bodies. But the most horrifying feature of the Gristleki was their shape. It was human. Even though they looked like skeletons with snake skin stretched over the bones, and even though claws sprang from their hands and feet, the creatures looked like they had once been men. Four scaly skulls slipped closer to Petra. Their faces had no lips. They had no eyebrows or eyelashes, as if they had been burned away. But their eyes were human.

One of them opened its toothless mouth, and Petra stared into the black hole. She tried to move, but her legs were rooted to the earth.

"Petra!" Astrophil was shouting in her ear. "Listen to me: you have to run. Do you hear me? *Petra!*" He gripped her earlobe so hard that blood trickled down her neck.

She took a step backward. The second step was easier.

A Gristleki smiled, showing its gums.

The other Gray Men had already borne away their first prey. That had been far too easy. These four hoped that the girl would put up more of a fight. They all smiled now encouragingly.

Petra had only two options: the forest or the town. Even in her fear, she couldn't lead these monsters to the homes of people she had known all her life.

She sprinted for the trees.

The Gray Men watched until she disappeared. Then they dropped to the ground and began to race on all fours. They poured after her like liquid poison.

Petra's heart pounded hopelessly in her ears, and every breath she took ripped at the back of her throat. She tried to run faster, but her legs were hot and weak. She stumbled.

A hand seized her. It spun Petra around, rasping up her arm. She stared at the scaly claw as it scraped along her skin, tearing ribbons of blood. The creature opened its mouth and its tongue slipped out. The Gray Man could smell the stink of fear. It looked at the girl's throat, where sweat mingled with a thin line of blood. Then it leaned forward and licked Petra's neck.

Something inside her snapped, and she began to scream. Petra felt like she was splitting apart, and with all of her heart and mind she cried, *"HELP! HELP ME!"*

For the first time in her life, Petra fainted.

WHEN SHE regained consciousness, she was lying on her stomach and her face was pressed against something soft. Her left arm and the side of her neck burned. She felt something twitch on her shoulder blade, shifting under her cloak: Astrophil.

She opened her eyes, lifted herself onto her elbows, and saw that she was on a large velvet bed. She murmured, "Where am I?"

Before Astrophil could reply, a voice said, "You're in my home."

Petra knew that voice. She spun around in shock.

"You're in London," said John Dee. "You're safe."

4

Blood of the Shadowdrake

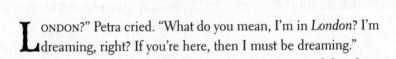

"L ONDON?" Petra cried. "What do you mean, I'm in *London*? I'm dreaming, right? If you're here, then I must be dreaming."

"I am afraid you are not," Dee said, standing several feet from the bed, tall and inscrutable.

"Explain to me what's going on!" Petra exploded. "What am I doing here? Where is my father? What were those . . . *things*?" She was ashamed when her voice broke.

"Impatient as ever, I see. The answers to your questions can wait. Your wounds cannot. They should be seen to first, my dear."

"I am not *your dear!*"

She jumped to her feet and ran to the door. She yanked at the handle, but the door wouldn't open. She glared over her shoulder.

Dee had not moved. He regarded her coolly.

"Let me out."

"Not in your condition."

"My condition?" she asked warily.

"You have been poisoned by the touch of the creatures that attacked you. You will probably die. You certainly won't do yourself any good with your theatrical hysterics. This will only cause your heart to beat more quickly, which will pump the poison through your bloodstream. Who knows," he said idly, "how long you will last?"

Petra, please sit down, Astrophil said.

He can't be telling the truth. It is not possible for me to be in London. It would take months for me to travel to England! So I'm supposed to believe him when he says I've been poisoned?

I believe him. And you are in London.

She was stunned into silence.

Petra, the spider continued, *I saw everything that happened while you were unconscious. John Dee did indeed save your life. Having done that, it would not be rational for him to harm you now, and he is clearly interested in doing you some good. You cannot risk the possibility that he is correct about the danger your wounds pose.* His voice shook.

She looked at her torn forearm. The gashes throbbed, just like her neck. Her entire left arm felt tight, swollen.

She faced Dee. "All right. How about this: I'll be calm, but I want answers."

"A bargain? You are in no position to negotiate anything. Perhaps I do not wish to answer your questions. Perhaps I do not care whether you are calm or not."

"You care," she stated. "You're just being tight-fisted with information. Like always."

He tilted his head, considering. "Very well. I agree to your bargain. Sit."

She sank into an overstuffed brocade chair. She wouldn't have admitted it, but she was glad to sit. Her head was swimming.

"Is my father in London, too?" she began.

"No."

"Where is he, then?"

"I do not know. Now, now, Petra, don't erupt into accusations. I thought we agreed you were going to be still, polite, and attentive."

"The word I used was 'calm.' I didn't say 'attentive,' and I *never* said 'polite.' Now, *where* is—?"

"I truly do not know. I could, however, find out. I certainly can make an educated guess as to where he is. So can you, unless the poison has begun to affect your brain."

She briefly closed her eyes. "The prince. Salamander Castle."

"Of course. Though I would probably specify that your father's location is in the dungeons. If, that is, he is still alive."

"But you'll find out, right?" Her voice was desperate.

"Yes. Not now, however. And I will not share that information for free. Next question?"

"I *need* to know—"

"Next."

"Answer my question!"

"My presence is doing you more harm than good." Dee glided to the door and placed his thumb on the latch. "I shall speak with you later. My doctor will be with you shortly."

"Wait." Petra stared at the brocade pattern on the arms of her chair, unnerved to see that the design was familiar. Those stitched red flowers had been in her dream. She fought against panic and dizziness. "I need to understand what's happening to me."

He nodded. "Yes. It is a topic that interests us both." He drew a chair forward and sat down across from Petra. "I am a man of great patience, but every admirable quality has its limits. I will appreciate seeing just how calm, attentive, *and* polite you will be as our conversation continues."

Petra took a breath to steady herself. "Tell me what those creatures were."

"The Gristleki. They are more commonly known as the Gray Men."

"But what *are* they?"

"An invention. Surely you remember the name Fiala Broshek? Sometime during our stay at Salamander Castle, a man called Karel had the misfortune to be delivered into her hands. Fiala Broshek is a surgeon with a rather interesting set of morals. She decided to use Karel for one of her experiments.

"Your education has been limited, to say the least. So I imagine you've never heard of a Shadowdrake, a particular breed of dragon that breathes darkness, not fire. Fiala Broshek paid a warrior to kill a Shadowdrake and collect its blood. She then cut the wrist of Karel, drained him of every drop of human blood, and gave him a transfusion of Shadowdrake blood. This brought the dead man back to life, if *life* is the word you wish to apply to such a creature. The operation had intriguing effects on the human body, as you witnessed firsthand. The surgeon repeated this operation with several other subjects."

"How did you get this information? From spies?"

"Just so. Are you interested to learn how I saved you from the Gray Men?"

She nodded.

"I decapitated them," he said.

Her jaw dropped.

"That means that I cut their heads off," he added.

"I know what it means!" Remembering the speed of the Gray Men and their burning touch, she said hesitantly, "All four of them?"

He smiled.

His message sank in. However terrifying the Gray Men were, John Dee was more dangerous. At least four times more dangerous.

She almost dreaded the answer to her next question. "If I'm really in London, how did you bring me here?"

"With the aid of my daughters. Judging by your shocked expression, you don't think of me as quite human, do you? Yet I *am*, Petra, and I have a family. My daughters, who are about your age, possess remarkable magic. They can manipulate passageways through space. In less than the time it takes for you to cross a street, I can step from London to Bohemia. Anyone can, anyone who knows precisely where to enter a passageway created by Madinia. She is able to tear Rifts in space. Margaret can close them."

"So Margaret and Madinia will help me go home." Petra's chest felt tight, just like her throbbing arm. "Won't they?"

"No."

A numbness crept over her. She couldn't tell if it was because of the Gray Men's poison or Dee's reply. But then Petra remembered something. She was so relieved, she laughed. "Wait. Wait a minute. The night I left Salamander Castle you told me you would grant me one favor. Remember? Well, I want it now. I want you to let me out of here. Send me home!"

"I didn't save your life for you to toss it away. If you return, you will be hunted down."

"You promised me! You—"

"Petra." He sighed. "I already granted you a favor. You called upon me for help."

"No," she whispered. "I didn't call *you*."

"Our minds are connected, and I heard when you called. I brought you here, and now you are safe. I promised you one favor. One."

"But you can't keep me here!"

"I can and will."

Petra struggled to rise out of her chair, but could not. She saw her fingers twitch, but did not feel them move.

"Hmm." Dee tapped a finger against his lips. "Paralysis. Finally. The poison has worked a little more slowly than I would have expected. But then, perhaps the Gristleki prefer to keep their victims mobile for a time. Paralysis does make their sport a little too easy." He rose to his feet. "Or perhaps you are stronger than I believed."

"Please!" she choked out. "I just want to go home."

"You have no home." He turned away.

Petra's eyelids slipped shut and the image of the brocade flowers bloomed beneath them, red like the flames that had consumed the house she was born in.

Dee closed the door behind him.

Part of Petra wanted to relive her dream, to pound against that locked door. But now the poison seemed like a cure. When the room went black around her she was grateful that she could not move and could not feel anything at all.

5

The *Pacolet*

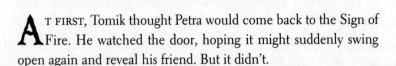

A T FIRST, Tomik thought Petra would come back to the Sign of Fire. He watched the door, hoping it might suddenly swing open again and reveal his friend. But it didn't.

Atalanta lay down. She rested her chin on her front paws and gazed up at Tomik with round, green eyes. "Why Astro go?" she asked mournfully.

"I don't know." Tomik shook his head. "I don't get it."

Lately, there were a lot of things that Tomik didn't get about Petra, like what she was thinking when she bit her lip, or shrugged, or made some other kind of gesture that meant she didn't want to talk about whatever he had asked.

Where Petra was concerned, one thing puzzled Tomik above all others: Prague. Why hadn't he gone to Prague with Petra? Why had he let her—*helped* her—travel alone to a city where the first thing she did was put her trust in a *Gypsy*?

Tomik looked at the shut door again. Something was wrong with Petra, that much was clear, but if Tomik left the shop unattended, his father would be furious.

Tomik's gaze fell on Atalanta. He made up his mind.

"Attie, I'm going to leave for just a little while. I'll lock up. Can you guard the Sign of Fire?"

She barked, leaping to her feet.

"Good girl. And . . . if somebody comes by who tries to get inside, who seems like he doesn't belong, try looking mean."

Atalanta leaned forward on her huge front paws and growled. A snarl ripped in her throat as her lips pulled back to show rows of pointy teeth.

Tomik patted her head. Atalanta immediately stopped snarling and licked his hand.

"*Mean*, Attie. Remember."

"Sorry." She bared her teeth again.

After Tomik locked the shop behind him, he took something out of his pocket. It was another Glowstone.

When the Kronos family began packing their things to move far away, Tomik saw the danger Petra was in and decided he would try to protect her, whether she liked it or not. He hadn't lied to Petra, exactly, when he gave her a Glowstone. His invention was better than any candle for seeing in the dark. But it was more than that. It was also designed to track Petra, and she *definitely* wouldn't like being tracked or tricked.

Tomik weighed the Glowstone in his hand. He turned to the left, in the direction of the Sign of the Compass. The crystal in his hand flickered with a faint blue light. So Petra had gone home, then. Tomik put the Glowstone back in his pocket and walked down the shop-lined street. It was oddly empty for what was usually the busiest time of day.

Tomik smelled smoke.

"Move out of the way!" someone shouted.

Tomik turned around. Two men rushed past him, buckets swinging from each hand.

He ran after them. "What's going on?" he called.

"Fire!" one of them replied. "The Sign of the Compass!"

Tomik raced alongside the men. He tried to bottle up his fear, but then he saw the skinny house. It was a tower of flame. Men and women circled it, passing pails of snow and flinging them into the roaring fire.

That's never going to work, Tomik thought with a moan. The people looked like sticks, their buckets like acorns. Flames flashed along the thatched roof.

Tomik pulled the Glowstone from his pocket. There was no mistaking it: the crystal's blue light was stronger. Petra had come here.

Tomik ran up to the men and women trying desperately to put out the fire. He spotted Tomas Stakan, blackened with soot, pitching snow as quickly as he could. "Father!"

"Tomik, what are you doing here? Who's in the shop?"

"No one," Tomik said hesitantly. "But Attie's guarding it."

"*What?* What were you *thinking*? Go home, now!"

"No." Tomik grabbed a bucket.

"I don't have time to argue with you. Look at that." His father stabbed a finger at the Sign of the Compass. "Our friends could be inside that house. We have to put out the fire!"

"Then let me help!" Tomik scooped up a bucket of wet snow and stepped toward the crackling wall of flame.

This time, his father didn't stop him.

The men and women of Okno heaved snow and wet earth into the fire, but they knew they were fighting a losing battle. The fire had already consumed the ground floor by the time the first help had arrived, making it impossible for anyone to enter the building. Now even the roof was ablaze.

Tomik couldn't allow himself to think. He moved mechanically, passing buckets, filling some, emptying others. He knew his father was next to him, but they didn't speak.

Then there was a sickening crack, like the sound of a spine breaking, as the beams of the house split.

"It's caving! Back! Get back!"

Somebody shoved Tomik, pushing him yards away from the fire.

There was a crunching sound of falling timber as the Sign of the Compass began to collapse, the fire rushing down to hollow out the inside of the house.

Tomik felt an arm around him, but couldn't look away from the flames, even though they hurt his eyes.

"Tomik," his father said.

Tomik turned. A tear traced over Tomas Stakan's sooty cheek. "I'm sorry," his father said, and tried to hug him.

"Stop it!" Tomik struggled.

"Son, no one could have survived that. If they were inside the house—"

"They weren't! Petra was *not* inside that house!" But Tomik knew that wasn't true. His Glowstone had shown that Petra had come here, and his inventions always worked.

Tomik broke away from his father and began to run. He didn't pay attention to where he was going. He stopped only when he realized that he could no longer hear the crackling fire. Now a different sound filled his ears. A bird was singing.

Tomik had reached the edge of the forest. He blinked up at the trees and saw a sparrow in the bare branches. Suddenly angry— angry at the bird for thinking it had the right to sing, angry at himself, and at Petra, too—Tomik snatched the Glowstone from his pocket and drew it back to knock the sparrow right off its branch.

Something stayed his hand.

The crystal was an even brighter blue than before. Tomik stared disbelievingly.

He had designed the smooth crystal to shine a deeper blue as it got closer to its target, which was the twin Glowstone in Petra's pocket. The crystal could pick up traces of where Petra had been, which is why it had flickered as soon as Tomik left his shop in search of her. But it would react most strongly to wherever Petra had been *recently*.

Which meant that Petra was *not* in the Sign of the Compass when it collapsed.

Tomik laughed with relief. "Petra!" he called, and plunged into the woods. He followed the Glowstone with a light heart, as if he and Petra were small again, and playing a really complicated game of hide-and-seek. A serious voice spoke up inside, reminding him that he would still have to tell Petra that her home was in ashes. But he ignored that voice, growing happier with each darker shade of blue.

The smile on his lips faded when he smelled something rotten.

He inched forward. The stone burned more brightly. The stench grew worse.

At first he thought he was looking at animal carcasses. Yet the four headless corpses on the ground seemed eerily human, though their skin was scaly, and black blood poured from their necks.

With dread, Tomik realized that the Glowstone was leading him into the center of the ring of bodies.

Then a metallic glint on the ground caught his eye. Tomik crouched down and brushed at the snow, uncovering a tiny iron horseshoe. He recognized this—it was the necklace Petra had worn every day since she had returned from Prague.

Tomik picked up the rough trinket and inspected it. *Master Kronos didn't forge this*, he decided. *It's misshapen.* He turned the horseshoe over, and immediately eliminated the possibility that Petra had made it. A strange language was scratched into the iron. Tomik knew one word—*Kronos*—but the rest was gibberish.

Trailing from the horseshoe was a broken leather cord that looked as if it had been seared by something. Tomik sniffed a blackened end of the cord. *Not fire,* he thought. *Acid, maybe? Or*—his gaze jumped to a headless corpse—*something else?*

Tomik knotted the cord where it had broken, slipped the necklace over his head, and tucked the horseshoe inside his shirt.

He checked the Glowstone again. As if it were a compass, he turned north, south, east, and west. The blue deepened most when he faced south, so Tomik stepped that way over a body, careful not to let any part of him touch it. Headless or not, dead or not, those things smelled *evil.*

Tomik walked a few yards away from the bodies. *Whatever happened, Petra escaped,* he encouraged himself.

He was striding forward, his hand holding the Glowstone outstretched, when his forearm vanished.

With a surprised cry, he jerked back. His arm reappeared. There was his hand, the stone firmly in his fingers. There was his wrist, properly attached to the rest of his body.

"A burned-down house. Four headless monsters. Disappearing body parts," he muttered to himself, shaking his head. "Petra, you've got a lot of explaining to do. And I don't mean the shrugging-and-ignoring kind of explaining. I mean the sit-down-and-go-over-every-blazing-detail-so-I-can-be-sure-I'm-not-going-mad kind of explaining."

Tomik dropped the Glowstone into his pocket. Tentatively, he reached out his right hand.

It disappeared again.

This time, Tomik didn't leap back. He flexed his invisible hand. It seemed to function all right. It just wasn't *there.*

And, oddly enough, it was warm.

Tomik exhaled, his breath fogging the air. There was still slushy snow under his feet. He was definitely cold, but his invisible hand wasn't. *Summertime,* he thought. *It feels like summertime, wherever my hand is.*

Tomik took a deep breath, shut his eyes, and walked several paces.

He felt the sun beating down on his skin, and heard a roaring, hissing sound.

He opened his eyes.

Tomik was on a beach.

Squinting against the sunlight, he bent down to scoop up the white, sparkling sand. It was perfect. It was just the right kind of sand for making the clearest glass. It was also the kind of sand impossible to find in Bohemia.

Dreamily, Tomik poured the sand into his pocket. He walked to the water and dipped in his fingers as a foamy wave rushed forward to soak his shoes. He tasted his fingers. Salt.

Tomik checked the Glowstone. It glinted in the sun, but the blue light was gone. He put it back in his pocket and decided to admit something to himself.

He was totally, utterly confused.

So he did what most people in his position would do. He took off his shoes, tied the laces together, slung them over his shoulder, and walked into the sea. No land marked the horizon, though there was a ship anchored not far off. Still fascinated by the fine quality of the sand, Tomik reached down to grasp a handful of the wet grit.

He was so preoccupied with what was in his hand, and by the strange experiences of the day, that he wasn't prepared for yet one more unexpected turn of events. He didn't spot the small, empty boat someone had dragged up and left on the dry shore. He didn't hear the light padding of feet. In fact, Tomik didn't notice anything until something sharp and cold flicked against his neck: a knife.

"Now then, lad," a man's voice laughed in his ear. The man spoke in Czech, but his accent was heavy. "I wouldn't venture too far out if I were you. This sea's got a wicked current, and she'll drag you straight out into deep waters. Best step back, and bide awhile with us."

"Yeah," added a younger voice. "And show us what you got in your pockets."

A rough hand spun Tomik around. The man and boy standing before him had brown skin dusted with dried saltwater. Tomik gasped. "Sea-Gypsies!"

"Didn't anyone teach you not to call people names?" The man pressed the knife more firmly against Tomik's throat. "Even if the names are true?"

"*Especially* if they're true." The boy glared.

"Ever tried running in sand, my white lad?" said the long-haired man. "I would say you haven't. Let me save you the trouble of finding out what it's like, then. It's hard and it's slow. And where would you go?"

"And where've you been?" demanded the boy. "This is *our* beach. How did you get here?"

"I was looking for a friend . . ." Tomik replied haltingly. "I don't know how I got here. I was in a forest, and—"

The Gypsies exchanged a look.

"—and I somehow ended up here. I know that sounds, um—"

"Like a mess of bad lies? Lucky for you"—the man sighed, as if he had been handed one more worry on top of others—"I believe what you say."

The boy patted Tomik's sides, looking for a purse or weapon. Tomik cringed in distaste.

"He's got a jewel, Treb!" The boy had plucked the Glowstone from Tomik's pocket.

Treb glanced dismissively at the crystal. "I'm not sure, little cousin. Looks like glass to me."

"It is." Tomik strained away from the knife and tried to grab the

Glowstone. The boy jerked it out of reach. "It's just glass with some lead in it. Give it back."

The boy began to juggle the crystal, watching it flash in the sunlight.

"Stop that!" shouted Tomik. "You'll drop it! You'll break it!"

The juggler snorted. "Not likely."

"Give it *back*, you filthy little Gyp!"

The man slapped Tomik's cheek with the flat of his knife. Treb said menacingly, "Let me make something as clear as that shiny rock of yours that you're never going to see again. Since you seem to be somebody who'd like to keep all his ears and fingers and toes, I'll clue you in: *Gypsy* and *Gyp* aren't the friendliest words. We're Roma, and that's what you'd better call us. Now, why would I bother teaching you this small, but limb-preserving, lesson?"

"You tell me," Tomik said through gritted teeth.

"I will indeed. Let's take a stroll."

Tomik was pushed in the direction of the small boat he had noticed too late.

"That's ours." Treb nodded at the launch when they reached it. "And now let me introduce you to someone very dear to my heart." He pointed to the large, anchored ship with its layers of sails. "That's the *Pacolet*, as swift a brigantine ship as you'll ever see. You'll take care to treat her with respect, for she'll be your home."

"My *home?*"

"Oh, only for a short while," said Treb, but the reassurance in his voice was mocking. "Only until we reach Sallay, a Moroccan port town stuffed with lowlifes like us. Then we'll sell you. We'll get a fair price for a young slave such as yourself."

"*What?*" Tomik shoved against the man, but was quickly seized by him and the boy. He bit, elbowed, and kicked. But as the Gypsies wrangled his arms to his sides, Tomik realized that Treb must be telling the truth about their plans. They were not hitting back.

They were trying to subdue him without leaving any marks. They didn't want to damage their new property.

The boy pulled a length of rope out of the launch and bound Tomik's hands behind his back.

"You hypocrites!" Tomik spat. "You think I'm at fault for calling you what you are, when you're going to *sell* me? I have a life in Bohemia, and a family, and friends! I have—"

"A loud mouth." The man winced. "Pipe down, *gadje*, or I'll gag you."

"Truth be told," said the boy, "the word *gadje* ain't always polite, either. Depending on how you put it." He said something to the man in their language and they snickered.

"I think it's time we were off, little cousin, don't you?"

The boy nodded.

Treb prodded Tomik's shoulder with one finger. "Get in the boat."

6

Ask-and-Answer

THE CAPTAIN of the *Pacolet* frowned as he watched one of his sailors teach the *gadje* how to tie knots. Treb was farsighted, so even at a distance he could see that the boy was quick to learn. This didn't improve the man's mood.

"Someone's been fiddling with the Loophole," Treb grumbled to his young cousin. He shoved tobacco in a pipe with his thumb, then clamped the stem between his teeth. "It makes me jumpy, thinking that somebody else knows about our window into Bohemia. Somebody's widened the opening and, blast him, has turned that window into an open door."

"Troublesome," the wiry boy agreed. He leaned against the rope ladder running to the top of the main mast. "Not much we can do about it, though."

Treb scratched a match into a tiny flame and lit his pipe, puffing. "Do you think *he*"—he flicked his gaze meaningfully at the Bohemian boy—"knows why our secret seacoast now stretches right up to the doorstep of that village?"

"Guess you'd have to ask him. He seemed pretty clueless, though—wandering around on the hot sand dressed for winter, squinting at the sky like a rabbit coming out of its hole. My money says he didn't know what he was doing or where he was."

"How unusual for a *gadje*," Treb sneered. "But what if whoever widened that Loophole has his hands on the Celestial Globe? That seacoast's hardly common knowledge."

The boy shrugged. "Can't be the world's deepest, darkest secret either. Our people found it by accident. Sure as the sun rises, *somebody's* got that globe. Don't matter to me much, though, whether that somebody's the fellow who ripped open the Loophole or the emperor in his satin shoes or your pet parakeet."

"I don't have a parakeet, coz."

"Darn right you don't. Stupid birds. But you get my point."

Treb exhaled a cloud of smoke. "I certainly hope that the emperor doesn't have his old, dried-up fingers on the Celestial Globe. That'd make our job a lot harder."

"We'll find out soon enough who's got our toy. That's why I'm here, ain't it?"

"Right enough," Treb said. He ruffled the boy's hair and was rewarded with a grimace. "And I'm glad for it."

Treb's cousin stared up at the flag snapping in the wind and sighed.

"Something on your mind?" Treb asked. "Still upset we couldn't pay a call on your friend? I don't care how close she lives to the Loophole. Our mission's a secret one. You knew that when you came aboard. Anyway, she'd probably run screaming from the sight of a fierce crew of salty Gypsies."

"Not her."

"So that *is* what's got your rope twisted."

"Not exactly." The boy glanced at the starboard side of the ship, where Andras was smiling encouragingly as the *gadje* produced a perfect slipknot. "I'll be straight with you, Treb. I don't like the idea of selling that Bohemian at a slave market."

"Why ever shouldn't we?"

"Well, what'd we take him aboard for, if it wasn't to keep the

Loophole secret? We didn't want him spouting off to the Bohemian hill folk about it. So do we really want him telling his new master in Sallay?"

"He's not going to tell his new master anything. Somehow, I don't think he speaks Arabic."

"He seems like a quick study, though. Won't take him long to learn."

"Who cares if he does? By the time our blue-eyed angel knows how to say 'Yes, sir,' *we'll* have the globe, and *we'll* know where all the Loopholes in the world are, and how to get through them. Then it'll be fine by me if some Sallay gent knows how to find one hidden beach. And we'll earn a nice purse of gold for selling the boy." Treb frowned at his cousin. "You know all of this. And you're too canny to worry about it." He pulled the pipe from his lips and jabbed it at the boy. "Don't try to fool me, coz. I can see through playacting just as surely as I can spy a gull on the horizon. Something else is eating at you. Out with it."

"It's just . . . Treb, it isn't right. Our people were slaves once, long ago in the desert. What sense is it for us to sell somebody else on an auction block?"

Treb choked, coughing out smoke. "Oh, *laddie*." He pounded his chest. "And here I thought you were almost a man, not a wide-eyed baby still clinging to his ma's skirts. You feel *sorry* for our prize *gadje*? And what do you think he'd do in our shoes? What do you think all of Bohemia is doing to our people?" Treb's astonishment was turning into anger. "How many Roma have been locked up already in the jail cells of Salamander Castle? Where is Bohemia's mercy to *us*? You're lucky your clan left Prague a month ago. You shouldn't be whining over the fate of a *gadje*. You should be glad that your family's safe."

"Not my sis," the boy mumbled.

"It's thanks to her that we have the information we do. Who else has an inside look into the dealings of Salamander Castle? She's in a risky situation, to be sure, but she's doing her part. And don't worry: no one looking at her would guess she's a Roma. Sadie's lovely pale skin'll save her."

The boy shot his captain a dirty look.

"That was kindly meant, coz. Sadie's as much of my blood as you are. More, even."

The boy snarled, "So I'm only your cousin when you need me, is that it? And when you're searching for something to fling in my face, I'm just some foundling brat your aunt took in. I won't be both, so you better decide which way you want to see me, *coz.*" He began to stalk away.

Treb snagged him by the shoulder. "I didn't mean that. But Neel, *Neel,* don't fret over a *gadje* as if you were his nursemaid! I can't think straight when you talk so foolishly. You make me say things I regret. You've got a good heart, but it's misplaced. Remember, there's us and there's them. It's an ugly fact, but a true one, and as old as history. If you haven't learned that lesson yet, you'd better learn it now."

NEEL STOOD on the platform midway up the main mast, working the topsail. Next to him, Tas pulled and loosened the ropes, helping swing the sail into the right position to catch the wind.

It was a fine day. The wind was strong, and the salt air smelled so fresh Neel wanted to eat it. The muscles in his arms sprang up as he hauled on the sail.

With unease, Neel recalled his conversation with Treb, though he knew he shouldn't. If Treb had slipped and showed he thought his loony aunt from the Lovari tribe might have made some mistakes in having a half-*gadje* daughter and adopting a stranger's illegitimate son, Neel was used to this. Treb was only saying out loud what almost everybody thought. But what really got to Neel, and what made him grip the rope hard, was Treb's suggestion that he wasn't true to his people.

So Neel was in no mood to listen when Andras asked him for a favor.

Andras stood below on deck, his bald head and powerful shoulders gleaming in the sun. "Neel!" he hollered up the mast.

"Yeah?" Neel shouted back.

"I need you to do something."

"What?"

"Swap jobs with me."

"Huh? You're off duty."

"Well . . . I've been watching over the Bohemian."

"And you want to swap *that*? No way, Andras." Neel laughed. "I'd rather be working the topgallant sail. I'd rather be up in the crow's nest. I'd rather be in the *brig*, so long as that *gadje* wasn't in there with me."

"Oh, he's not half-bad."

Neel hooted.

"Honest." Andras spread his hands. "I wouldn't mind spending time with him, but he's real inquisitive. Keeps asking all kinds of questions, and my Czech's not good enough to understand even a small part of what he's saying. Poor lad's been swiped from his home. Least you could do is come down and explain to him what's going on."

"Nope. Not me."

Andras glared, his wrinkles cutting so deeply that they looked like scars. "I'm giving you an order."

"And you know where you can stick it."

"I outrank you!"

"I outsmart you."

Andras put his fists on his hips. "Don't make me come up there and shake you out of your tree."

"So Blue Eyes has got questions, does he? I should say so. But. I. Don't. Care. Find somebody else to hold his hand. I can't figure why you're bugging *me* to do it."

"You speak Czech better than anyone on this boat."

Neel shrugged and hauled on a rope. Treb spoke Czech as well as he did. Andras was just trying to flatter him. Well, it wouldn't work.

"*And*," Andras said with a wicked note in his voice, "we all know how fond you are of Bohemians. Why, who hasn't heard about your girl—"

"Friend!" Neel yelped. "She's a *friend*!"

"Ooo—ooo," Tas cooed.

Even the sailors clinging to the other mast were paying attention now.

"*Argh!*" Neel dropped the rope in his hands.

Tas swore, fumbling with his rope as the sail swung wide.

"Neel!" Treb was striding up the deck. "What in the name of the four tribes are you doing to my topsail?"

"Neel's distracted," Andras loudly explained. "He keeps thinking about—"

"Nothing!" Neel fastened the rope into place. "Andras, will you switch jobs with me?"

There was a pause.

"*Please?*" Neel begged.

Andras began climbing up the Jacob's ladder. When he reached the platform, he took over Neel's rope with a chuckle.

Neel said sourly, "For someone so old, your sense of needling others is right spry."

He flew down the ladder before Andras could laugh at him again.

• • •

"Oн." The blond boy's face hardened. "You."

Neel noted with satisfaction that the Bohemian was already burned by the sun. "That's right, Pinky. Looking red as a bloody dawn, you are. But a whole lot less prettier."

"I'm not talking to you. Get me somebody else."

"Is our prisoner making demands? You'll talk to who you can get, and be glad for it."

There was a pause. "I want to ask some questions."

"Get on with it, then."

"Yesterday, you said this ship is sailing for Morocco."

"Uh-huh."

"Where you're going to *sell* me."

"Yep."

"If I'm a prisoner, why did somebody let me out of my cage?"

"You mean the brig? That was Andras's idea. He talked Treb into it. Said you'd do no harm on deck during the day with the crew to keep an eye on you. Plus, we don't want you looking all pasty and sickly-like for the auction," Neel continued, ignoring the boy's staggered look. "That'd bring down your price. But we'll lock you up nice and tight each nightfall."

The Bohemian closed his eyes. "When will we reach Sallay?"

"A few days. Depending on the wind."

The boy's jewel-blue eyes flew open. "How is that possible? Yesterday I was in Bohemia. No boat can sail from Bohemia to Morocco in a matter of days. Of course, no boat could ever sail *anywhere* from Bohemia because we *have no seas!*"

"Well, that's what you get when you walk through a Loophole."

"Loophole?"

Neel studied him. "You really don't know how you ended up on that beach, do you?"

"A friend of mine's missing, in trouble."

"Looks like your pal ain't the only one."

"I tried searching the forest, but all I found was four headless monsters."

"Monsters? Are you telling tales?"

"Why would I lie? I mean, aside from the fact that you're a kidnapper who has ruined my life and definitely doesn't deserve the truth."

"Huh. *Monsters.*"

"Gray, scaly, and clawed."

Neel filed that information away to tell Treb. Slowly, he replied, "Look, I don't know anything about your beasties. But a Loophole's like . . . a shortcut. A way of hopping from one place to another. One minute you're in a Bohemian forest, the next you're off the northern coast of Portugal, not far away from North Africa, on a speedy ship like the *Pacolet*. There are Loopholes all over the world, but they're hard to find. Going through one's like threading a needle blind. You can't miss it by even a hair. My people happened upon your Loophole by accident, ages ago. We're a roaming sort, so we've discovered a couple of other shortcuts like this. It's rare for a fellow to just stumble through a Loophole, like you did. Guess you got lucky." Neel smirked.

A small, black-haired girl ran up the deck and dashed between them. Laughing, she raced along the bow and turned around to sprint to the other end of the ship. She pattered away.

Neel felt suddenly somber. "Are we done playing ask-and-answer? I've got work."

"One more thing . . . " The *gadje* gazed after the girl. "Why are there children on this boat? Babies, even? That girl's no more than three years old. I've seen old people on this ship, families . . . they can't be sailors. Don't they get in your way?"

"They do. But that ain't the point."

"So Sea-Gypsies always travel with their families?"

"Most of them aren't our relations. Look, Pinky"—Neel's voice sharpened—"there's plenty in this world you don't know a bit about. Your precious, white, mighty prince—"

The *gadje* raised his hand. "I hate his guts."

"Oh. Good. Because that sunken wreck of a human took it into his head to lock all us Roma up and swallow the key. Happened real sudden. Not a lot we could do about it, but we did what we could. The Maraki—the Roma tribe you so sweetly call 'Sea-Gypsies'—sent word for the free Roma in Bohemia to slip through the Loophole to the beach and gather there. The families on board had to leave behind their wagons and horses and I don't know what all." His throat tightened. He cleared it. "Treb and I had just loaded the last of 'em onto the *Pacolet* and rowed back to the beach in the launch to clean up. Wanted to hide any trace of campsites. No need for the Portuguese to notice something special about that stretch of sand. That beach is *our* secret. We were ready to leave when you turned up, and if you'd stepped through that Loophole fifteen minutes later, you and I never would have laid eyes on each other."

There was a pause. "Like you said," murmured the *gadje*, "I guess I was just lucky."

7

Madinia and Margaret

PLIP. PLIP. PLIP.

Petra opened her eyes, which were gummy from long sleep.

She felt something squirming on her neck. At first she thought it was Astrophil, but the sensation felt nothing like the cold prickle of his legs. It felt . . . fleshy.

Petra's brain seemed to be trying to tell her that the *plip-plip* sound had something to do with whatever was crawling on her neck—and, she realized, on her arm. She glanced down and gasped.

Fat black leeches teemed over her left arm. As she stared, one of them wriggled and dropped off, falling into a bowl placed next to the bed. *Plip.*

Petra reached to crush the insects, but someone caught her hand. A short, gray-haired man shook his head at her. Then he pointed to the leeches and smiled.

"What are you doing to me?" Petra shouted. "Get them *off!*"

The old man shook his head again, and replied in a language that sounded like hissing snakes.

English, Petra thought with a groan. She pulled weakly against the man's grip.

He *tsk*ed at her. He let her go, but then quickly doused a handkerchief with a strong-smelling liquid. He clamped the cloth over her nose and mouth.

Petra sank back into sleep.

Below her bed, Astrophil waited, growing hungrier as the days passed.

SOMEONE WAS STROKING Petra's hair. Only two people had ever done this: Dita and her father. Maybe her mother had, too, but Petra couldn't remember. She had been only a baby when her mother died.

Petra opened her eyes.

A woman was sitting next to the bed. Her hair was white, pulled back into a simple twist, but her skin was unlined. Her face held no expression. There was no tug of a lip, lift of a cheek, or furrow of a brow.

"Hello," the woman said in a flat voice. "I'm Agatha."

Petra, I am so relieved you are awake. You have been asleep for several days. Astrophil's words buzzed in Petra's mind. *I was so worried.*

Where are you?

I am hiding under the bed. It is very dusty. I do not think highly of the Dees' housekeeper.

Petra glanced at her left arm. The leeches were gone. The welts left by the touch of the Gristleki were healed, but fresh, fierce, and red.

She turned to Agatha. "There was a man here . . ."

"Yes. Dr. Harvey."

"He put *leeches* on me."

"He used them to suck the poison out of your blood."

"Who are you?"

"Agatha," the woman repeated. "Agatha Dee."

"Agatha *Dee*?"

"Yes. John Dee's wife."

I don't like her, Petra told Astrophil.

Petra, would you try to like her enough to ask for a favor? Because—the spider's voice grew embarrassed—*I am extremely hungry.*

Petra bolted upright. *Oh, Astro! You haven't had any oil in days! I'm so sorry, I can't believe I didn't think of this right away. You might have died.*

You might have, too, the spider said gently.

"Agatha?" Petra leaned toward the woman. "Could I have some brassica oil? Please."

"Is something the matter?"

"No, nothing. But I need brassica. A large jug of it. Now."

The woman's face betrayed no surprise at this unusual request. She walked to the door, unlocked it, and murmured to someone in the hallway. She turned back to Petra. "It will be brought to you shortly." She locked the door. "I am glad you are well," she said, though her voice sounded empty of any gladness, "and that I am able to help you."

Petra thought that Agatha might mean something more than fetching brassica oil. "Help me?" Hope fluttered inside her. "Will you help me get back to Okno?"

"No. I am here at my husband's request. He asked me to teach you English."

"Oh," Petra said resentfully. She knew what this meant. It meant that Dee intended Petra to stay in London for some time. "So when are you going to force the first lesson down my throat?"

Agatha Dee didn't seem offended, if only because she didn't seem *anything*. "It's done. You already know English."

"I—*what?*"

"Yes. You're speaking English now. You have no trace of a Czech accent. You know every word I do."

"You . . . used magic? Teaching—it's your gift?"

Agatha nodded.

How was Petra ever going to get away from *four* magically talented Dees? She frowned. "I'm surprised that Dee didn't make me learn English the hard way."

Agatha reached to lift Petra's chin. "Why do that, when everything else will be so hard?"

"LOOK AT THAT SCAR . . ."

Petra touched her neck and turned, her ponytail swinging over her shoulder. Her silver eyes measured the two girls. "The poison didn't damage my hearing."

"It might have done something to your fashion sense, though," said the freckled girl, raking her gaze over the trousers Petra had worn the day of the attack.

Petra crossed her arms, brandishing the burnlike wound that reached up to her elbow. "Why are you here?" she demanded. Speaking English felt effortless, like walking without thinking about the fact that her entire body was doing a balancing act with every step. "Do you want a tour of my jail cell? There's that awful bed I was stuck in for days, there's the chair in which I was interrogated by your interfering father—"

"And over there's a mirror"—the freckled girl pointed—"that you might think about using."

"Madinia," her sister murmured.

"What? Don't look at me like that, Meggie. The first step to recovering from an abysmal lack of style is to admit that you have a problem. I'm only trying to help."

"You Dees have a funny idea of *help*," Petra snapped.

"We just wanted to introduce ourselves, Petra," the quiet sister said. "I'm Margaret."

The freckled girl stuck out her hand. "Madinia." She waited for Petra to shake it. When Petra didn't, Madinia plopped down into the nearest chair, her silk skirts spilling around her. "Wasn't that a freakish scene in the forest? Petra, you should have seen it! Too bad you were passed out. But our dad was right in the thick of things, swinging away like a master swordsman. Those gray creatures were as skin-crawlingly creepy as anything I'd ever seen, but I wasn't afraid at all. Not a jot!"

"I was," said Margaret.

"Poor Meg! I know what you're thinking, but you shouldn't blame yourself. Why, anyone could have made the same mistake. *I* wasn't petrified out of my wits, but *anybody* could have—"

"Madinia!" Margaret turned a furious gaze on her sister. "You have no wits!"

"That is *so* unfair! Why're you—?" Madinia glanced at Petra, then back at Margaret. "Oh."

"What mistake?" Petra asked. "What're you talking about?"

"Nothing," said Madinia.

"Maybe I'll mention this conversation, then, the next time I speak to your father."

"Please don't do that," said Margaret. "I made an error, but we fixed it. No harm done."

"We think," said Madinia.

"You know, if you hadn't been so excited—"

"If you hadn't been as jumpy as a tail-stepped cat—"

"This room is *my* jail cell," Petra interrupted. "Give me an answer or get out of it."

Margaret took a deep breath. "Madinia's magic can tear holes in space. Mine can close them."

"Old news."

Madinia was offended. "They are rare gifts."

"And the odds are very, very small that a person who can create a Rift will know someone who can sew it back up," Margaret added.

"A Rift?" Petra asked.

"Oh, that's just one of the many words people use," Madinia said. "They're also called Gates—"

"Or Lacunae," her sister supplied.

"—Loopholes—"

"—Portals—"

"—Alleys—"

"So?" said Petra.

"So," Margaret replied, "over the centuries, people with Madinia's magic have left Rifts all over the world. And they can be dangerous. Imagine what would happen if somebody was riding a horse across the French countryside and galloped right into the Indian Ocean. Or what if the Ottoman army was marching through the desert and then suddenly walked into London's Smithfield?"

"They'd be crushed by our forces!" Madinia thumped her fist on the arm of the chair.

"If the Rifts are such a big problem," Petra said, "why don't you just travel the world and close all of them?"

"I'm not a *maid*," said Margaret. "I've got enough work cleaning up after Madinia. Anyway, Rifts are very hard to find. It'd be like searching for one particular leaf in a forest. Even so, Dad says I must always close up a Rift Madinia makes, just in case. But . . . when we went to rescue you, Madinia and I screwed things up."

For a moment, Madinia looked like she might protest her innocence, but then she said, "Dad pinpointed your location, Petra. I was supposed to tear a gateway to it. But I didn't know that there was already a Rift, an ancient one, close by. Look at the weak cloth of your trousers. See that hole? Well, what would happen if you made a new hole right next to it? *Rip*. You'd end up with one roaringly big gap."

"Once we stepped through"—Margaret twisted her fingers together—"and saw the Gray Men, all I could think of was getting out of Bohemia. I forgot to patch up the Rift. Or maybe I wouldn't let myself remember because I was such a coward."

"You were just rattled," her sister consoled.

"Be glad you were unconscious," Margaret whispered to Petra. "It was a terrible thing to see."

"I saw enough," said Petra.

"Anyway"—Madinia sat up straight—"maybe we slipped up, but we fixed the problem. We snuck out of the house a couple of days ago. We went back to the forest—your country's shriekingly cold, Petra!—and Meg sewed up the Rift. The whole thing. Even the gap that was there before I magicked it. So, no problem."

"Nothing you need to tell our father about, Petra," Margaret said. "Please? Because Madinia and I came to see you for another reason."

"Dad wants to chat with you in his library," Madinia told Petra. "You're so lucky! He never lets *us* in there."

Petra looked at the sisters, considering. She said, "You wouldn't have to worry about me keeping your secret if you sent me home."

"We can't do that," said Margaret.

"Our dad would punish us!" Madinia protested. "We wouldn't be allowed to leave the house for the rest of our lives, and the winter ball is just around the corner!" She frowned at Petra. "I think you're very selfish to even suggest that we do such a thing."

Margaret said, "We're not going to send you back to Bohemia. We know it's not safe for you there."

"Yes," Madinia chimed in. "That, too! We saved your life, remember? I think you owe us a little confidentiality."

Petra reflected. "I'll keep your secret," she promised, deciding that if she had learned anything from her past encounters with Dee, it was that hidden information is a powerful weapon.

At this thought, her hand strayed to her left hip.

There was nothing there. The sword was gone.

With panic, Petra realized she had been so distracted by poison, leeches, and Astrophil's hunger, she hadn't noticed that her sword was missing. Had it been lost in the forest? Had Dee taken it?

"You said that Dee wants to see me," Petra said urgently.

"Kind of immediately," Madinia replied. "He said it's important."

"We're supposed to show you the way to his library," Margaret added.

Petra nodded. "I'll go. But I need a minute alone."

"I hope it's to make yourself look a little less grotty," Madinia said.

Margaret nudged her sister. "We'll wait for you in the hall, Petra."

When the door shut behind them, Petra called softly, "Astrophil?"

The spider slipped out from under the bed. His eyes glowed a deep green from the brassica oil he had gulped down an hour ago.

Petra walked over to the mirror. She told herself she wouldn't flinch no matter what she saw. She looked in the mirror, and stood still.

There were shadows under her eyes, and a long, thin red weal stretched from her left collarbone to her jaw. The scar was an almost perfectly straight line. Almost.

At the base of her throat, the scar was interrupted by a horizontal curve of untouched, pale flesh. Something had protected her skin from the Gristleki's burning tongue.

My necklace, she realized, and touched the white line where the leather cord had been. Losing the necklace was the least of her worries, but Petra still bit back a sob. Would she lose everything that she cared about?

Astrophil was walking up her leg. He leaped to her elbow. *Look at me, Petra.*

She did.

We will find a way to return to Okno, the spider said. *I promise.*

Petra attempted a smile, but it flickered and died. She pulled the tie from her ponytail and shook her brown hair over her shoulders, hiding the scar.

Astrophil crawled up, and perched on her right ear. *I think you look lovely with your hair down, anyway.*

"Hmph," was Petra's reply.

8

Ariel

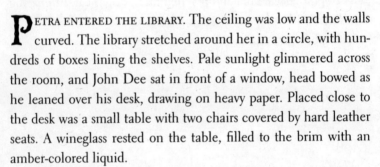

PETRA ENTERED THE LIBRARY. The ceiling was low and the walls curved. The library stretched around her in a circle, with hundreds of boxes lining the shelves. Pale sunlight glimmered across the room, and John Dee sat in front of a window, head bowed as he leaned over his desk, drawing on heavy paper. Placed close to the desk was a small table with two chairs covered by hard leather seats. A wineglass rested on the table, filled to the brim with an amber-colored liquid.

John Dee looked up. "Sit there, Petra." He pointed a long-nailed finger at the table. "I will attend to you shortly." He dropped the thick charcoal pencil from his hand and reached for a thinner one. He bent again over the paper. His hand moved in little tics now, as if he were adding detail.

Go on, Petra, Astrophil encouraged. *I do not wish to be here any more than you do, but we will get nowhere locked up in that bedroom.*

Petra slowly crossed the room and sat in one of the chairs.

For several minutes, there was no sound except the scratching of Dee's pencil on paper. Finally, he set the pencil on the desk. "Drink the wine."

She hesitated.

"My dear, would I bother saving your life only to drug or poison you later? You are still weak from your illness. The wine will do you good."

Petra sipped the thick liquid. It slid down, heating her throat. It was delicious, and she was surprised to find that her wounds throbbed a little less. She drank again. The wine tasted like honey.

Dee turned away, and went to stand behind his desk. He looked out a frosted window. "Well," he began, his breath fogging the glass as if his words had a life of their own. "What are we going to do with you?"

This seemed like a trick question to Petra.

"I have been trying to sketch your character." He plucked the paper from his desk. "It is incomplete, to be sure, yet I judge my illustration to be a fair one. Would you like to see it?"

Petra pushed away the wine. She shook her head.

He came close and slid the drawing in front of her. What she saw made her knock over the wineglass and spring to her feet. "You *thief*!"

"I thought you *liked* thieves. One Roma boy in particular. And did you not become a thief yourself when you broke into Prince Rodolfo's Cabinet of Wonders?"

"Give it back!"

On the paper, bleeding golden wine, was a drawing of a rapier-like sword.

"Your father," said Dee, "is a man of extraordinary talent."

"Don't you dare—"

Petra, Astrophil interrupted. *My English is embarrassingly rusty, so perhaps I have misunderstood something. I know grammar is not your favorite subject, but would you tell me if John Dee just used the tense I think he did? The present tense?*

" 'Is'?" Petra whispered.

Dee nodded.

"You're sure my father *is* alive?"

He nodded again.

Petra sank back into the chair. Dee sat across from her.

"Do not bother asking for more information," he said. "I will not give it to you. Yet."

"Then why am I here?" Petra said dully. "So that you can play with my head? Why don't you just scry me, then, and scramble my brain for good?"

"I have no intention of doing such a thing," he snapped. He paused, and seemed to gather his thoughts. "Petra, you are astonishing. Not only because of the talent I believe you possess, but because you are so stubbornly blind to it. If I compare you to your father's sword, it is because you are equally rare. I command many men and women—"

"Spies."

"—and I doubt I could name one who would be able to accomplish what you did last autumn. Though, I grant you, they would have failed with far less noise than you caused with your success. I asked you to meet me today because I wish to make a trade."

She waited.

"I would like to satisfy my curiosity about you," he continued, "and I need your help in obtaining answers. It will require a ritual, and it will be dangerous, but you will be safe if you promise to obey my instructions. If you are not willing to do so, you shall place both our lives in jeopardy. For your obedience, I will trade *this*." He tapped the wine-soaked drawing.

"The sword already belongs to me."

He smiled. "Finders, keepers."

Petra looked at the sketch. The golden liquid had warped the lines of the sword. "I want my sword back in the *exact* condition it was in when I arrived. I'll know if it's been damaged."

"Of course."

"And it'll be *mine*. I can use it whenever I want, wherever I want. You can't take it back."

"I wouldn't dream of it. I honor my word."

"Then can we just do this ritual thing and get it over with? What do I have to do?"

"In the future, Petra, you might try to learn the details of a bargain *before* you agree to it. Just friendly advice. As for the ritual, it involves summoning a spirit. I have questions to ask concerning you. I will ask them of Ariel."

"Who's Ariel?"

"*What* is Ariel," he corrected.

"*What* is your problem? Can't you answer a simple question?"

He sighed. "There are four kinds of spirits, one for each element: earth, air, fire, and water. Ariel is a spirit of the air, and air is a tangle of several noteworthy things: change, dance, song, and knowledge. Yes, knowledge. For much of what people know is heard or said. Words are breathed, and anything spoken out loud is heard by air spirits. This includes history, prophecies, and rumors. Ariel might know what we do not, or confirm what I suspect."

He waited, but Petra didn't ask the obvious question. She wasn't sure she really wanted to know whatever it was that Dee suspected about her. "Can you consult any kind of spirit?"

"No. Most don't come when you call, and if they do, they make certain you regret it. Ariel is under an obligation to me. I rescued it. If I call, it will come. Now, Petra, follow me into the center of this room."

She let Dee lead the way, for she didn't want to walk at his side. But she couldn't help being curious. "How did you save Ariel?"

"Ariel angered a water spirit by dancing itself into a tempest off the coast of an Atlantic island, sucking the sea high up into the air. When Ariel tired of dancing, the water spirit imprisoned it inside a bubble of sea spray, which I burst. Stay here, Petra." She stood in the center of the room as Dee walked to a bookshelf. He tucked one box under his arm and opened another, a deep square one. He reached inside the shelved box and brought out his fist. Glittery powder trailed from his closed fingers. He began to draw a circle around Petra with the dust.

He stepped inside the circle and opened the box he carried with him. Inside was a feather, matches, and a small, brown lump of incense. He passed the feather to Petra, then struck a match and lit the incense, setting it on the ground. He gestured at the twinkling line bending around him and Petra. "Dust from a fallen comet," he explained. "Understand, Petra, that Ariel doesn't need stardust or feathers or incense to find its way here. These objects are not even purely associated with air. After all, even birds must land on the earth from time to time. I use these objects to help *me* concentrate. They are helpful only because I *consider* them to be allied with the air, not because this is wholly true."

In spite of herself, Petra was intrigued.

"Ariel knows all languages," Dee continued. "We will both know what it is saying. But that doesn't mean we will be able to *understand* the words we hear. Clarity isn't Ariel's strong suit."

Smoke from the burning incense spiraled into the air. He looked at it, swept his gaze along the curve of comet dust, and glanced at the feather in Petra's hand. "One last thing," he said. "*Be silent.* I cannot stress this enough. You might not like taking orders from me, but I assure you that you'll like it even less if Ariel rips you into bloody shreds and scatters the pieces to the four winds."

Dee stood still, closed his eyes, and began to murmur.

After several minutes of this, Petra fidgeted.

This is quite fascinating, Astrophil commented.

I'm glad one of us is entertained.

Petra, it would be to your advantage to pay attention. Do you realize that Dee must be an extremely powerful sorcerer?

He's an extremely powerful pain in the—

Witnessing this spell is an opportunity I doubt you would have even if you attended the Academy. Have you not noticed that Dee seems to be trying to teach you?

Teach me what? How to close my eyes and speak nonsense? Because I can do that already. The only thing he's done since we walked into this room is to try messing with my mind.

Yes . . . but he seems to be doing it in a very, hmm, instructive way.

They broke off their conversation, for a blue-green light began to gleam in front of Dee. It grew larger, sparking like a candle sprinkled with pepper. It stretched taller and swelled, and then it took a shape that made Petra blink.

Hovering before her and John Dee was a creature that was half woman, half dragonfly. Her turquoise hair streamed in stormy ribbons, and a set of wings flowed from her elbows. From the waist down, her body tapered into a point that looked as sharp as a shimmering blue-green needle.

"Ariel is a she!" Petra was startled. "She isn't an it or a what!"

"Shh," said Dee. "Ariel, tell me about the girl."

"Sutton Hoo," chimed the dragonfly-woman.

"And she doesn't speak Czech," Petra continued. "Or English. Dee, you spin a fancy tale but that doesn't make you anything other than a liar!"

"Sutton Hoo is a place in England," Dee told Petra. "Now *be quiet.*"

"King of the air-swimmers," Ariel hummed, "changed into gold."

"Yeah," Petra muttered. "This is *really* helpful. Bet all your questions are answered now, Dee."

"*Petra Kronos,*" Dee said sharply. "You will anger Ariel if you cannot be still and listen! If you care nothing for your own life, show some respect for mine!"

Petra snorted. Then she began to giggle uncontrollably.

Petra, Astrophil said shakily. *Do calm down. I can spare a few legs, but you only have two, and they work best when attached to your body.*

Dee gripped Petra's shoulder. The urgency on his face only made her laugh harder.

Ariel chuckled, too. "Chimera," she said.

"She is?" Dee asked.

Petra stopped laughing. She stepped away from Dee.

"Chimera," Ariel repeated. "A silver-singer. A dream-thinker." She cocked her head and looked slyly at Petra, her snaky hair twisting. "Murder, betrayal, black teeth, a tree dressed in robes, the heavens pressed into a ball, a dirty metal river." Her last word was a hiss: "Assassin."

She drifted close to Petra, and she raised her wings around the girl's head, shielding her from Dee's sight. Ariel's mouth drew close to Petra's left ear, where Astrophil clung. Petra stiffened. Would Ariel tell Dee about him? Petra needed to keep the spider hidden from the spy. Dee had proven months ago in Salamander Castle that he would threaten someone she loved for his own ends, and Petra refused to risk Astrophil's safety.

The chill of Ariel's skin rippled off her in icy waves. Petra shivered, stared at the blue-green wings, and didn't know what to do.

"Greetings, web-spinner," Ariel whispered.

"Hello." Astrophil's voice was tiny.

"Secret-keeper, heed my words and save your lady: never trust a poet."

Ariel lowered her wings. Petra was relieved when the spirit turned to Dee and breathed no word of the spider, saying only, "Liberty for truth is a fair exchange, deep-searcher."

He nodded. "Go, then."

The spirit wrapped her dragonfly wings around her body, dwindled into a slender oval, thinned to a point of light, and vanished.

"Well." Dee stuffed his hands inside his pockets. He began to pace, his feet breaking the circle of stardust. "Ariel seems to like you, Petra, though *why* is beyond my comprehension. You reckless fool. *Laughing* at Ariel. Do you think I invent threats for my own amusement? Why can't you heed a simple word of warning?"

"Why should I believe anything you say?"

Dee stopped abruptly.

"I was laughing at *you*," Petra said.

Dee opened his mouth, but then shut it.

"Anyway, Ariel wasn't at all like you said," Petra continued. "There were no tempests. And Ariel *is* a she," Petra returned to her earlier point. "Kind of insecty, but definitely a she."

" 'It' is more appropriate. Ariel doesn't always look like that. It appeared that way because of you. Because of what you are."

Petra raised an eyebrow. "I'm a dragonfly?"

"You are a chimera."

"Right. And is a chimera someone who kicks her captor in the shins, causing him to fall down, conk his head, and lose his memory, making him forget that he was ever a pompous sneak? Because that *does* sound an awful lot like me."

"Petra, sit down. There are things we must discuss."

"No. There are games you want to play, and I'm sick of it."

"No more games." Dee reached for his waist and seemed to unbuckle the air. He offered his empty hands to her.

She took the invisible sword, and the weight of it calmed her a little.

"I ask you again to sit, Petra. Allow me to explain what you are, for truly there are few of your kind in this world."

9

Riddles

"I HAVE A BROTHER with four legs and a big hat," said one of the children sitting in a circle at the stern of the ship. "What's his name?"

"Too easy!" cried a boy in a red shirt. "Everybody knows that one! It's a table!"

Parents hovered near their children as they challenged one another with riddles. A few feet away, the *gadje* sat cross-legged, staring intently at the cluster of people. Two sailors worked close by. Klara was coiling rope and Brishen was scrubbing dried fish scales off the deck, but they both listened to the children's game.

"I've got one," Klara said, flicking back her braids. "My sister is tiny, thin, and has a long tail that trails behind her."

"I know," Brishen said, "it's a—"

Klara elbowed him.

He gave her a guilty look. "A squid?" He winked at her.

"A *squid*?" the children yelled. "It's not a squid!" "What kind of idiot would think *that*?" "Brishen, you've been out in the sun too long!"

"Maybe, maybe," he said. "But what is it, then?"

They fell silent. Then one girl raised a timid hand. "Um, Klara, is your sister . . . a needle?"

"That's right!" Klara sang.

Neel was watching this from a distance, his arms folded across his chest as he leaned against the port side of the ship. He noticed that the blond boy was running his fingers absentmindedly through a patch of sand by his feet, but his gaze never wavered from the riddlers. Neel wondered what the *gadje* found so interesting about a game he couldn't possibly understand. The children continued to chatter in Romany.

"My sister has a big belly, two long hairpins, and rocks herself to sleep every night."

"A ship!"

"I have a brother," began the boy in the red shirt, "who has many round eyes and a mouth that opens sideways. He has a home wherever he goes."

There was a pause. Neel guessed what the answer was. Judging by the faraway looks on the parents' faces, they were thinking the same thing.

Everyone was astonished when the *gadje* cleared his throat. His accent was thick, but he spoke in perfect Romany: "Is it a wagon?"

"I THINK HE'S CUTE." Klara chewed on a dried carrot.

"You would," Ashe said. She passed the flatbread down the table. "Cradle-robber."

A few men looked up from their stew, alarmed by this conversation.

"Not *that* kind of cute," Klara said. "Cute like a little lamb. A lamb who says, 'I is thirsty. May have tar to drink?' "

The Maraki chuckled.

A young boy set down his bowl of stew. He grinned, showing baby-tooth gaps. "He asked me how to say 'I'd like bread to eat.' I told him the Romany words for that are 'I slurp fish guts raw.' "

Nicolas reached across the table to muss his hair. "Good lad."

Andras sliced a lemon. He bit into a wedge and pulled the yellow rind from his teeth. "Don't know why you're all mocking one of the few *gadje* who's actually trying to learn our language."

"A dog can sit and beg," said Neel. "Doesn't make him a man."

"What's he trying to learn Romany for, anyway?" someone asked.

"He's sucking up to us."

"He's just trying to get by."

"He's plotting something," said Neel. "That's what I'd do."

A father of five whose family had been rescued by the *Pacolet* remarked, "I don't like the boy any more than most of you, but I still can't believe we're *selling* him. Our people don't do that. When in the history of the Roma have we ever traded slaves?"

Everyone looked at Treb. "New times"—he tossed a raisin in his mouth—"new measures."

"We could just keep him on board, Treb." Brishen leaned forward. "He's young and fit. He'd know the ropes soon enough. He doesn't complain, and he seems like a helpful sort."

"All part of the act," Neel said. "I'm Lovari. I'd know."

"Not everyone's as underhanded as you," said Nadia. "Just because you broke into the Bohemian prince's toy chest and can never shut up about it doesn't mean—"

"Neel saved his clan with those stolen jewels." Andras pointed a carrot at her.

"Well, while we're discussing people who don't belong, why don't we talk about *him*?" Nadia retorted. "Neel's Lovari! He said so himself! Why is he suddenly one of us now?"

"Nadia," Brishen whispered, casting his eyes at the Loophole Beach families, "show some tact. Not everyone here is from our tribe."

She bit her lip. "I didn't mean—all I meant is that Neel is

counted as one of the *Pacolet*'s crew. He gets a vote in our deci-sions, just as if he were Maraki. But he *isn't*."

"Neel's here as a favor to me," Treb said. "End of story. Now, as for the Bohemian lad, I want one thing as clear as a rain-washed sky. There will be no vote on his fate. I'm your captain, and what I say on this matter goes. Tomorrow we'll arrive in Sallay. We'll sell him in the market, and he'll fetch a fine price, too. Then we'll stock the *Pacolet*'s larders and sail on. If some of you have gotten fond of him, that's not my problem. I warned you not to. That lit-tle lamb's for eating."

TOMIK'S CELL was darker than dark. The brig was at the very bot-tom of the ship, in the hold. He wondered what was swimming on the other side of the hull's wooden wall: sharks, whales, or just a school of tiny fish startled by the great ship sailing past them? He imagined the fish darting away, their scales flashing.

On Tomik's first day aboard the *Pacolet*, he threw up. Repeat-edly. He felt like his stomach was trying to crawl up his throat, and his brain sloshed in his head. When Andras unlocked his cell door and led him up onto the deck, Tomik was stunned by the sunlight. The wind stole his seasickness and flew away. From that time for-ward, he spent every minute he could on deck, letting his skin soak up the salty air. He studied the ship, trying to understand how the sails worked. He listened to the crew, learning their language. He tried fishing, though that wasn't a success.

Tomik could almost fall in love with life aboard a ship. In differ-ent circumstances. *Very* different circumstances.

On hands and knees, he felt his way across his cell. In one cor-ner there was a bowl of food. In another, a chamber pot. During his first night of captivity, Tomik had confused the two, which wasn't very pleasant. But tonight he didn't crawl in the direction of either corner.

His fingers brushed against a small pile of sand. Sitting up straight, he emptied his pockets and felt more grains sifting down onto the pile. It wasn't much, but it would have to be enough. Andras had said they would reach Sallay tomorrow.

Tomik pressed the sand under his hands. He wasn't sure if this would work. He had no fire. But, then again, he did have the heat of his will.

THE MORNING BEGAN with an argument. Two sailors were yelling at another one. Finally, Treb stepped in, pushing the three apart.

"They're fighting over you," said a voice at Tomik's side. It was the boy from the beach, the one who spoke Czech so well. "Klara and Brishen just refused to be part of the group taking you to the slave market. Seems to offend their delicate natures."

Tomik shrugged. "People don't like slaughtering livestock, but they'll eat the meat."

"You ain't the first to make a comparison like that, little lamb."

"Stop using nicknames. It's just something you do so you can forget I'm a human being."

"Why no, Pinky. I call things as I see them. Anyway, you never did tell me your name."

"Like you care," Tomik scoffed. He walked to the railing of the ship and looked out. He was transfixed by what he saw.

The boy went to stand next to him. "Oh. Sallay."

The sea was bursting against the rocks around the harbor. The port bristled with ships, and their masts thrust into the sky like a forest of tall trees. "There are so many boats," Tomik murmured.

"Plenty of rigs," the Gypsy agreed. "You got every kind of ship in that port: carracks, caravels, galleons, pinks, junks, snows, lateens—"

"Are all the sailors on those ships like you?"

"What d'you mean? You mean, are they all Roma? Nah. But most of us who dock in Sallay are trying to see where we can pick up extra gold on the waves."

"Pirates."

"Not many sailors like that word, and those who own up to it . . . well, you don't want to meet *them*. The ones who stop lying to themselves are the real danger." The boy worriedly rubbed his forehead. "Look, I'm not jumping for joy at the thought of selling you. It's not the way I think things should be. But Treb's our captain, and it's his call. Doesn't mean he lacks a heart, though. Him and me have got business to attend to in the city, but before we do that we'll make sure to find you a good home. We won't set you up on the auction block. We'll ask around, see where the slaves are happy. I'll sort it out with Treb. He owes me."

Tomik made no reply.

"And I'm sorry," the Gypsy muttered. "For whatever it's worth."

"Not much," said Tomik.

THE *GADJE* WAS QUIET as the small group of Maraki walked along the dock. His hands were bound behind his back with a cord of stout rope. Treb had tied the knots himself, since Andras had given him a dark look when asked. The sailors made their way into the market, which sprang up just beyond the docks that brought so much trade.

If you could name it, you could buy it here: camels, indigo, American corn, eastern jade, weaponry, spices—and people.

Neel had been to North Africa before, but never to a city that hummed with so much life, with scents that he wanted to bury his face in, and wares that were so tempting. He was just thinking about stealing some fruit when Tas shouted, "He's gone! The *gadje* disappeared!"

The sailors halted.

"What do you mean, he *disappeared*?" Treb bellowed. The Maraki scanned their surroundings. The Bohemian had vanished. "You were supposed to be watching *him*, not the Persian silver and the Moroccan ladies, you lackwits!"

"But he was tied up!"

"Nope." Neel bent to pick up the frayed rope. "He sawed through it."

"With *what*?" Treb raged. "His fingernails? One of you slipped him a knife, you sad, worthless, pathetic lot of guppies!"

Neel examined the rope. There was blood on it. Ignoring the Maraki as they traded blame, he scanned the ground and saw a drop of red in the dust a few feet to the left.

He squeezed past people, searching for blond hair amid the bobbing river of dark heads. He was beginning to worry that he had followed the wrong trail when, several stalls ahead, someone knocked over a cage of birds. Amid the squawking, Neel heard the stall owner cry in Arabic, "Get back here, you white devil!"

Neel sped up, sprinting past Turkish rugs piled several feet deep. Finally, he spotted it: the yellow head of the *gadje*, dashing behind a donkey.

Neel could run quickly, but he had an even more valuable talent. The tips of his fingers itched. As he shouldered past the donkey, Neel felt his fingers begin to grow. To anybody's eyes, even his, Neel's hands seemed to be the same length as always, but they stretched invisibly beyond his bitten nails. Neel's ghost fingers unfurled, reached forward, snagged the back of the *gadje*'s shirt, and hauled him close.

The boy wheeled around and punched him in the face.

Neel staggered back. His head reeled in pain, but his ghost fingers didn't let go. Feeling the Bohemian twist against a grasp far stronger than Neel could ever have with mere flesh and bone, he blinked and tried to focus. "You rotten little—!" The words died in his throat as his vision cleared.

The *gadje* was holding a knife. It was as clear as ice.

"I don't want to—I want—" the Bohemian stammered. "I just want to get out of here!" He slashed the knife down on Neel's arm.

Blood spurted. Shocked, Neel let go but then toppled into the *gadje*, knocking him to the dirt. The two boys struggled against each other, shoving and kicking. Dazed, Neel was wondering which way was up and where, exactly, the knife had gone, when several hands pulled him away.

The Maraki surrounded them. Andras grasped the *gadje*, who was smeared with Neel's blood. Treb supported Neel.

"He took a bite out of you," Treb muttered to Neel in Romany. He pulled aside the torn flap of Neel's sleeve, exposing the long, throbbing knife cut. "You all right?"

Neel tried to stand up straight. He turned away from Treb to glance at the *gadje*, whose shirt had also been ripped open. The blond head hung down. Suddenly, it jerked up, and gave Neel a glare that was equal parts hate and misery.

A look like that might have struck Neel to the heart, but he was distracted by something else: a small metallic object was swinging from the Bohemian's neck.

It was a miniature horseshoe.

Neel's ghost fingers seized the *gadje*'s throat. "Where did you get *that*?"

10

The Owl of Sallay

"**B**ELONG—MY FRIEND—" the *gadje* choked. "Petra."

"How did *you* get that necklace?" Neel demanded. "Where is she?"

"Don't know—"

"Neel! Let him go!" Andras ordered.

"Who are you?" Neel shook the boy.

"Tomik," he gasped.

Neel's ghost fingers snapped open.

"My name is Tomas Stakan." The Bohemian rubbed his throat. "Tomik, for short."

Tomik. Neel knew that name. Petra had always said it with a homesick sound in her voice. Tomik had made the magical glass spheres that saved Neel and Petra as they escaped from the prince's castle. With a hand pressed on his bleeding arm, Neel scuffed the market dust with his sandal, and his toes knocked against something hard. He crouched down and brushed away the bloody dirt. The knife was gleaming and clear, its hilt rounded and smooth, its blade small but wicked. A knife made out of *glass*? Neel glanced at Tomik, and felt a grudging respect.

"We can't sell him, Treb," said Neel.

"Why ever not?"

"Because he already belongs to a friend of mine."

ANDRAS CINCHED A STRIP of cloth around Neel's arm.

"You sure are a sorry sight, little cousin," Treb said. "The right side of your face is as raw as fresh meat, and whether you like scars or not, that cut on your arm'll be a keeper. It hurts to look at you."

"No one asked you to." Neel leaned back against a leather pillow.

"Here." Treb handed him an earthenware cup of coffee.

Neel sipped, looking across the tent at Tomik, encircled by the Maraki. The *gadje* was silent after his long story. He looked down, tracing a thin cut on his wrist. It must not have been easy to cut the rope that had bound his hands.

"Are you still up for seeing Vulo about the globe?" Treb asked Neel.

"Ready as ever."

"Good lad!" Treb beamed. "You know how important this is."

"Yeah. I know."

"Not just to me, but to *all* the Roma."

"Treb, I *know*."

"Of course you do. But before we visit Vulo, there's still the question of what to do with the Bohemian—Tomik, you call him? I couldn't be prouder of you, Neel. You caught him while the rest of us were trying to see through sun and dust. Now, I know you said you wanted to keep him aboard the *Pacolet*, but that's a poor reward for your efforts. If we were to sell him, you'd get some of the profit—"

Neel set down the cup. "Petra'd never forgive me."

"Sure she would, if she likes you better than him. She wouldn't say a word against you."

"You don't know her."

"Well, if you want to choose a couple of Bohemians over the welfare of your own people—"

"Treb, quit it with the Roma guilt trip already, will you? The *Pacolet* was doing just fine, money-wise, before we ever picked up Tomik. We don't *need* an extra purse of gold. Anyway, this isn't about choosing between people."

The captain folded his arms across his chest. "What's it about, then?"

"A plain and simple deal."

Treb raised his brows.

"You invited me to come aboard the *Pacolet*," Neel said. "You asked me to help find the globe. I wanted to do it, and asked nothing in return. Sailing with the Maraki, the risk, the thrill—that's my kind of thing. I didn't even mind the thought of laying my healthy brain on the line. But now that's got a price. I help you, and we keep Tomik on board with us. *And* we go back to Bohemia to look for Petra."

"That's absurd."

"Nothing wrong with seeking payment for an honest day's work."

"Neel, I hate to wake you when you're dreaming, but what's family for if not to tell you when you're being stupid? Face reality, little cousin: if what Tomik says about your friend Petra is true, then that means one thing: whether by fire or beast or the Bohemian prince's executioner, she's *dead*. If you think otherwise, you're living in a fantasy."

Neel's yellow-green eyes narrowed. "It's my fantasy, then. You give me Tomik and Petra, and I'll do whatever it takes to steal the Celestial Globe. That's the deal."

Treb stood, looking down at his cousin with disgust. "You can keep the blond lad, but the *Pacolet*'s going nowhere near Bohemia.

We're not chasing after a ghost. And that's my final say on the matter."

THE MARAKI walked down the streets of Sallay, past orange walls of baked earth that rose on either side. Cube-shaped buildings were stacked one on top of the other. Along the roofs, the monkeys chased the cats and the cats chased the monkeys. People of all colors and countries strode the streets, bartering, begging, thieving, and selling.

"Is there anything to this city *except* the market?" Tomik asked Neel. The Bohemian's freed hands were stuffed in his pockets.

"Nope." Neel snatched a date as he brushed past a fruit stall. "That's what I love about it. There's always something going on. And behind every one of those haggled deals is a story. Say you've got a nice rig. You spy a heavy Spanish boat and board her, find yourself a load of gold ripped from the Americas, and sail off with it into deeper waters. You gotta unload the gold somewhere, right? But are you going to do it in Europe, where someone'll look at you twice, thrice, and before it's four times you're in jail waiting for the hangman? Not likely. In Sallay, gold's just gold, not something that once belonged to the Spanish who stole it from the New World."

"So the New World really exists, then? America's not just a myth?"

"Oh, it's there all right. Haven't seen those lands with my own eyes. But just because you can't see something doesn't mean it ain't there."

Tomik glanced at him. "You've got some kind of magic, don't you? *You* were choking me. I couldn't feel any hands on my neck, but I could barely breathe. And when we were fighting, I couldn't break away."

"How much did Petra tell you about me?"

"I know you're an expert *thief*," Tomik said with disdain, "and that you're great at picking locks. You helped Petra break into the Cabinet of Wonders so you could raid it for gold and jewels. Other than that, Petra hasn't said much about you."

"Well, all I know about *you* is that you weren't there with her in Prague."

Tomik pressed his lips together.

"And that you've got a gift for glass," Neel added reluctantly, "that kind of saved our hides in Salamander Castle."

Tomik flicked a hand, as if tossing Neel's words away. "And you—do you possess some kind of mind control? Is that why I couldn't continue punching your face in? Because, in a fair fight—"

"Says the *gadje* with the knife to the unarmed man! If I could order minds around I'd lie to mine and forget I ever had any interest in saving your snobby self from a lifetime of cleaning Moroccan privies!"

"Sorry," Tomik muttered.

Neel rolled his eyes. "Sure you are. The only thing you're sorry about is that I got invisible hands that can knock you flat. Well, your fate's a sad one, but you'd better learn to live with it. Yeah, I got a gift, one only those with Roma blood inherit. It's called Danior's Fingers. I can steal a purse with no one feeling a thing. And you couldn't do my ghost hands any harm, so don't even think about it. Even if you'd slashed the air with that shiny knife of yours, you wouldn't have been able to chop off one invisible pinkie. And the more I concentrate, the farther my ghost hands stretch. I work at it. Gets easier as I get older."

"I'm an adult," Tomik said. "Are you of age?"

"More or less. Listen, fall back with me a bit. Let the Maraki walk ahead of us."

Curious, Tomik slowed his pace. The gap between them and the backs of Treb and the others widened. Goats milled around the boys' legs, braying and baaing.

Neel's voice dropped. "Their Czech's not great, but Treb speaks it decently. I don't want them to listen in on this."

"'This' what?"

"This secret. A plan."

"I'm not sure why you picked me to be your confidant, but if you're so concerned about privacy, should we really talk around *him*?" Tomik nodded at the shabbily cloaked goatherd who walked close by.

Neel snorted. "The chances that fellow speaks Czech are slimmer than a starved snake. We're in *Sallay*. He's a *goatherd*. Your country is the size of a bug on the map of Europe. Think a little." Neel tapped his head. "I'm just worried about *them*." He nodded at the sailors' retreating backs.

Tomik shrugged. "It's your secret."

"Look, it ain't necessary for us to *like* each other."

"Good."

"But you're Petra's friend."

"Since the day she was born."

"Do you think she's dead?"

The expression on Tomik's face was that of somebody facing a question he had done everything in his power not to consider. He remembered how the light of the Glowstone had vanished on the beach. "I don't know," he admitted.

"But if you knew she was alive," Neel pressed, "what would you do to find her?"

"Anything."

"Would you help me track her down?"

"Help *you*?"

"No need to sound all cowardly," Neel said with scorn. "The risk'd be nothing to you."

"Is your Czech so bad that you have problems with the translation of 'anything'? If the fact that I'm stuck in Morocco with a band of Sea-Gypsies and a herd of stinking goats"—he pushed away one that was chewing on his shirt—"isn't proof enough that I'd do whatever it takes to make sure Petra's safe, I don't know what else would convince you. I'm just . . . confused. I mean, what do you care? You and Petra were partners in high-risk crime, but you helped her because there was something in it for you. Petra's said that you're a friend. But what was she to you but a golden opportunity?"

"She sure was. Maybe not the way you think, though."

Tomik's eyes measured Neel. "All right. What can I do to help find her?"

"Have you ever heard of the Mercator Globes?"

Behind them, the hooded head of the goatherd raised a little. Neither boy noticed.

"No," Tomik said, bewildered. "What does that have to do with—"

"The Loopholes. Remember the Loopholes? How I said they were all over the world? Gerard Mercator was Flemish: a *gadje*, but a real savvy one. When he discovered that there were ways to leap from a river to a mountain, from one country to the next, he decided that the knowledge of where all the Loopholes are, where they lead, and how to wiggle through them would be more valuable than any price he could name. He spent his life traveling until he was rimed with sea salt and his skin was as brown as a walnut. And he must've had a magic way to him, for he crafted two round maps with the power to guide anyone through hundreds of Loopholes: the Terrestrial Globe and the Celestial Globe. From what we know about Mercator, he was a jealous, grasping sort of fellow, and he didn't want anyone to navigate the Loopholes unless they went to him first. Course, there were plenty of folk who would have been pleased to swipe that power out from under his nose, but Mercator was a step ahead of them. You know how it's a bad idea to keep all your gold in one place? Well, that's why Mercator made two globes, and why you've got to have both to make them work properly. The globes aren't small, and it's harder to steal two hefty things than one, so at least Mercator knew that even if someone managed to steal just a single globe from him, that thief would still have no luck with the Loopholes."

"And I care about this because . . . ?"

"Because the globes are why we're in Sallay. Mercator had a taste for traveling, but being a wanderer is a Roma's *life*. The Roma found that beach to Bohemia centuries ago, and other Loopholes like it, without the help of any *gadje* globe. We found them because we were destined to, because we know the world like no other people. The way we figure it, the Mercator Globes belong to *us*. And, since the Roma are a right tricky sort, we just so happen to already have our hands on one of them."

Unseen by the boys, the goatherd inched closer.

"And what does Gerard Mercator say to that?" Tomik asked.

"Nothing. He's dead. *What?*" Neel said, catching Tomik's look of accusation. "He died in his fluffy old featherbed, all right? The Roma don't stoop that low. But we want that second globe. There was a meeting of the leaders of the four tribes—the Lovari, Ursari, Maraki, and Kalderash. The *Pacolet* was given the job to find the Celestial Globe. You see, the Terrestial Globe shows where the Loopholes are, but we can't figure out which is connected to which. We know for sure that a Loophole's a two-way street: each one goes to another location, just like the one on the Portuguese beach connects to that Bohemian forest you were mucking about in. Well, you can guess that it's kind of important to know where you're headed before you leap through a Loophole. Over the years, a few brave Roma have studied the Terrestial Globe, and tried out the Loopholes marked on it, to see where they led. But most of the explorers never returned. Probably stepped from a nice, safe place into a volcano and oozed into fiery goo, or something. And it wasn't even easy for those Roma to enter the Loopholes in the first place, because of the way they're mapped on the Terrestrial Globe. That globe is speckled with Loopholes, and a speck seems pretty small, but it's the same size as a dot that marks a whole city. To go through a Loophole, you've got to enter its *exact* location. You can't just be in the right city. You've got to stand on the right cobblestone in a specific street. You can't just be in the right forest. You've got to step on the right blade of grass.

"With the Terrestrial Globe, we know more or less where the Loopholes are. But more or less ain't good enough. Now, the Celestial Globe's a big mystery, and we don't know what it does. We're hoping that, with both globes combined, we'll be able to figure out not just the rough idea of where a Loophole is, but how to find its exact entrance, and where you're going to end up after you enter it.

"The *Pacolet* has been searching for the Celestial Globe, and our sources pointed to North Africa. Imagine what it would mean for the Roma to slip through Loopholes to wherever we like. We would get rich with good trade. We wouldn't face problems like what we've got with your prince."

"You would be able to wage war," Tomik observed warily.

"Huh? Oh, right. I guess I see why you're saying that. The Mercator Globes *would* go a long way to surprising an enemy. Wouldn't be too bad a plan to turn up on someone's doorstep with a load of troops. But war's always about land, one way or another, and the Roma's a nation with no real country. We make our home wherever we please. So why would we bicker and kill over territory? In the history of the Roma, we've never fought a battle. If we had, you'd know it."

"I still don't see what this has to do with—"

"I've explained why the Maraki are in Sallay, but not why *I'm* here. We know that the Celestial Globe's in these parts, but North Africa's a big place, so . . . we're going to see a scryer. That's my part in all this. I'll help scry to find the exact location of the Celestial Globe. When that's done I'll do my best to steal the globe out of whatever hiding place it's in. After my expert thieving in Salamander Castle"—Neel straightened his shoulders—"I got a reputation to uphold."

"A reputation for being an idiot! You're going to scry? *Willingly?* That's like diving off a cliff when you've no clue how deep the water is!"

"*Pfft.*" Neel waved his hand. "It ain't that bad."

"Have you ever done it?"

"Well . . . no. But Treb needs someone young enough, and someone he can trust. Who better than his own cousin, who also has a fierce talent for busting into locked and guarded places?"

"But a scryer needs a *child* to be a medium. You've got some growing up to do—"

Neel made a noise of protest.

"—but you're not exactly a child," Tomik continued. "Look, it's none of my business. It's yours, and your mind. If you want to lose it staring into a mirror and speaking a bunch of nonsense that no one'll probably be able to understand anyway, go ahead."

"Ain't you the cautious type. There's no fun in *you*. And you're forgetting the very thing we've been talking about this whole time: Petra."

"We have *not* been talking about Petra! We've been talking about globes and Gypsies and some dead man named Mercator! If you cared about Petra, you'd scry to find out about *her*."

Neel heaved an aggravated sigh. "That's my point."

"It is?" Tomik gaped. "So you . . . you're going to ask the scryer where Petra is?"

"No, you are. I'm going to be tranced out and speaking lots of gobbledygook, like you said. The Maraki will let you in the room. They'll want to keep an eye on you, and they'll think you don't know enough Romany to understand what's going on. And you don't. It's one thing for you to play a kids' riddling game. It's another for you to figure out a scrying—which, from all I've heard, is hard enough to follow when it happens in your own tongue.

"But I'll teach you a few key Romany words. When Treb's done questioning me about the Celestial Globe, you jump right on in. You don't have to worry about understanding whatever I say in response, 'cause I'll remember that when I snap out of the scrying. That's how these things work, right? The kids who scry always remember what they see in the mirror."

"That's the problem. Sometimes they never remember anything else."

"You want to know what's happened to Petra? You'd better start studying how to ask."

Tomik was so focused on learning a quick lesson in Romany, and Neel so intent on giving it, that neither of them saw that the goats had disappeared. Nor did they notice that the herder still walked behind the boys, trailing his tattered cloak.

TREB RAPPED ONCE on the door.

"Who's there?" called a low voice in Arabic.

"Who do you think?" Treb replied in Romany. "Treb of the Maraki, captain of the *Pacolet*, with his sailors."

The door opened, and there stood a short, round man with enormous dark eyes, leathery skin, and black hair that stood up in tufts.

"Hello, Vulo," said Treb.

"Welcome," the man replied in their language, and waved the captain inside. He watched as the Maraki filed in behind Treb. Vulo nodded at Neel, identifying him as the boy who would scry, the one who had become the subject of many Romany stories.

Vulo's thick eyebrows lifted when he saw Tomik. "A *gadje*? How surprising."

"You're too right about that," said Treb.

"Are you sure that you wish to have the boy—Indraneel, correct?—scry in front of an outsider?"

"Not to worry," Treb said. "That white lad's no master of Romany. All he knows in our tongue is 'wagon,' 'I drink tar,' and 'Fish guts are yummy.' Anything we say'll be just a wee bit over his head. He stays."

"As you see fit," Vulo replied doubtfully.

At their host's request, the Roma sat on the floor. Neel tugged at Tomik's elbow, gesturing for him to follow the others' lead.

Treb glanced around him at the hard-packed earth covered by a brightly woven rug, round windows like those found in a Roma wagon, and white-painted walls. "It's a fine house," he said as Vulo served them coffee. "But don't you miss the roaming life, Vulo? Don't you feel . . . boxed up? You're a Roma."

"They call me the Owl of Sallay." Vulo blinked his large eyes. "And every owl needs a nest."

When each of the guests had placed his tiny cup on the ceramic tray Vulo offered, the short, round man turned to Neel. "Are you ready, Indraneel?"

"Neel," said the boy.

"It's best to use proper names for any occasion when the mind is opened, and when one's very identity is at stake. Don't you know that?"

"I guess," Neel muttered.

"You all appreciate the dangers of scrying," Vulo addressed his guests, "and I presume you care about Indraneel. Remember that the longer I maintain mental contact with him, the greater the risk to his mind. Keep your questions short and simple. Scrying is unpredictable at best. Indraneel might say that an ostrich has stolen the globe and sits on it like an egg. If you don't understand whatever answer he gives, I don't care. Keep your peace. Now, inform the outsider." Vulo pointed at Tomik.

Neel translated. When he finished, he gave Tomik a meaningful look.

The Bohemian nodded.

Vulo drew Neel into the center of the rug. The Maraki and Tomik ringed themselves around the pair, sitting cross-legged.

The Owl of Sallay placed a mirror on the ground, uncorked a tiny jug, and poured olive oil on the flat, silver oval. He and Neel knelt on either side of the mirror. Vulo smeared the oil until the entire mirror gleamed greasily, and then reached to grasp Neel's face.

Neel pulled away, and looked at Treb. Nervousness flickered in the boy's eyes.

"You'll be all right, coz," said Treb. "Vulo's an expert scryer. That's why we came to him."

"Treb's correct," the Owl said soothingly. "Don't be afraid."

"Who said I was?" Neel shot back.

Vulo placed his oily hands on either side of Neel's face. "Just look at me, and relax." Vulo ran his thumbs across the boy's cheekbones. Neel stared back. He blinked once. A minute passed. He blinked again. Two minutes passed. Finally, Neel's yellowy eyes were wide, and as flat as coins. His face was empty of any expression.

"Look in the mirror, Indraneel of the Lovari."

Neel did.

"What do you see?"

"Nothing." Neel's voice was hollow.

"Are you sure? What do you see?"

"My face."

"Good."

"A blue wall. A golden bird."

Vulo pursed his lips. Without tearing his eyes from Neel's, he said, "Treb, I worry that the boy is seeing random images, which is dangerous to his sanity. I want to wake him quickly. Ask your question."

Suddenly anxious himself, Treb stammered, "Where . . . Indraneel, where is the Celestial Globe?"

Neel didn't reply.

There was a rustle from an unexpected corner as Tomik leaned forward and asked in Romany, "Where is Petra Kronos?"

"Shut that *gadje* up!" Treb yelled.

Tas clamped a hand over Tomik's mouth, staring at the Bohemian in shock.

"London," Neel intoned. Then he said an English word: "Cotton."

"What do you mean, 'cotton,' and why are you speaking in English?" Treb leaped to his feet. "Where's the globe, Neel? Is it in London?"

"London. Cotton."

"The globe or your blasted friend?" Treb pressed.

"Enough." Vulo released Neel. The boy slumped forward, his jaw hitting the mirror with a crack.

"There now." Vulo lifted him up. Neel's head lolled.

"Is he all right?" Andras asked worriedly.

Vulo frowned at Treb. "I *told* you not to push him."

Treb's face tightened with shame. "I know. I didn't mean to. It's his fault!" He hauled Tomik to his feet and shook him. "Why couldn't you keep your mouth shut?" he snarled, not caring that he was shouting in Romany, and that the boy looked confused. "If you've hurt Neel I'll—"

"I'm fine," Neel mumbled. "Just woozy, is all."

Treb dropped Tomik.

"Looks like I got another bruise." Neel rubbed his chin. "Why's everyone so determined to uglify my good-looking face?"

Outside Vulo's house, just below a rounded window, the goatherd listened to the relieved laughter of the Roma. He slipped away from the wall. As he walked away from the Owl of Sallay's house, he stepped ever more quickly.

"YOU'RE EARLY."

"Yes, Master Novak." The goatherd stepped forward, and lowered his hood. His face and hands had been dyed with walnut juice, to blend in with the dark-skinned Moroccans, but his features were European, and he spoke Czech. "I have news."

"Another tale of piracy?" Novak sighed, leaning back against his chair. "How dull. What is the point of being a spy if no one has any interesting secrets? I might as well go back to Prague."

"I'm here to tell you about something *very* interesting. And Prince Rodolfo will think so, too."

Master Novak had an ordinary face, the kind you forget minutes after seeing it. But now his eyes flared with intensity.

"I heard someone in the market talking about the Mercator Globes," the goatherd continued. "I thought they were just a myth, but—"

"Tell me everything."

The goatherd did. "I couldn't understand them once they began speaking Gypsy, but the ship's called the *Pacolet*, and its sailors already have the Terrestrial Globe."

Novak pursed his lips. "Only one Mercator Globe? One is worthless. You need both to navigate through Rifts."

"One is better than nothing," urged the goatherd. "Having one globe means that you're close to possessing both. And if you have the Terrestrial Globe, no one else can use the power of the globes combined."

Novak considered this. He nodded. "I'll send a letter to the prince."

"But mail travels slowly, and we cannot wait for the prince's response! That could take a month or more. The Gypsies might be sailing from the harbor even as we speak. Let's chase the *Pacolet*, capture it, and snatch the globe."

"Very well," said Novak. "We'll hunt the Sea-Gypsies down like brown foxcs." He stood. "Ready my ship."

11

A Bargain

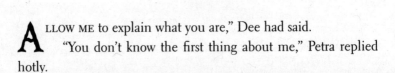

A LLOW ME to explain what you are," Dee had said.

"You don't know the first thing about me," Petra replied hotly.

"Do you know what my greatest skill is?" Dee asked. "Research. On November 17, 1584, at approximately four o'clock in the morning, a woman named Marjeta Kronos gave birth to twins. Am I correct?"

"Why do you have to stick your nose in business that *isn't yours?*" Petra bolted for the door, but the knob wouldn't turn. "And why is every door in this house locked?"

"Oh, I did that. I said that my greatest skill is research, but of course I possess several others. Being able to lock a door by merely thinking about it is just one of my talents, and one of the least impressive."

"People can only have *one* magical talent." But then Petra reconsidered. "Though . . . you can scry. You made some kind of connection between our minds. *And* you can call upon spirits."

"So it would seem."

"You also killed the Gray Men."

"Yes," he said, "though I did that through very skilled swordsmanship, not magic. I must be modest."

"And you can magically lock doors? None of that fits together."

"No, it doesn't, my dear. Not if you truly believe that a person can inherit only one magical gift. I'm not saying it's a bad rule to live by. But no rule is without exceptions. I am an exception. And so are you."

Petra found a chair and sank into it. "A chimera, right? Is a chimera some kind of . . . magical mixture, like Ariel was half dragonfly, half woman?"

"Yes. When I was young, it became clear that I had powers most didn't. But as I grew up and began to undergo training, it seemed obvious to everyone that I wasn't like other children with magical abilities. I was an oddity."

"Imagine that," Petra muttered.

"No tutor my parents hired could pinpoint the nature of my talent. Was I a scryer? A shape-shifter? Could I see in the dark? Drink fire like water?"

"What can you do, then?"

"Oh, I am sure the details would bore you."

"Can you . . ." Petra stumbled over a question she needed and feared to ask. "Can you read minds?"

"No."

"But the link between our minds—"

"Is that, and nothing more. Through it, I can know your location. You could do the same with me, if you bothered to learn how. If I say something to you, using that link, it is not very different from communicating out loud. I cannot guess your secret thoughts. They are behind a closed door, and I do not have the gift to open it."

"You could be lying to me."

"You could trust that I am not."

His brown eyes held hers, and for such a muddy color, they were piercing. Petra looked away.

Dee continued, "Naturally, when my daughters were born, I watched to see how they would develop. They turned out to be normal—well, 'normal' in the sense that they each have only one talent, like ninety-nine percent of the magical human population. Like your father, your dear friend Tomik Stakan, and the long-fingered Roma boy."

"I'm going to stop asking how you know these things."

"A wise decision. Because you won't get any answers."

Petra remembered something. "Ariel called you a 'deep-searcher.' "

"Ah, you noticed. I do search deeply. I gained the habit when I traveled the world as a young man, looking for clues about my own abilities. I saw things you couldn't imagine, and things you wouldn't want to. I met the wisest people, the craftiest, the kindest, the laziest, the lost, and those who would cut my throat as soon as cough. I've never given up the study of people—what they need, want, and are willing to do. When Madinia and Margaret were born, I became interested in twins, and I discovered that this kind of birth is the most likely to produce chimeras. Especially if one child dies."

"My twin brother was stillborn," Petra admitted.

"And what did Ariel call you? 'Silver-singer.' 'Dream-thinker.' What have you inherited, Petra? Ariel's first name for you is easy to understand. Your father has an extraordinary gift for metal. You shattered the Staro Clock's metal heart."

"I don't know how I did that. That was an accident."

"Forgive me if I don't believe you."

"Really," she insisted. "The heart probably had some kind of automatic destruction mode and I triggered it."

"Yes, of course," Dee said.

Then he snatched a knife from the folds of his cloak and flung it at her.

Without thinking, Petra plucked it out of the air. She stared at the knife in her hand and dropped it to the floor. "You could have killed me!"

"But I didn't. Come, don't pout."

"Pout? You threw a *knife* at my *head*!"

"I was reasonably certain you would dodge it. I *am* impressed that you managed to catch it without doing your fingers any harm. Your gift for metal is obvious. Why deny it? Because you can't make that blade rise off the floor and dance a waltz like your father could? That is hardly surprising. As a chimera, you possess more than one magical talent. Consider them separately, and you might find that they each seem weaker than they should be. Combined, however, you will have something rare, and very powerful. Now, what might your second talent be, dream-thinker?"

Petra didn't respond.

"I wonder," Dee said. "Have you ever had a nightmare that came true?"

She remembered the red brocade flowers.

"Perhaps you heard something that no one else did?"

The scream of the Gray Men, throbbing in her bones.

"Or felt something that wasn't there?" Dee suggested.

Neel's ghost fingers, untying the purse tucked under her shirt.

"I believe that you are gifted with mind-magic, Petra Kronos."

"No," she said.

"Consider the evidence. For example, you and I enjoy a strong link between our minds."

"*Enjoy?*" Petra choked.

"And I forged it easily, Petra, so easily that I confess I was astonished. When you called for help, it was loud, unmistakable, insistent: a clarion call. That takes talent, and usually training."

"I told you before: I didn't mean to do that. I wish you'd leave me alone. What am I to you? Just some Bohemian nobody you arm-twisted into doing your dirty work. You saved my life, but your weird and totally unwelcome responsibility to me is *over*. I have to get back to my country. I've got things to do, and a father to find."

"I think not. You asked me for help, Petra. I interpret that to mean protecting your life and making certain you're able to do the same. Let me train you for a year, and then I'll return you to Bohemia."

"A *year*? Never."

"Or you can be locked in a room in my home indefinitely."

"A month," she bargained.

He just looked at her.

"I don't even have a month!" said Petra. "The prince arrested my father!"

"Mikal Kronos is in no immediate danger of dying."

"Are you sure?"

"Yes."

There was nothing to make Petra believe Dee was telling the truth—nothing, except that she desperately wanted to believe him.

"Nine months," Dee offered.

Petra hesitated. "Six."

"Nine, and when you leave London I'll give you all the information I have on your father."

"Done," she said.

They didn't shake hands.

"This will not do." Astrophil wrung his legs. He and Petra had returned to her bedroom, and servants locked the door behind them. "I must learn English. You must get me books. I understood only a third of what you were saying."

"Maybe I could steal something from Dee's library," Petra suggested.

"You will do no such thing! He might catch you, and he is far too clever not to wonder why you are interested in English grammar when you already know the language perfectly. There must be another way. Befriend his daughters."

"The snipey Madinia and the cowardly Margaret? I don't think so."

Astrophil paced across the floor. "I need to be able to advise you. I cannot do that if I am unable to understand what people say. I will study the English language. You, Petra, must go along with Dee's plan. For the moment, you have no other option. Be cooperative. Meanwhile, we will do everything possible to create a window for escape. We'll gather all the information we can about this house, the people living in it, and the city. Now, I know you do not like the idea of mind-magic—"

"It's creepy."

"Study it anyway. If that is what allowed Dee to forge the link with your mind, and if that link is what makes him able to locate you, then you could—"

"Learn how to break it." Petra took the hope she had felt a moment ago, and a new sense of determination. She wove them together in her heart. She was not so different from her father. Like him, Petra had always been able to take comfort in a good plan.

THE NEXT DAY, a servant whisked into Petra's room. "These are for you, miss." She held out a pair of clean trousers and a loose shirt. "My stars and pincushions, but Master Dee has strange ideas."

"What do you mean?" asked Petra.

"Why, you need a proper dress! And the idea of putting you in a room alone with young Kit! And Mistress Dee says no to none of it. Of course, she's not exactly in her right mind."

"What's wrong with her?"

The maid leaned forward. "Sits around like a wooden doll all day, doesn't she? With that empty face. She'll talk to me like she's surprised I exist—and not in that typical 'I'm a grand lady and you're dirt' kind of way. More like she doesn't really know what's going on, or doesn't care. Hurry along, now. The master won't like it if you're late to meet Kit."

"Who's Kit?"

"Dress yourself, and then you'll find out, won't you?"

DEE WAS WAITING for Petra outside a door on the top floor of the manor. Astrophil, peeking from behind the curtain of Petra's hair, had counted three floors. Petra had tried to look out the windows as she and the servant, Sarah, walked past them, but all she saw were more houses and narrow streets caked with snow.

Dee dismissed Sarah. "Good morning," he said to Petra. "Today will be your first lesson. After some consideration, I decided that where fencing is concerned, you are not ready to receive lessons from me, so I have hired someone to train you. I will give you lessons where the . . . ah, more subtle aspects of your abilities are concerned, because I know of no better instructor. One word of advice before we enter the practice room. Don't reveal anything of yourself to anyone in London, especially not to the young man you are about to meet. We will keep your identity secret. Your name is Pamela Dee—"

Petra gagged.

"—a distant cousin, recently orphaned, and now living on my charity." Dee opened the door.

The room was huge, with a scuffed wooden floor and weapons with various pointy, deadly-looking parts lined the walls. In the center of the room stood a boy. Petra was tall for her age, but he was taller. His brown hair was cut close to the skull. His face was longish but pleasing, with deeply set eyes, a straight and narrow nose, and a pointed chin.

"Christopher Rhymer," Dee introduced, "is admirably able to

teach you fencing. He is a prodigy. You're lucky to be able to learn from him. Christopher, this is—"

"Petra," she said, and was glad to see the irritation on Dee's face.

"That's an unusual name," said the boy. "It sounds foreign."

"Her parents were odd people," Dee said smoothly as he crossed the room to a low table where a sword rested. He handed it to Petra, and she saw that it was an exact replica of her father's sword—except, of course, that it was visible. And the blade was blunt. "This is yours," Dee told Petra. "Make certain you deserve it."

He left the room.

"I'm known as Kit to my friends." The boy cocked his head as he considered Petra. "That'd mean you."

She hung back warily.

Kit nodded at the closed door. "He's a frustrating piece of work, isn't he, our Master John Dee? He keeps you guessing, all the while with a little smile on his face. When he claims to tell you the truth, you can never even half believe it. It makes him good at his job, though."

"I guess. If you want to be an expert spy, I suppose you have to practice being a liar."

"Hey, now." He raised a hand in defense. "I was once a spy."

"*You?*"

"Oh, yes. I began training in the profession when I was little. There's honor in espionage, Petra." He hastened to soothe away her dislike. "It's a fine way to protect your country, to keep it safe from plots within and warring foreigners without. Don't judge what I did. Not until you know something about it."

"You said you *were* a spy. What made you quit?"

"I didn't quit. I was forced to retire. Dee's right—I am a prodigy," he said matter-of-factly. "I wasn't just gifted at spying. I was *extraordinary*. I don't have any magic, but I had a natural talent for discovering things people were desperate to keep hidden. I was successful at every mission given to me. But I couldn't keep my mouth shut about it. I'm great at worming out secrets, yet I can't seem to be secretive myself. I strutted, and became . . . noticeable. Not a good thing in my job. My *former* job. And fencing?" He hefted a sword and looked at the blade. "Again, too much skill, too little modesty. I beat everyone who dared to duel with me." He checked to see if she thought he was exaggerating. "Truly. Though . . . well, I never did fight Dee. I don't even know if he's good with a sword or not. And there lies the difference between him and me. When I walk into a room, everyone knows who I am: a skilled spy, a frighteningly good swordsman, and a braggart. When Dee walks into a room, everyone's on their toes. They don't know which way to look. So here I stand—fifteen years old, barely an adult, and already retired. I'm no longer part of Queen Elizabeth's society of spies. I just teach swordplay for my bread. Dee's done me a favor by hiring me to teach you. He pays well."

"But isn't Dee . . . noticeable, too? *I* know he's a spy. Can it really be such a secret? Why isn't *he* forced to quit?"

"You've guessed correctly, Petra: everybody knows Dee's a spy. Everybody. But you see, he's on the queen's council. So if he travels as an ambassador to another court, its ruler *expects* that Dee's there to gather information. Dee just recently returned from a trip to Bohemia. I'm sure Prince Rodolfo knew full well that Dee sought his secrets. The only question in the prince's mind would have been: how *much* does Dee know, and what will he do with that information? Maybe the prince even *wanted* certain tidbits to make their way to Queen Elizabeth. In that case, all he had to do was feed them to the English spy in his court. Politics is a game of open secrets, Petra. Why, just three months ago, an English sailor named Drake decided to turn pirate. His ship pounced upon a

Spanish galleon and stole a mind-boggling sum of gold. Drake returns to London and presents his treasure to Queen Elizabeth, who is delighted. But King Ferdinand of Spain is less than happy and writes to the queen demanding his gold and Drake's head. Queen E claims she has no idea what King F is talking about. King F knows that she does. See? It's all part of the game."

"Why don't you play it, then?" Petra asked. "Couldn't you be an ambassador one day?"

"It's kind of you to suggest it, even if you disapprove. Yes, you do. I can see it on your face. But the idea you present is a greasy pole, and I don't want to try climbing up it. Anyway, I'd still have the same old problem: I can't be discreet. Everyone knows Dee's a spy, but nobody can guess *what* he knows."

Petra appraised him. "You *are* chatty."

"You see?" He laughed. "Even you think I'm unfit for the job. I just . . . well, I'm trying to be honest with you."

"Thanks, Kit. I appreciate it."

"I'm sure you *won't* appreciate losing to me, though." He gestured for Petra to draw her sword. "And you will. Badly. I'm not allowed to go easy on you. You're several years behind. If you wanted to do something with a blade other than hack at bushes, you should've begun long ago. We'll be using real weapons, not practice ones made of wood. The blades are blunt, but they'll still hurt if they hit you. Lessons will be fast and you'll have to work to keep up. Basically, you're in for a trouncing."

"Maybe I'm better than you think," said Petra.

"I doubt that. We're friends now, right? So let's have no lies between us. Use whatever advantage you can against me, but I'll still beat you."

He did. Repeatedly. First he showed her how to hold the sword, thrust with its point, and shuffle her feet to meet or duck away from him. Then Kit lunged immediately into an attack.

Petra tried to connect magically with her sword, to direct it as she wanted. But Kit moved too quickly for her to concentrate, and he kept shouting at her: "Use your *wrist*!" "No! Don't drop your guard!" "That's *pathetic*!" The flat of his sword rapped against her arms, legs, and sides. The tip of his blade often stopped just short of her neck and heart. She was dead several times over.

This is making me dizzy, Astrophil complained from his hiding spot under Petra's hair.

Finally, Kit called a halt to their practice. Petra was trembling. *I hate that I'm so weak, Astro*, she thought.

He tried to comfort her. *Some of it is due to your illness.*

Some, but not all. She hadn't even used her injured left arm. It was the muscles in her right that ached. When Kit grabbed a pitcher of water and poured some for Petra, she had trouble raising the glass to her lips and her hand shook.

Kit studied her. "Tomorrow, wear your hair up, or I'll chop it all off. It gets in your face. Anyone can grab a fistful and jerk your head back for a blow to the neck. But if you promise to keep your hair out of the way, I'll let you keep it. I know girls have their little vanities."

"You don't know me very well," she said.

He paused. "I suppose you're right. And I was wrong about you where one thing is concerned, Petra." Kit took the glass from her, then reached to shake her hand. "You are better than I thought."

12

The Death of the West

PETRA HAD NEVER been afraid of the dark, but all she could think about was that the door to this strange bedroom was locked. Astrophil was sound asleep under the bed.

Petra felt small and empty, like an old, dented thimble.

She missed her father. She remembered how he would hold her when she was little, how he smelled smoky—the coal of his smithy, the candles of his study. She would press her face against his chest and his voice, usually so quiet, would rumble under her ear.

Petra held the pillow against her cheek, and tried to sleep.

"YOUR HIGHNESS, do you have my daughter?"

"Why would I tell you that?" The prince lifted a perfumed handkerchief to his nose. He had forgotten how much his dungeons stank.

Mikal Kronos was on his knees in the dirty straw. "Please, take my eyes, if you will only—"

"If I wanted your eyes, old man, they would already be mine. But they are last year's fashion."

"I could rebuild the clock's heart," Mikal offered.

The prince squeezed his handkerchief, recalling his plans to seize the Hapsburg Empire through a clock that could waste fields, strike towers with lightning, and flood cities. How his brothers would tremble! How foolish they would look!

"Yes," the prince said, and folded the handkerchief into a neat square. "I suppose you could."

PETRA READ THE NOTE, fury boiling in her stomach. She smashed the paper into a ball and flung it into a corner of her bedroom.

Astrophil, perched on the frame of an oil painting, watched the paper whiz past. "What did it say?" he asked.

"It said no."

Well, not in so many words. Across the top of the note was Petra's scrawl: "I DEMAND to be let out of this room. My door is always locked." Below this was Dee's response: *Unlock it, then.*

Petra took stock of her surroundings, as she had so many times. The one window showed a snow-covered garden many feet below. Several paintings of old, shriveled-up people hung on the bedroom walls. Astrophil liked them, because he could hide behind the frames if anyone opened the door. Petra hated them, because she was sure that everybody in the house thought they were hideous, too, and that this room was where the Dees kept everything they didn't like but still wanted to own—including her.

Petra's angry gaze fell on a pile of crumpled trousers and shirts. They were sweat-stained from days of practicing with Kit. Up until a moment ago, when Sarah had delivered the note, Petra had thought that the clothes were a sign that Dee was trying to win her over. He had noticed, Petra had thought, that she preferred trousers. She readily wore them, transferring Tomik's Glowstone to the pocket of each new pair.

But the note, combined with the fact that Dee hadn't seen her since he had introduced her to Kit almost a week ago, made her think that, after all, he probably couldn't care less what she thought of him.

She began to pound on the locked door.

"Petra!" Astrophil chided. "What happened to our carefully considered master plan? The one where you pretend to be a good, likeable girl so that we can gain people's trust and find a way to escape?"

"All—part—of—the—plan," Petra muttered in between kicks at the wooden door.

It flung open.

"Heavens, child!" Sarah gasped. "What is the matter?"

"I want to see Madinia and Margaret."

PETRA CONFRONTED THE GIRLS when they entered her room. "You haven't been to visit me."

"Who has time?" Madinia said airily.

"You didn't seem to like us," Margaret told Petra.

"*And* we've been busy," Madinia insisted. "Why, we have to buy dresses for the queen's winter ball. We've walked all over London until our feet were achingly sore. And I have just been in *rapture* with my lute lessons—"

"You hate playing the lute," said Margaret.

"You're right, I do!" Madinia laughed. "I'd like to break my lute over Master Bassano's head. That squinty old beast!"

"Why did you send for us, Petra?" asked Margaret.

"I'm bored," Petra lied.

"Me, too!" said Madinia. "What shall we do?"

"You could show me around your house," Petra suggested. Perhaps she could run right out the front door . . .

"That's your idea of fun?"

"Well, we could hunt for secret passageways or something," Petra tried.

"And then play dice on the rugs?" Madinia sneered. "I'm not a *child*."

"You shouldn't leave your room, Petra," said Margaret.

"Why? Does your dad have a pet monster in the hallway?" Madinia giggled.

"Or is your family keeping something secret from me?"

Madinia stopped laughing. She looked at her sister.

"It's not that," said Margaret. "But if Dad insists on your door being locked and guarded, he must have his reasons."

Guarded? Petra hadn't known that. "Maybe," she thought out loud, "he thinks *I'm* dangerous."

"Maybe you are." Margaret spoke so seriously that Petra regretted her last comment. Why did she always have to say whatever she was thinking? Now Margaret was suspicious.

Petra needn't have worried, however.

"Ooh, dangerous!" Madinia trilled.

Petra decided to focus her efforts on this sister. Thinking of the pile of dirty clothes and the one thing Petra knew for certain about Madinia, she said, "Well, your father can't have a good reason for denying me dresses, can he? Look at what I'm forced to wear." She pointed.

Madinia's jaw dropped. "You"—she seized Petra's hand—"are coming with us *this very second*."

"You're too skinny!" Madinia scolded.

Her dress sagged on Petra. The only place where the dress wasn't too loose was around her shoulders, where it was too tight.

"And *tall*!" Madinia sounded as if Petra were to blame for this problem. "That dress is at least three inches too short on you."

I wish I could see this properly, Astrophil commented from his post on Petra's ear.

You've got a mean streak, Petra accused.

"At least we can put a ruff on your neck to hide that hideous scar." Madinia reached for a starched, frilled collar.

Petra pushed it away. "I'm not wearing that. I already agreed to put on this stupid cage." She kicked at the hoopskirt, a bony structure underneath the dress that made the skirt stand out like a bell.

"Petra, you're my project! You have to do what I say!"

Why am I doing this? Petra moaned to Astrophil.

I haven't the faintest idea. You were the one who seemed to think that playing dress-up was part of the plan to escape. And how is that, exactly?

"Leave her alone, Madinia," Margaret said. She was sitting at the edge of the huge, curtained bed that she shared with her sister.

"She looks like a stick!"

"She looks fine. She's just different."

Petra gave Margaret a grateful glance. "If neither of you has dresses that will fit me, couldn't we go into the city to buy one?" she suggested.

Ah-hah, said Astrophil.

"Absolutely not," said Margaret.

The gratitude Petra had felt toward her was replaced by something ugly. "Why not? Is the city too big, bad, and scary for you?"

Margaret crossed her arms. "*You* are not allowed to go out."

"Just because Dee says so. Do you even know why? Do you even care? You're his *slaves*, both of you. Some people have fathers who are kind, who listen to what their daughters have to say, and who would risk their lives to protect them!" Petra's eyes began to sting. "What kind of father forces his daughters to kidnap someone?"

"We were trying to help," Margaret said.

"I keep hearing that, but it never sounds like anything but a lie!"

Madinia's face was flushed. "Try this on for truth," she hissed. "Our father loves us, and yours is nowhere to be seen."

Blindly, Petra turned to walk out of the room. Hot tears spilled onto her cheeks.

Petra, said Astrophil.

That was all he said, but it was enough. She halted, not looking at the twins. "I can't stay locked in one room practically every hour of the day. I can't. Tell—would you ask your parents to let me out?"

"Dad's busy." Madinia stamped a foot.

"You have a mother, too!"

There was a silence. Then Petra felt a hand on her shoulder.

"I'll ask her," said Margaret.

PETRA WAS SURE that Kit noticed her red-rimmed eyes, but he didn't say anything. For someone who had once been a spy, Kit didn't ask a lot of questions. On their second day of practice, Petra had walked into the room with her hair in a ponytail (and Astrophil gratefully abandoned to the dizzy-free environment of her bedroom). The scar on her neck had been exposed and Kit's eyes had sharpened with curiosity. Then he looked away.

He wasn't quiet, though, when it came to telling Petra how terrible she was at fencing. Today he bashed the rapier out of her hand with one blow. It clattered on the floor.

"Usually you swing your sword like a drunken farmer who's been drafted as a foot soldier. Today you're still that farmer, only somehow you've developed a death wish, too," Kit said.

Petra shrugged.

"You are aware that normally you hang on to your sword, even if I kill you in a hundred different ways?"

She shrugged again.

"Petra, it's not easy to keep your grip when you're up against me, and the fact that you can—*usually*—is promising."

"So?" she said listlessly.

"So . . ." He took a breath, and then barreled ahead like someone who couldn't stop himself. "Are you going to tell me what's wrong?"

Petra did—a little bit. Dee had warned her not to tell anyone in London about who she was or why she was there. She didn't trust Dee, but she knew common sense when she heard it. So all she told Kit was that she felt like a prisoner in Dee's house. "And Dee said . . . I thought . . . I thought that Dee was going to give me lessons."

"Really? What kind of lessons?"

"I'm not sure," she hedged. "But I haven't seen him since the day I met you."

"He's been busy, I hear."

"With what?"

"I'm not sure," he said, mimicking her earlier words. "He's been meeting a lot with Walsingham."

"Who's Walsingham?" Petra asked.

Kit blinked. "I used to work for him. He is England's master of spies. Sir Francis Walsingham is the secretary of defense."

"Oh."

"And the fact that he is the secretary of defense is something that anybody raised in this country, as you supposedly were, should know."

Petra scrambled. "I've led a very sheltered life."

His gaze flicked to her scars. "I'm sure."

"I've never cared much about politics."

"And your attempts to explain yourself only convince me that you are hiding something. Why would Dee keep his orphaned cousin locked up in her room, only to be let out for *sword practice*, of all things?"

Petra didn't answer.

Kit sighed. "Get out of here. You're going to be worthless today. I think you'll find that, because I'm letting you out of practice early, the servants who usually escort you won't be waiting outside the door. If you run to Dee's library, you might catch him before Walsingham turns up for their weekly meeting. Maybe if Dee sees your face when you ask him for a little freedom he won't be able to say no. And, Petra, I'm happy to answer any questions you have. But be warned: someday you might have to answer *mine*."

PETRA RUSHED to Dee's library, glad that she had a good memory and an even better sense of orientation. Luckily, she didn't encounter any servants before she slipped down a winding staircase to the floor below. Her hand still gripped the rope railing and her foot had touched the last stone step when she heard voices drifting in from the corridor.

"John! You're needed immediately."

"Good afternoon, Francis. Step into my library, and we can discuss the matter."

"There's no time for that. The queen needs you *now*. It's the West—"

"Gabriel Thorn?"

"He's dead, John. You—"

"Petra," Dee suddenly called. "I know you're there. Stop skulking in the shadows. Step forward."

She did.

Dee was standing just outside his library door next to a thin man with a short, pointed beard.

"Who is that?" demanded the man who could only be Francis Walsingham.

"A distant relative, and a nosy one, too," said Dee. "Well, Petra, I suppose that from this day forth you won't be able to blame anyone for being a spy without feeling a little hypocritical. One of my daughters' winter cloaks is in my library. You shall borrow it. You are coming with us."

"We're going out? Really? Where?"

"The queen's residence in London. Whitehall Palace."

13

The Queen's Swans

I REALLY DON'T UNDERSTAND," Walsingham said through clenched teeth, "why *she* is to come with us."

"No doubt there are many things you don't understand," Dee replied.

"And why must we take your carriage? We'd get to the river faster on foot."

"This one"—Dee tilted his head toward Petra—"might try wandering off. To look at the shops. I'd find her, of course, but that would waste our time."

Walsingham threw up his hands and climbed into the waiting carriage. Dee gestured for Petra to follow.

When all three of them were inside, Walsingham reached to slam the door shut, and the carriage jerked forward. As the horses began to trot, the leather and wood frame of the carriage shook so hard that Petra's teeth rattled.

Petra could smell Walsingham's hair oil. She wrinkled her nose.

He saw her do it. "The idea of taking a *young girl* along on such a politically delicate matter . . ."

"You know better than to underestimate youth. What about Christopher?"

"Kit has his uses."

"Indeed."

It was chilly in the carriage, and Petra was grateful for the cloak, though fetching it had meant she'd had no time to run to her bedroom for Astrophil. She rubbed at the fog on the cold glass carriage window until it squeaked. Through the clear circle she could see stately manors giving way to rows of shops. People were brushing snow off stalls piled high with winter vegetables. "Where are we?"

Walsingham spluttered. "She doesn't even know where we are? John, I hope she's not one of your brain-addled charity cases, because the council will *not* like—"

"Careful." Dee didn't raise his voice. He didn't move an inch. But Petra was still reminded of the moment when she had learned that Dee was capable of beheading four vicious monsters.

Walsingham shut his mouth.

Dee turned to Petra. "We live on Throgmorton Street. This is Cheapside, where most of the trade in London takes place. If you are ever on the hunt for news about someone or something, there is no better place to seek it than where people buy and sell goods—unless it's where people drink. Taverns are excellent sites for gossip. So are the Liberties, but no one will talk to a stranger there."

"What're the Liberties?"

"Home to a pack of lawless scoundrels," said Walsingham. "And foreigners."

Dee explained, "For a reason that many people claim is a mystery but which surely has a great deal to do with the mayor's pockets, and the money put in them, the Liberties is an area of London that does not answer to the city's laws."

"Are we going to the Liberties?" asked Petra.

"No, my dear."

Petra had begun to notice that Dee called her this when he deliberately wanted to irritate her—or, maybe, when she had irritated *him* with her ignorance.

"I told you," he continued, "that we're going to the palace. We're taking Grass Street south to the River Thames, by the London Bridge. From there we'll hire a boat."

Petra turned back to the window, though it had misted over again. She had looked away to hide her surprise from Dee—surprise that he was taking her on a trip to see a dead man *and* supplying information about London along the way, as if the idea that she might be asking questions to prepare for an escape had never entered his head. But he *must* have thought of that. He wasn't stupid. She wished she had been able to take Astrophil with her. He would have known what to make of this.

Petra considered telling Walsingham that she was being held captive in Dee's house. But Kit's former master seemed just as bad as Dee, as far as Petra could tell, and she doubted he would believe her. It was better to stay quiet. If she didn't say anything, then maybe Dee wouldn't suspect—

The carriage halted, and Walsingham flung open the door. As he strode toward the river bank he called, "You there, oarsman!"

Dee didn't move from his seat, so Petra didn't either. "Why did you tell him my name? You said to keep it secret."

Dee gave a slight shrug. "You told Christopher. You might as well have told the entire town." Dee paused, and said, "I see you've unlocked your door."

"What?" Petra was confused. Then she realized he was referring to his note. "No, I didn't."

"I disagree. I have spoken with my wife. You will be given the same freedom as our daughters. You will dine with them. You may go for walks with them, and attend functions or visit places that I would deem suitable for Madinia and Margaret. You will be given the same weekly allowance they receive, which you may spend as you see fit. Do you know why I have agreed to this?"

Petra was stunned. "I have no idea."

"None? Why, the answer is simple, my dear: if you were to get lost, which is easy to do in a new city—"

"I never get lost."

"If you were to go missing, then you needn't worry. As long as the link between our minds exists, I can find you and bring you back to my manor. You might, however, find my methods to be unpleasant."

Petra followed Dee to the wharf, because it was clear that she had no other option. When she stepped into the boat, she came to a conclusion:

It would be a fine thing to outwit John Dee.

THE BOAT SLIPPED through the fog and Petra watched swans glide past in the blackish water of the Thames.

The oarsman noticed. "You're thinking that them birds would make a tasty meal, aren't you, lass? You oughtn't. They belong to the queen."

"I was thinking that they're pretty."

He shuddered. "Mean creatures, and strong. They'd break your arm if you let 'em."

"I paid you to row, not talk," ordered Walsingham. "We've wasted enough time."

"I doubt the West will be any deader when we arrive," said Dee.

"Oh, the West *this* and the West *that*," Petra said impatiently. "Isn't his name Gabriel Thorn? Is the West some sort of nickname?"

"No." Walsingham was offended, though Petra didn't see why. "It's more of a title. A way that the queen's council shows respect for its most important members. It's—"

"A nickname," said Dee.

"There are thirteen members of the council." Walsingham turned to Petra. "I am one of them. Dee is another. But throughout Queen Elizabeth's reign, there have always been four members whose voices have more weight. They are her North, South, East, and West. Robert Cecil became the North when his father, who used to hold that position, died. Francis Drake recently became the East. He's a great favorite with the queen."

"Who's the South?" Petra asked.

"He is." Dee nodded at Walsingham.

Petra looked at Dee, wondering why he wasn't one of the queen's favorites, and how he felt about it.

"So the West is dead," she said. "Big deal. Why are we rowing through the freezing fog?"

"Well, I don't know why *you* are," Walsingham told her. "But *we* are going to Whitehall because the queen requested our presence."

"I gather, then, that Gabriel didn't die in his sleep," said Dee.

"You're taking the news rather coolly," said Walsingham.

"And how should I take it?"

"I just thought you'd care, one way or another."

Petra snorted. "He doesn't care about anything but himself."

Walsingham was shocked. The oarsman suppressed a smile. Dee's expression didn't change. For a moment there was no sound but the dipping of oars in the water.

Walsingham cleared his throat. Ignoring Petra, he said to Dee, "A servant found the body in the palace library. The corpse was a little stiff, but not totally rigid. The West can't have been dead for more than a few hours. I've already inspected the body, and there are no signs of any struggle. He has no bruises on him." Walsingham shrugged. "Gabriel Thorn was too great a lover of wine. I'd say the old man's heart just gave out."

"Yet the queen ordered you to send for me," said Dee. "And you were anxious that I come."

"The queen says jump, I jump. So do you. The death seems natural, to be sure, but you're supposed to confirm it."

"Here we are," said the oarsman. Behind him, a covered dock appeared out of the mist. It looked like a little wooden house jutting over the water. The oarsman rowed the boat to a set of stairs leading out of the house and down to the river.

A servant skipped down the steps to offer his hand. The two men got out of the boat, and began walking up the stairs when the servant reached to take Petra's elbow. She jerked away. "I don't need help." But the river looked dark and cold. She hoped she wouldn't slip. She stood up.

"Stay a moment, my lovely lass," the oarsman said.

Petra turned to look at him.

"You're a bold one, I can tell. And them silver eyes of yours seem awful deep. Mine've seen a lot, too, rowing from one bank to the other. Take my word: don't go poking around politics, especially when there's already one dead body. Men like that"—he jerked a thumb at the cloaked backs of Dee and Walsingham, retreating into the dockhouse—"they're swans. They seem grand. Give 'em cause, though, and they'll fly at you. They'll break you."

"I know," said Petra. She planted her foot firmly on the stairs and stepped out of the boat. "But thanks for the warning."

PETRA FOLLOWED DEE and Walsingham down a long hall crowded on either side with small, decorative shields. She leaned forward and rapped a knuckle against one.

"That's not a toy." Walsingham knocked away her hand.

"It's made of pasteboard! I didn't break it, and wouldn't mind if

I did!" Petra was tired of being bullied, and was just about to say so when Walsingham spoke again:

"She's a little savage, John. She has no manners—or, if she does, they're bad."

"She's curious," Dee said. "It's part of her charm."

"Francis," called a hunched man waiting at the end of the hallway. "A word, please."

As Walsingham walked away, Dee explained the meaning of the colorful shields. "They're gifts to the queen from her knights. Notice the various animals and trees. They are symbols that refer to a knight's family. As you see, each shield bears a short poem that either brags about the knight's status, praises the queen, or does both. Walsingham's shield is somewhere on this wall." He waved a hand.

"Where's yours?"

"Nowhere. I am not a knight, nor will I ever be."

Petra examined him. He didn't seem to mind being passed over by his queen. She looked at the shields—they were bright, flashy. They called attention to themselves. Dee didn't. But Petra thought Dee was probably more powerful than a dozen knights with silly pasteboard shields.

He stood patiently.

Petra ignored him, walking down the hall, studying the shields. One of them caught her eye. The shield showed a tree, and dangling from its branches were socks, scarves, hats, coats, trousers, and dresses. Beneath it were these lines:

> *To My Queen*
> *My finest cloth shall dress your land*
> *And warm it ever at your command.*

Dee looked over Petra's shoulder. "A wretched poem, though there are worse."

"Whose is it?"

"It belongs to Sir Robert Cotton. The entire shield plays on his last name. Cotton, cloth, clothes—"

"I get it," Petra interrupted. Then a thought struck her. "Ariel. She talked about a tree dressed in robes, just like the picture on the shield."

Dee glanced at Petra, and his face held a new expression. It almost looked like respect. "Yes."

"But what does that have to do with me?"

"I don't know," Dee said abruptly. "Ariel mentioned a great deal of things, including the possibility of murder. And here we stand, ready to view Gabriel Thorn's body. We—you, especially—would do well to consider Ariel's words."

What else had she said? Petra remembered the spirit's warning to Astrophil: *Never trust a poet.* Petra's gaze swept down the corridor, over the two-line scraps of verse on each shield. There were *hundreds* of poets here.

Dee asked, "Would you like to find out why I brought you to Whitehall Palace?"

She did. She couldn't help it. But she lied. "No."

"That was a rhetorical question," said Dee. "Follow me."

WHITEHALL PALACE SPRAWLED. Petra was used to the splendid but simple form of Salamander Castle, with its square-shaped rooms and orderly hallways. Whitehall felt alive, as if every night, while its occupants were sleeping, it sprouted another room that grew at an impossible angle.

Petra followed Dee into a chamber with a high, vaulted ceiling. She felt swallowed up by the space. "What is this place?" she asked, and her words echoed.

"The Watching Chamber," Dee replied. "Balls are held here."

"So it's for dancing, not watching."

He glanced at her over his shoulder. "There is always someone watching."

Dee led her down a corridor. At the end was a closed door, in front of which stood Walsingham and the man with the hunched back, who gave Petra a keen but not unkind look. "Who is this?"

"My ward," Dee replied.

"I'm Robert Cecil." The man took Petra's hand and gently patted it. "I think you should wait here. A dead body is not a proper sight for a young lady."

"I agree," said Walsingham.

"I don't," said Dee. "Petra is here to assist me."

"I am?" Petra asked.

"I've had enough of your eccentricities, John," Walsingham said. "I'm off to the kitchen to question the servants. I doubt that you and your little assistant will discover anything new about the body. But try, by all means."

He walked away, his shoes clapping against the stone floor.

"He's a competent man," Robert Cecil said, watching Walsingham go. "But the queen requires *your* opinion on the death of the West, John."

The three of them stepped into a library. Leather bindings, mostly in red and green, gleamed on the shelves. Astrophil would have been awestruck, but Petra felt disappointed. She was wondering why, when she realized that there was nothing remotely magical about Whitehall Palace—not like Prague's castle, which overflowed with glorious objects and enchanted rooms. This palace made Petra wonder what it was hiding.

Then she saw Gabriel Thorn's body slumped in a chair.

"He was here from ten o'clock until about eleven o'clock in the morning," said Cecil. "He had reserved the library for his private study. No one came in, as far as we know."

Dee studied the body, looking carefully at the face and mouth. "Petra."

She stayed by Robert Cecil's side. The body's skin was already gray, and it seemed to Petra that her scars burned.

"There's nothing to fear from a dead man," Cecil said gently.

"That is not always true," said Dee. After this discomforting statement, which did little to make her forget about the Gray Men, Dee ordered, "Petra, come here."

Not wanting him to think she was nervous, she did.

"Many poisons are metallic," Dee began.

"I know that," Petra snapped. "Do you think my father wouldn't have warned me about the dangers of metal?"

"Then put that knowledge to good use and tell me if anything about Gabriel Thorn looks unusual."

"He looks dead."

"Very insightful, my dear. If your eyes have learned so much, imagine what your touch could do."

Petra recoiled. She understood what Dee was suggesting. She remembered Tomik asking her to hold the Glowstone and guess what kind of metal it contained. She slipped her hand inside her pocket and wrapped her fingers around the only thing, besides Astrophil and her father's sword, that she had left of her home. She didn't squeeze Tomik's Glowstone, just felt its smooth shape. She often clung to it when she was lonely.

Or afraid.

"I'm not touching a dead body," she stated.

"You do not have to, if it is too distressing," Dee said. "By all means run away and hide."

Petra knew that what he said was a trick, but it worked anyway. She wanted to be brave, and she began to wonder if Dee was correct about her magical gift. Maybe she was special.

She found herself stepping forward. Quickly, before she could change her mind, she laid her palm on Gabriel Thorn's wrinkled forehead. It was cold and hard.

"Don't think about what you're touching," Dee said. "Think about what it holds."

Petra remembered the Thames, and how opaque the waters were. Somewhere below the river's surface was a bottom—muddy, old, and far from the sun. She forgot about the curve of the skull beneath her palm.

The image of a bright, twisting liquid floated in Petra's mind. She recognized it. "Quicksilver."

"Good," said Dee. "Keep your eyes closed."

She hadn't realized that they were.

"This will be more difficult," Dee continued. "Can you tell me how long the quicksilver has been inside the blood? A long time? Since late this morning, or early?"

Petra's lips automatically formed the answer: "A little after ten o'clock."

"That's enough." Dee lifted her fingers from the West's forehead. Petra snatched her hand away, and cradled it in her other palm. It was cold. She blinked at Dee, and the world felt unsteady.

"It is, of course, only her word," Robert Cecil said.

"I'll take it," Dee replied. "What Petra says is consistent with certain signs on the body. Notice how pink Gabriel's cheeks are."

"That could be from wine."

"True. He does smell of it. But then, where is his bottle? Where is his glass? If nobody entered the room, these items should be here."

Cecil was silent.

"Gabriel's mouth and gums are also a bright red," Dee continued. "This, and the high color of his cheeks, are symptoms of poisoning by quicksilver."

Cecil sighed. "I'll tell the queen."

"The key, I believe, will be discovering *why* Gabriel reserved the library this morning, and if he was indeed alone."

Cecil passed a weary hand over his forehead. "How distressing. Gabriel wasn't always well liked, but it's difficult to imagine that anyone would wish him dead. Well, except . . ." He glanced at Dee, and then cleared his throat in embarrassment.

Except you. Petra was sure that's what Cecil had been about to say. She remembered Walsingham's comment to Dee: *I just thought you'd care, one way or another.* Was Dee glad that the West was dead?

With the face of someone eager to change the topic of conversation, Cecil said rapidly, "Now, John, while I have you here, would you be so good as to look at a draft of a law being considered by Her Majesty? I'd like to know your thoughts on it before the council meets." He led Dee to a table near a window, and pulled a sheaf of paper in front of them.

As the two men leaned over the table, Petra stepped away from the West's body. She didn't want to linger near the corpse, but she thought about what Tomik would do in a situation like this. He would be thorough. He would look for something that everyone else had missed.

Petra glanced down at the thick carpet, and saw a tiny, tear-shaped seed by the leg of the chair. She bent down and picked it up. It looked like an apple seed, except it was a dusky orange, not brown.

Petra put it in her pocket and felt a sense of satisfaction. She had noticed something Dee hadn't.

Still warm with the glow of this small triumph, Petra decided to act upon a sudden idea. After a glance at the two men, who were engrossed in conversation, she scanned the shelves until she found what she wanted: a small, compact book on English grammar. She tucked it under her arm, then carefully pulled the cloak around her shoulders.

Petra Kronos had stolen from the queen of England. Astrophil would be pleased, and Neel would be proud.

DEE WAS QUIET as the oarsman rowed him and Petra away from the dockhouse. The fog had lifted, and Petra could now see the palace and the fields of dead trees around it.

It was colder than before, and snow began to fall. Petra shivered under her cloak. The silence made her uncomfortable. She was bursting with questions, and finally she couldn't resist. "Why did you bring me to Whitehall?"

"You might have thought Ariel's words were nonsense," he answered, "but I never did. When Walsingham came to Throgmorton Street with the news that a councillor was dead, I recalled Ariel's prediction of murder. That warning came when I asked the spirit about *you*. Clearly, the death of the West is connected to you in some way."

The chilly feeling that crept over Petra had nothing to do with the cold. "But I didn't know Gabriel Thorn."

"That may not matter."

"Did he know the prince?"

Dee paused before replying. "I do not think so. I don't yet understand why Gabriel died, or what you have to do with that fact. But events at Whitehall confirmed my suspicion that Ariel's words about you were not random. In the Shield Hall—"

"The Cotton tree," Petra supplied. "The tree dressed with robes."

"Yes. And then there was the dirty metal river."

Petra looked at him blankly.

"Think, Petra."

She remembered the quicksilver, a liquid metal that flows without being heated. "But quicksilver isn't dirty. It's shiny."

"It's poisonous. That is dirty enough."

"Oh." She didn't speak for a moment, then lunged into a question that had been bothering her. "Why haven't you been giving me lessons?"

"I just did, in the Whitehall library."

"But you didn't before. You've been ignoring me."

He didn't give the response that Petra expected. Dee didn't say he had been busy. Instead, he replied, "The unfortunate thing about being a teacher is that it is impossible to make a pupil learn something if she doesn't want to do so."

Petra heard herself saying, "But I do want to."

His eyebrows lifted.

"I mean," she amended, "I might want to. But nine months is too long." It had always been too long, but Petra had made that agreement thinking she could escape well before the end of that period.

"Anything worth learning takes time," Dee said.

"I don't have time."

"Then what do you propose?"

Petra considered the things that she knew about John Dee. He enjoyed bargaining. He constantly challenged Petra, whether by mocking, tricking, or entrapping her. He seemed (Petra forced herself to admit it) intrigued by her. He might care about the death of the West, and whatever Petra had to do with it.

"I propose," Petra began, "that we stick to our original agreement. Except—"

"Except?" He was amused.

"Except that if *I* solve the mystery of who killed Gabriel Thorn, you will send me home to Okno right then and there. With all of my possessions," she added, thinking of the sword.

Dee laughed.

"And," she added, "you will break the link between our minds."

"That part is not negotiable. A mental link like that can be broken only by the person who forged it, or by whoever owns the minds that are connected. I will not sever that link, which means that you are the only one left who can. Somehow, I don't think I will be teaching you how to do that."

"But do you agree to the rest?"

"Why not? You proved at Salamander Castle that you excel when properly motivated. This agreement may make you a more willing pupil. But, of course, our bargain will be binding only if you discover who killed Gabriel before *I* do." He let this sink in. It wasn't likely that Petra could beat Dee in a race where all of his connections and experience would give him more than a head start.

But Petra had what she wanted: a chance.

She nodded. The oarsman looked at her with disapproval, but Petra ignored him, and he didn't say anything, because he was used to being ignored.

14

On the Ratlines

NEEL SPUN a little golden hoop between his fingers. He had stolen it in Sallay, along with a bolt of crimson cloth for Sadie.

On the night the *Pacolet* left Sallay, almost two weeks ago, Neel had eaten almonds until his stomach cramped. Today, looking at his sister's red cloth made him feel even worse. He remembered their farewell. While the rest of the Lovari praised Neel's theft from the Bohemian prince, Sadie had been silent and furious. When she finally spoke, it was to say that she was staying in Prague.

Neel had teased her. He sang songs about a castle stablehand who must have stolen her heart (he didn't realize that he might have been singing the truth). She grew angrier and angrier until finally the very intensity of her emotion made her laugh.

She hugged him. In a low voice, she said, "If you had been caught, they wouldn't have just killed you."

Neel wished she were here, not holed up in Salamander Castle, smuggling messages through white traders the Roma trusted. He missed her. Sadie was good. A bright flame that made everyone around her glow.

Neel didn't feel like a good person.

He opened the earring.

Then a pair of feet appeared on the ladder leading from the hatch in the ceiling.

"Neel, what are you doing down here?" demanded Nadia. "You should be working with the rest of us."

"You should be working on catching Brishen's eye, 'cause that'll never happen on its own," he sneered. He set the pointed end of the open hoop against his left earlobe.

"You'll get an infection if you do it like that," said Nadia.

He pushed the earring through. He heard as well as felt the tiny pop when it went through his flesh. He pinched the hoop closed, and blotted the blood between his thumb and forefinger. His earlobe throbbed, but he didn't mind. It felt as angry as the rest of him.

"My fire's burning just fine, so why don't you mind yours," Neel told Nadia, using the Lovari expression.

"The Maraki don't have campfires. We live on ships."

"I'm not Maraki, and you know what I meant."

"I'm sorry." Her voice was rough in that way that some people have when the only way they can apologize is to harden themselves first. "I'm sorry for what I said the night before we reached Sallay. I didn't mean it. It doesn't matter who's in which tribe. We're both Roma." She sat down on the hammock next to Neel's. "I know what your problem is."

He kept his expression carefully blank.

"It's him," said Nadia.

Neel collapsed into his hammock and covered his face. "I *hate* him," he groaned.

"Then why is he on this ship? You're the one who made us keep him."

Neel knew that, and didn't understand why all of his reasons for doing so now seemed pale and insignificant next to his resentment. It hadn't been right to sell Tomik as a slave, and Neel could work with the *gadje* if he had to, just like when the two of them had plotted out the scrying in Sallay. But now this handsome white outsider, who also happened to be Petra's oldest friend, was here to stay—*and*, to Neel's dismay, Tomik had become the darling of the *Pacolet*.

At least Nadia didn't seem too keen about him. "If I go on deck," he asked her, "will you leave me alone?"

"Yes." She reached into Tas's kit and pulled out a bottle.

"What're you—"

"Hold still," she ordered, seizing Neel's head. "Or you really will get an infection." She uncorked the bottle with her teeth and poured alcohol on his ear.

He shrieked.

IT MIGHT BE SURPRISING that Tomik was a favorite aboard the *Pacolet*. After all, its sailors had been ready to sell him into slavery, and their captain was disgusted with him. Even as Treb set the course for England, he complained to anyone who would listen that the *gadje* had screwed up the scrying, and that if they were chasing a phantom instead of the Celestial Globe, it was all Tomik's fault. But from the first day that Morocco disappeared on the horizon, the Maraki adored Tomik with that easy feeling that comes from being relieved of guilt.

They also saw that Tomik was dedicated. He learned Romany more quickly than anyone would have guessed. He studied the parts of the ship, and never stopped asking questions. At first the Maraki pretended to be annoyed by this, but they soon gave in to feeling flattered.

Tomik's sunburn darkened into a tan, his hair was streaked into an even brighter gold, his laugh was open, and he seemed to have forgotten that the sailors had once been his captors. The only person Tomik avoided was Neel, which everyone thought was strange, since Neel had raged at, badgered, and insulted the Maraki into keeping him.

The *Pacolet* had left the Loophole Beach families in Sallay to make their own way in life, since independence was important to the Roma and the ship had been a temporary (and cramped) solution to their problems. Neel and Tomik then became the youngest people on board, if only by a couple of years. It is perhaps natural, then, that Tomik became the pet of the Maraki, who showed him the same affection they would have toward a puppy taking its wobbly steps.

It didn't occur to Neel that he himself was treated differently because the Maraki considered him an equal.

While Neel was below deck, slapping the bottle out of Nadia's hand and cursing her, Tomik was making a discovery.

There was little wind that day. After the *Pacolet* had left Morocco, it sailed west past the Canary Islands. The ship would eventually turn to the northeast and England, but not before it had sailed far out into the Western Ocean. This route meant that the *Pacolet* could take advantage of good currents and the trade winds, which made the journey faster. But you can't trust the wind. It has its lazy days just like the rest of us.

Tomik had little to do. He stood next to the railing, sweat trickling down his back. He was hot and bored. He had offered to fish with the Maraki who weren't working the sails, but they had waved him away, telling him to take a nap in the shipmates' cabin. Tomik left them, but he didn't go below deck. That's where Neel was. Tomik looked at the empty blue sea and wondered what to do.

He didn't want to think about his family and Petra. He knew the Stakans would worry and grieve. But he wasn't dead, and he wasn't in danger—none that he knew of, at least. Still, Tomik would imagine his family in tears, and Attie howling at the door, and a wave of guilt would overcome him.

So he avoided remembering the Sign of Fire. He also tried not to think about Petra, because just as Treb worried that the *Pacolet* was sailing toward her and not the globe, Tomik feared that the opposite was true.

Tomik pulled the horseshoe necklace from underneath his shirt and studied it. Neel seemed to have forgotten about it. This surprised Tomik, because it was obvious that the trinket meant something to him. Tomik didn't guess that this was exactly why the other boy acted as if it didn't exist.

He flipped the horseshoe over. In tiny letters, and in a formal tone that was unusual for Neel, the horseshoe said, *This is Petali Kronos. Be kind to her, for she is bound by blood to Indraneel of the Lovari.*

Tomik didn't understand all of this, but he understood what mattered.

"Blood," he muttered, with a fresh flare of jealousy. "That's nothing compared to thirteen years."

Tomik trusted his friendship with Petra like he trusted his lungs to breathe and his bones to bear the weight of his body. But reading the horseshoe made him feel like spoiling for a fight.

That was when Neel, who was feeling much the same way, slammed into Tomik's shoulder as he strode across the deck.

Tomik's chest hit the railing. He gasped in pain.

"'Scuse me," said Neel sweetly, and kept walking.

"Guess I'm not surprised." Tomik's voice was quiet, but there was no wind, so it carried.

Neel turned to face him. "Say what you mean," he said, switching from Czech to Romany. "If you can."

"Walk away," Tomik haltingly replied in Neel's language. "Your gift."

Neel stepped closer. "Speak more clearly, lambkin."

"Bohemia—your fault."

Neel laughed. "I've been blamed for many things, most of 'em true, but no one's caught me ruining a whole country."

Tomik shook his head.

"What happened in Bohemia is my fault?" Neel still had a smile on his face, but it was dangerous. "Which is what, exactly? Did your crops fail? Do you feel the need to blame some Gypsy for it? Or maybe you're thinking of something a mite more personal? I know you can't blame me for Petra, 'cause her getting attacked by the prince's beasts happened on *your* watch, not mine. Wait—silly me, here I'm assuming that you *have* some kind of watch, that you might look out for her, since you're supposed to be her friend. But I can't help remembering that you were nowhere in Prague when she was alone and needed someone, and found me."

Tomik shook his head again. He summoned all of his concentration to make what he had to say count, and cut deep. "No. Roma, on Loophole Beach. All Bohemia. *That* is your fault. Why prince lock up Roma? You stole. Prince search *you*. You are—you make mess. You walk away."

The Maraki weren't sure who threw the first punch, but no sooner had the words left Tomik's mouth than he and Neel were a yelling, twisting mass of limbs.

Two hands reached in, grasped both boys by their hair, and yanked them apart.

"A nightmare, that's what this is," said Treb. "I keep thinking I have an extra purse of gold and a cousin with brains, and then I realize I've got *this*." He shook the boys and they winced. "Neel, why are you more trouble when you actually get your way? This mess is your fault."

"It isn't!" he shouted, not realizing that Treb hadn't heard the whole exchange between him and Tomik. Treb was referring to their fight, nothing more.

Treb released them, and they staggered.

"Go to the crow's nest, both of you," he said. "You can yowl at each other all you like up there."

"Treb!" Neel protested.

"Don't whine at me, coz. I know you can't stand him. *I* can't stand him. But if you won't learn how to hate and be silent about it, then shimmy on up there and get it out of your system and *out of my way!*"

Tomik didn't understand this conversation. The Romany words were said too quickly. But he couldn't miss what was expected when Treb hauled him up by his shoulders and set him on the ratlines, the ladderlike structure made from ropes that stretched from the deck to the top of the mainmast.

Treb pointed to the sky. "Up."

"Maybe he'll fall," Neel said hopefully.

Treb reached for him.

"Don't get grabby with *me!*" Neel leaped for the bottom rung of the ratlines. "I'm going!" He swung himself up and began to mount the ropes, passing Tomik.

Every day on the *Pacolet*, Tomik had seen sailors climb the ratlines to reach the sails on each of the two masts. The sails were square-shaped, and grew smaller as they neared the top. Neel passed the course sail. He looked back. "Careful!" he called. "Or you'll go splat and dead!"

Tomik decided that he didn't like heights.

The rope creaked beneath his hands and feet. He followed Neel, and began to climb along the topsail. The rocking of the boat grew more violent the higher he went, and the crow's nest still looked like a brown speck he would never reach.

Tomik squeezed the rough rope until it began to blister his palms. His right leg shook with the strain of his fear. The deck was far below. He froze.

Neel clambered inside the crow's nest and looked down. "I spy a coward!"

Tomik lunged ahead. His foot slipped, sending his leg into space. The rope snagged the back of his knee. Tomik straightened, caught his breath, and continued to climb. The ratlines angled closer to the mast now, and he climbed past the topgallant sail.

Tomik hauled himself into the crow's nest, which was little more than an open wooden barrel, and he collapsed on the floor.

Neel was lounging—as much as the small space would let him. The crow's nest tilted back and forth. "Remember," he said, "we still got to go back down."

Tomik glared.

"It gets easier," Neel said, his voice losing its mocking edge. "A fellow can get used to anything."

Tomik stood up and leaned over the edge of the barrel. The deck below looked like a slipper. The horizon was a hazy line. His pulse was just beginning to slow when a seagull flew by and dropped a white-green glob on his head.

Neel roared. His entire body trembled with laughter, and tears leaked out of his eyes.

"It's not funny," Tomik said.

"Is—too—" gasped Neel.

Tomik considered chucking Neel out of the crow's nest, but then was struck by how absurd this situation was. He knew he looked ridiculous, with gull droppings oozing through his hair. And Neel did, too, squirming with giggles. In spite of himself, Tomik smiled.

He sat down next to Neel. "I don't really think it's your fault."

Neel stopped laughing. "I don't either."

"I just said that about Loophole Beach to make you mad."

"Well, it worked."

"But I still don't like you."

"Oh, Tom." Neel wiped away his tears. "Warn me the next time you're gonna break my heart."

TOMIK WASN'T SURE how long they were up there. He didn't doze off, but he didn't feel awake either. The crow's nest rocked, and every time Tomik opened his eyes he was surprised by how far he was from his village and everything he knew.

"We're going down," Neel said abruptly.

"We are?" Tomik replied, still dreamy.

"Yeah."

The wind had come back, though it was gentle. It fluttered through Tomik's hair as they climbed down the ratlines. Neel was right—this did get easier, and by the time Tomik's feet hit the solid wood of the deck, he was steady.

Kiran was nearby, gutting a fish. He tossed the bloody sac of organs overboard and looked at Tomik. "Well done."

That was all anyone would ever say about Tomik's first time on the ratlines, because the entire ship was about to prepare for battle.

Neel raced across the deck, heading aft. He reached Treb and Andras. "I think we're being followed."

Treb pulled the pipe from his mouth. "What makes you say that?"

Neel pointed at a dot on the water.

"Hmm," said Treb.

"Might be nothing," said Andras.

"Might be. Might not."

"You bet it's not," said Neel. "They've been following our path for a few hours now."

Treb frowned. "I don't have time for pirate games."

"The ocean's a big place," said Andras. "We can outrace them."

"We'll leave 'em in our chop," Neel agreed.

"In this wind?" Treb scoffed. "It's as soft as a lady's breath.

Depending on what kind of ship that is, she could gain on us. We can't risk engaging an enemy ship. With the Terrestrial Globe on board . . ."

The three of them looked at one another.

Treb narrowed his eyes. "Did someone blab our secret in Sallay?"

Andras was stern. "What do you think?"

Neel suddenly remembered the goatherd. "Well, it wasn't me!"

"Neel," threatened Treb, "if I've got a reason to, I'll hoist you up into the rigging by your toes."

"That ship," said Andras, looking over their shoulders, "is definitely gaining."

"If they want the globe, it could be to our advantage," said Treb. "They won't risk firing on us. Any ship that holds the globe would be too valuable to sink. If they're after our prize, they'll pull up alongside the *Pacolet* and board her. They'll try to cut us down one by one with swords. But if they're your average pirates, we can expect cannon fire. We'll give 'em as good as we get."

"They could be friendly," said Andras.

"In *these* waters?"

"We shouldn't sink a ship if it means us no harm."

Treb snorted. "Were you always this soft?"

"They could even be Maraki," argued Andras. "We can't see what flag they're flying."

Treb paused, considering.

Andras pointed at a far-off knot of dark blue. "There's a storm coming. The wind'll pick up."

"Right," Treb said. "Here's what we're going to do. Neel, set up the drogue. We'll let them believe we're a slow ship run by inexperienced sailors. They'll get close, and we'll see what they're all about. If we're being chased for the globe, we'd better find out that our secrets are not as safe as we think. We will *not* let them board. Andras, get Garil to ready the cannons."

Andras started to walk away.

Treb called, "Tell him to aim them *high!*"

"WHAT'S HAPPENING?" Tomik asked Neel.

"Nothing."

Tomik scanned the crew. They were bristling with swords. "Nothing looks a lot like something."

"Then maybe you ought to get below deck and stop pestering me with questions you know the answers to."

"I can figure out what's going on. What I want"—Tomik crossed his arms—"is details. And my knife."

"What?"

"My glass knife."

Like every other sailor onboard, Neel had many more important things to do than stop and stare. But that's what he did.

Both Neel and Tomik sensed that this was going to be a recurring theme with them—trying to figure out who owned what, and who owed what.

"All right," Neel said. "Follow me. You can help."

They descended into the belly of the ship until they reached a large wooden door that yawned wide. Nicolas stepped out of the room. There was a sword in his hand, a long dagger at his waist, a knife in his boot, and a second sword strapped to his back.

Neel raised an eyebrow. "How are you going to move with all that?"

"Like a well-armed man," Nicolas answered, and left.

The air in the room was tangy. It smelled of the oil burning in the lamp that hung from the ceiling, and of well-kept wood, leather, and steel. Weaponry poked out of thrown-open trunks.

Neel unlocked a canvas-lined box and took out the glass knife. He handed it to Tomik. Not having a better place for it, Tomik tucked it into his belt.

"Can't you make some of those glass bombs?" asked Neel. "Like Petra used in Salamander Castle?"

"Sure." Tomik shrugged. "Just give me several days, a brassica-fueled fire, a glass-blowing pipe, some—"

"Forget it." Neel walked deeper into the dark recesses of the room, Tomik at his side.

On the floor lay a peculiar object. It was large, long, and shaped like a cone. Its shape had been made by attaching animal skins to a metal hoop, stitching them together, and drawing them down to a point. Ropes braced the cone, running along its sides and coming up over the hoop. A foot above that, the ropes were knotted together to an iron ring.

"Get that end," Neel ordered. "We have to set this up before the ship gets close enough to see us." They lifted the thing and carried it out of the room like they might carry a body.

They brought it up on deck, where the wind had already begun to blow strongly. Tas and Kiran were waiting for them at the stern of the ship. The men quickly went to work, attaching heavy chains to the pointed end and a long length of rope to the ring. The other end of the rope was securely fastened to a bolt on the deck.

"It's called a drogue," Neel said, just as Tas and Kiran heaved the object overboard and the coil of rope at their feet began to unwind. Most of the rope slipped into the waves behind the *Pacolet*. The rest of it lay in a taut line.

Tas and Kiran nodded at the boys and lifted themselves onto the ratlines, heading for the sails.

"The drogue's going to slow us down," Tomik stated.

"Yep. The *Pacolet*'s quick on the wind, but the drogue'll make those other fellows think we can't outrun 'em. They'll get confident, they'll get close, we'll find out what they want. If they're not very nice, we'll cut the drogue and hightail it out of here—after we do a little damage, if need be."

This struck Tomik as a dangerous strategy. "So it's a *good* thing that ship's gaining on us?"

Neel looked troubled. "We'll see."

The *Pacolet* slowed, the sky darkened with the coming storm, and the mysterious vessel drew close.

Treb and Andras stood at the port side of the ship. Sailors thronged behind them, armed and wary.

"They're not Maraki," said Andras.

The other ship, which bore no Roma flag, sliced across the water. It fired a warning shot. It wasn't the thud of cannon fire, but the crack of a pistol.

"I guess they're not friendly," Andras said.

"And they've got guns," Treb muttered with jealousy.

"Newfangled, unreliable things," Andras consoled. "The bullets don't go where you want 'em to even half of the time."

"And the other half?" Treb shook his head. "With a shot like that, they mean business. But not enough to fire a cannon and sink us. Go aloft, Andras. I need you up by the topsail on the mainmast. Catch that wind, and hold it tight until we're ready."

Andras walked to the mast and began to leap up the Jacob's ladder.

The enemy ship drew closer. Its narrow body was swift on the waves, its sails looked new, and the deck held enough people to tell Treb that the Maraki were outnumbered. Treb waited. The ship pulled up to the *Pacolet*, and the two vessels sailed side by side.

"Where's your captain?" someone yelled.

With some surprise, Treb registered that the words were in Czech. "What do you want with us?" he shouted back.

"I think you know!"

"Maybe I'm a little slow."

The other man laughed and pointed with his sword at the *Pacolet*. "I can see that. Let me explain, then, what's going to happen. Your ship's practically dead in the water, she's so slow. You can't escape from us, and we're prepared to board your boat and kill you all. But it doesn't have to be that way. You've got one thing, and one thing only, that we want. Surrender it, and we'll let you go. We'll do you and your ship no harm."

The wind began to blow fiercely, and far-off thunder rumbled over the ocean.

"If you come aboard my ship, you might win against us," shouted Treb. "But I think you won't, and many of you will end up bleeding in the water for sharks to eat. What do we have that's so precious you'll risk that?"

"You know perfectly well!" snarled the Bohemian captain. "Give us the globe or give us your lives!"

"You'll get neither!" In Romany, Treb called, "Neel! Cut that drogue loose!"

Neel pulled his dagger from its sheath and sawed at the rope that bound the drogue to the *Pacolet*. The rope frayed, but wasn't breaking fast enough. Neel could see the other ship edging up to the *Pacolet*. It wouldn't be long before the Bohemian sailors leaped across the divide.

For a split second, Tomik thought about surrendering himself to his countrymen. Then a gunshot rang out, and he saw Klara clutch her arm.

Tomik brought his glass knife down on the rope. It flashed in the air, and sliced the rope in one clean stroke. The rope spun away into the water.

The *Pacolet* surged forward, its sails puffed full of stormy wind. As lightning stitched across the sky, the Maraki up in the rigging did everything they could to harness the wind's power. They hauled the sails into the best position to give the *Pacolet* the distance needed for their next move.

"Fire!" yelled Treb.

The Maraki at the cannons lit their fuses. The cannons began to boom. Chain shot and bar shot flew into the air and struck the enemy ship, tearing through its sails, splitting its yards. The Maraki aimed for the ship's rigging, and finally they got the hit they wanted most of all. The foretop mast—the highest point of the Bohemian ship's mainmast—shattered. Chunks of wood rained down.

There was a clap of thunder. The storm was here.

In the sudden rain, the Maraki didn't look back at the chaos they left behind them—or, if they looked back once, they didn't do it again.

"What will happen to them?" Tomik asked Neel as the *Pacolet* hurtled over the waves. "Will they sink?"

"No. We could've punched a hole right through that ship's gut. We didn't. We just wanted to cripple her, to clip her wings so she couldn't fly after us. So we aimed our cannons high at their rigging. That ship won't sink, but she can't sail."

"What will they do?" Tomik persisted.

Neel paused. "I don't know."

THE STORM WASN'T as bad as it seemed, and the *Pacolet* rode it out.

The bullet had only grazed Klara's arm. The wound was bloody but shallow, and Brishen cleaned it.

When the sky was clear again and the waves calmer, Tomik walked up to Neel.

"I'll give you this"—Tomik offered the horseshoe—"for the crystal you took from me."

Neel agreed.

It was a fair trade.

15

The Terrestrial Globe

T HE DAY AFTER THE BATTLE, the wind changed. It blew from the east, and was as hot and dry as air in a brick oven. This wind has a reputation: it's called a levanter, and it's mean. The Maraki stowed the sails, because a levanter could blow them off course. It blew them off course anyway, carrying them farther out into the Western Ocean than they ever wanted to be. It was late January, and this time of year in that particular region of the sea meant one thing: storms, and lots of them. Serious storms. Storms that could chew you up and spit you out.

But Neel had more important things to worry about than the weather. He was reminded of this when Treb's hand reached out of a dark passageway and seized him.

"Hey!" yelped Neel.

"I'd like a word with you, little cousin."

"Ever hear of asking? Your habits are getting right rude."

"They're about to get ruder." Treb pushed Neel into the room where they stored all the food. There were sacks of barley, dried fruits, dried meat, dried vegetables, and, most valuable of all, large casks of fresh water.

Treb shut the door behind them. He struck a match and lit his pipe. The red glow of the burning tobacco was the only light in the room.

"Why all the secrecy, Treb?"

" 'Cause you seem to be a little short on it."

"Is this about the globe?"

Treb didn't reply. Neel could hear the crackle of the tobacco as it burned.

"And you got to lock me up in the pantry to ask me about it? Come on, Treb. Everybody on this ship knows what we got, and what we're after."

"There is one thing I don't want my sailors to know," said Treb.

"Yeah? What?"

"How little faith I have in you."

"Those sailors were Bohemian," Neel pointed out. "Bo-hee-mee-un. Seems to me you should be hassling someone else. Someone blond."

"So you think Tomik tipped off those sailors. Now why would he do that?"

"To be rescued by them. To go home."

"Hmm. Yes, that does make sense. Or it would if I hadn't seen Tomik cut the drogue loose."

Neel didn't reply.

"You're talented, coz," said Treb. "But what are your skills? Thieving and lying. Not exactly things that inspire confidence in you. So far all you've done is put our mission at risk. We need the Celestial Globe, and you need to help me get it if I'm going to be able to trust you again."

"Maybe I don't *want* your trust," Neel shot back.

"Don't think that hasn't occurred to me."

Treb stalked out of the pantry, and left Neel in the dark.

● ● ●

"THE CAPTAIN wants to see you," Andras told Tomik.

Tomik nodded wordlessly. He had a pretty good idea of why he'd been sent for. He followed Andras toward the stern of the ship, and the captain's quarters.

Tomik paused nervously outside Treb's door. Maybe he had made the wrong decision. Maybe he shouldn't have cut that rope. "Klara?" he asked.

"She's fine." Andras put a hand on Tomik's shoulder and opened the door.

Treb was seated on an intricately carved, satin-backed chair that must have cost a fortune. He leaned across an elegant table to knock the ashes of his pipe into a brass bowl, glanced at Andras, and flicked his gaze at the door. Andras left.

Tomik didn't want to look at Treb directly. He stared at the satin arms of the chair, which were water-stained.

"We plucked it from the sea," Treb said in Romany. "There are storms that smash other ships to pieces, but not the *Pacolet*. We're scavengers. Most of our wealth has been taken from the dead. Sometimes we come across things bobbing on the waves: trunks, furniture, bodies. This, for example, was found in the pocket of a corpse." Treb reached into his coat, pulled out a tube, and passed it to Tomik.

Tomik inspected the leather cylinder, noticing the glass lenses on either end. He peered through the smaller lens.

Treb began, "It's a telescope. For seeing—"

"I know," Tomik said. "For far away." He passed the telescope back. "I fix it."

"It's not broken."

"I make better," Tomik insisted, and wished that he knew Romany well enough to explain how.

The captain smiled, and for a moment Tomik thought Treb wouldn't ask the questions he dreaded.

"I'd like to show you another, more important treasure," Treb said, "but first you have to tell me something. How did those Bohemian sailors know that we carried the Terrestrial Globe? Did you somehow make a Bohemian friend in Sallay? It looks suspicious, see, that the ship that attacked us was sailed by your countrymen."

Tomik was silent.

"Now, I'm not blaming you. Not necessarily. Maybe somebody else had a big mouth. Somebody who also speaks Czech. I know that somebody wasn't me. But perhaps . . . oh, I don't know, let's say my cousin dropped a word or two he shouldn't have. Know anything about that?"

It would be so easy for Tomik to accuse Neel. But then Tomik thought about Petra, and what she would do in a situation like this. He imagined her silver eyes blazing. She would say, "Don't you dare, Tomik. You owe him."

So Tomik pressed his lips firmly together.

"I'll feed you to the little fishies," Treb warned.

Tomik shook his head. "You will not."

Treb stood, and grabbed Tomik by his collar. "What," he snarled, "don't I scare you?"

"If you want to kill me, I am already dead."

"True." Treb released Tomik's shirt. "But I've got more than half a mind to throw you in the brig and keep you there morning, noon, and night. You wouldn't like that, would you?"

"No."

"So you'll tell me?"

"No."

Treb chuckled. "Then it's a good thing I know the answer already. And it's a good thing for you, lad, that you can keep a secret."

Treb opened a trapdoor that had been so well disguised, Tomik hadn't been able to tell the difference between it and the wooden planks of the rest of the floor. Treb hauled up a leather chest, which he unlocked, then he lifted out a round bundle of cloth about two feet in diameter. Cradling it in his arms, he stepped in front of Tomik and set it on the table. He unwrapped the cloth.

Tomik's eyes widened in wonder.

He had seen maps before. Maps of his country, even of Europe. But he had never seen his whole world arranged across the surface of a large sphere.

He saw his home, crowded by neighboring countries. Bohemia was so small.

He saw Morocco, guessed the *Pacolet's* location on the ocean, and was amazed at how far he had traveled. He found the island of England with its squiggled shape, and knew how far he had to go.

Tomik reached out and spun the sphere. The brown of the continents and the blue of the water blurred together. With a finger, he stopped the globe. His skin prickled. He lifted his hand away, and saw a red spark. It was in Bohemia and, he guessed, was the general location of a Loophole. There were red points of light all over the globe.

Tomik remembered his own words to Neel in Sallay: *You would be able to wage war.*

Treb noticed the worry that crossed the boy's features. "This globe isn't much use without its twin, but whoever possesses both Mercator Globes will wield a great deal of power," he admitted. "They could be dangerous in the wrong hands."

"Destroy this one, then," Tomik said in Czech. What he had to say was too important to be misunderstood.

"Oh, no." Treb wagged his finger. "Don't be so noble, Tom. It's drastic, and dumb. The globes belong to the Roma."

After many years of being friends with Petra, Tomik recognized unreasonable stubbornness when he saw it. He looked away from Treb, and back at the globe. He noticed the lines that crossed the sphere and cut it into squares. He had seen latitude and longitude lines before on the flat surface of maps, and knew that they were used for judging distance and travel. But they seemed different on a round shape.

"It looks as if someone has thrown a net over the world," he said.

"Now all we have to do is haul it in."

WHEN TOMIK AND TREB emerged from the captain's quarters, the sails lay flat. There was no wind. Treb turned in a circle, looking at the sky from every direction. "Stow the sails!" he suddenly shouted up at the Maraki in the rigging. "Do it now!"

"Why?" Tomik asked.

"Because if we don't they'll be ripped to shreds," Treb muttered. He strode up to Andras. "Why didn't you tell me about this before?"

"I wasn't sure—"

"You don't have to be sure! If you can't figure out how to prepare for a tempest, then at least give me fair warning when one is squalling up, and leave the thinking to me! Tell Garil and Marko to lash the lifeboats to their skids. Get below deck and bring Nadia, Kiran, and Ashe with you. Take him, too." He nudged Tomik forward. "Have them latch any portholes shut and reinforce them with wooden planks. Batten all the hatches. We can't take on any water."

Tomik was so preoccupied with the fact that he had just been treated like a member of the crew that he didn't think about being worried. After all, the *Pacolet* had sailed through storms before. But then Tomik spotted the dread in Andras's eyes, and realized that whatever was coming, it was no ordinary storm. The sea was still. The wind was dead, the horizon dark, and the sky tinged with green. An eerie quiet surrounded the *Pacolet*.

"What do we do?" Tomik asked Ashe as they went below deck. Ashe entered the rope room, and passed Tomik short lengths of cord knotted loosely into slings. He copied what she did, and slipped the rope over his head so that the slings crossed his chest, running from his left shoulder to his right hip.

"You heard the captain," she replied. "We close the hatches, we—"

"No, after that."

"This is a tempest, Tom. If we had the drogue we'd set it up to slow us down as we hit the waves. But it's gone. The only thing we can do is lock everything tight, tie down anything loose, blow out the lamps, stay below deck, and hope we don't get smashed to pieces." She grinned at him nervously. "Whatever you do, don't stand too close to me. With the waves, you'll probably puke."

Even below deck, Tomik could hear the wind begin to wail. They went into the pantry and starting using the rope to secure casks of food and water.

Suddenly the ship tilted. Ashe and Tomik tumbled into each other. A small barrel fell and split, showering raisins across the room. Then, with a wooden scream, the ship leaned in the other direction. Tomik slipped across the floor and hit a cask. It cracked, springing fresh water.

"No!" Ashe dropped to her knees and pressed her hands against the leak. "Get some pitch, Tom! We need to seal this up!"

But then the *Pacolet* hit a giant wave. The ship shuddered, and the oil lamp hanging from the ceiling fell to the pantry floor. The lamp burst into a fireball.

Tomik crawled toward Ashe, pulled her hands away from the

cask, and smashed his fist against the leak. The wood shattered, water gushing across the floor and over the fire.

The room plunged into darkness.

"Why did you do that?" Ashe wailed.

"There are other water casks," he reminded her.

"But we don't know how much we'll need after the tempest, or even where we'll end up! We could be blown halfway to America! Fresh water is the difference between life and death on the sea!"

"So is fire," Tomik pointed out.

Ashe couldn't argue with that. If the *Pacolet* caught fire, it wouldn't matter how many casks of water they had.

Tomik heard her scramble to her feet. She cursed. "My matches are wet."

Tomik reached into his pocket and pulled out the Glowstone. He squeezed, and pale blue light filled the room.

Ashe squinted at him. "Aren't you full of surprises." The corner of her mouth lifted, and some of the anxiety left her face as she tugged him to his feet. "Come on. Let's finish before things really get bad."

By the time they reached the mess hall, where the Maraki had agreed to wait out the storm, almost all of the sailors were huddled together. They had already blown out the lamps, and they sat in the dark as the *Pacolet* rolled back and forth on the waves.

Trying hard to walk steadily, Tomik stared at the floor in the light of the Glowstone. He didn't see the looks of amazement.

"What is that?" breathed Klara.

"I made it," Tomik said. He passed the Glowstone to her. He was wobbling on his feet, and desperately wanted to hang on to something. He grabbed the edge of the table and sank down onto the bench.

"I'm glad we didn't sell you." Nicolas clapped Tomik on the shoulder.

Tomik gulped. He leaned over and vomited.

"I take that back." Nicolas stepped away.

"Here." Someone shoved a pail under Tomik's chin and he threw up again.

"Better?" Ashe asked.

Tomik nodded, red with shame.

"I doubt you'll be the only one using this bucket," Stevo comforted. "The tempest won't stop anytime soon."

"Where are the others?" Ashe looked around the room.

"Treb, Andras, Kiran, Tas, and Oti are still on deck, stowing the sails."

"Still?" Ashe's voice rose.

"We can't let the wind tear up our sails, or we'll be stranded out here."

Tomik glanced up. "Where is Neel?"

"Who knows." Nadia rolled her eyes. "He's probably holed up somewhere feeling sorry for himself. Treb raked him over the coals today."

"That was supposed to be a private conversation," Klara said.

"Like you can hide anything on this ship!" Nadia flung up her hands. "What am I supposed to do, pretend I didn't hear about it?"

"Yes," Klara replied.

The *Pacolet* slammed into a wave and several sailors were thrown to the floor.

Brishen stood up. "We have to look for Neel."

Just then, the Maraki who had stayed on deck walked into the room, soaked with rain and sea spray.

"The sails?" Brishen asked.

Treb scowled.

"We had to leave some of them," Andras said. "The tempest was too wild. We got below deck a while ago. We've been in the hold, making sure the *Pacolet*'s not taking on seawater."

"Did you see Neel?" Brishen asked.

Tas frowned. "No. Why?"

Treb scanned the room for his cousin. He swore. "That lad is more trouble than he's worth."

"Why is everyone acting like Neel's playing some kind of game with us?" cried Klara.

"That's what he does." Nadia shrugged.

"He could have been swept overboard!"

"Then he's gone," Nadia said.

Without thinking, Tomik stood up and staggered out of the room.

The Maraki fell silent. They were so used to Neel taking care of himself, and to his habit of challenging people twice his age, that most of them found it hard to think that he could be in danger. Yet as they watched Tomik walk away, fear flared in their hearts. The Maraki leaped to their feet and began to search the ship.

The last thing Tomik wanted to do was to go on deck, but when Nadia said *he's gone*, he realized two things:

Neel was reckless, and he might be Tomik's friend.

And then there was Petra's voice, echoing in Tomik's mind: *You owe him.*

So there was only one place Neel could be: in the heart of the storm, doing something stupid. And Tomik had to find him.

He fumbled with a batten and unlocked a hatch.

Tomik wasn't surprised to find that the people who knew Neel best were standing right behind him.

"Move!" Treb reached over Tomik's head and shoved at the hatch. Then the captain boosted Tomik up through the hole.

Tomik slid over the wet surface of the deck. He scrambled to his feet and clung to the railing.

Treb, Andras, and Brishen pulled themselves out of the hatch.

The sky was black, the *Pacolet* creaked and moaned, and the rain stung Tomik's face.

Treb looked up into the rigging. "No," he whispered.

The shreds of one sail whipped in the wind, but the rest had all been stowed. A small, dark figure was climbing down the ratlines.

The *Pacolet* hit a tall wave, and water curled like a white claw over the bow.

The ship leaned, and Neel's legs slipped from the ratlines. He fell, but then dangled in midair, his hands hovering a few feet below the rope. He was hanging on to the ratlines with Danior's Fingers. Then, with an acrobatic move Lovari children are taught as soon as they can walk, Neel swung the lower half of his body until his feet found the rope.

When he jumped onto the deck, his wet, black hair was flattened against his cheeks and he looked exhilarated. He grinned at Treb.

"I'm going to kill you," Treb said, and reached to embrace his cousin when the ship suddenly tilted at an alarming angle. Neel tumbled and flew just a few feet past Tomik. His head hit the railing.

Tomik rushed forward. The *Pacolet* continued to lean left, and Neel's limp, unconscious body was toppling overboard when Tomik grabbed him. Neel hung over the water.

The ship rocked back to the right. Tomik's arms felt like they were going to pop out of their sockets, and he knew he couldn't hold on.

But he didn't have to. Several hands reached for the rope slings still crossing over his shoulder. Andras and Brishen pulled Tomik away from the railing, and Treb dragged his cousin onto the deck.

The rain poured down, and blood flowed from Neel's temple onto the wooden planks.

● ● ●

WHEN NEEL WOKE, the storm was over. He was in the captain's quarters, and sunlight streamed through the portholes. He shut his eyes. His head was ringing with pain.

He heard Treb's voice: "Good morning."

"There ain't much good about it," Neel groaned.

"Oh, I don't know. The sun's out. We're still alive. We're so off course that I barely know how to begin setting us back on track for England, but all in all I'm a fortunate captain. And a fortunate cousin."

"The sails? I lost one."

"You lost your blasted mind, is what you did. Sails can be patched up, Neel. It wasn't worth the risk."

Neel opened his eyes again.

Treb smiled.

"He's awake?" Tomik was standing in the doorway.

"Go away," Neel mumbled.

"Tom can go wherever he likes," Treb said. "He's officially in my good graces after saving your life."

"You did?" Neel blinked at Tomik.

Tomik crossed the room to Neel's bedside. "Now we're equal," he said, knowing that this wasn't exactly the right Romany word.

"We're even," Neel corrected, and offered his hand.

For the moment, that was all they needed to say—and, indeed, all they could say, for soon after they clasped hands, Neel's relaxed and slipped to his side. Tomik and Treb let him sleep, and went on deck to survey the damage.

The captain looked up at the rigging, shaking his head. "Some of the braces snapped," he said, referring to the ropes that controlled the sails. "Plenty of repairs to be done."

"How long will it take to reach England?" Tomik asked.

"A while."

16

The Statue of Life

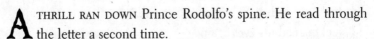

A THRILL RAN DOWN Prince Rodolfo's spine. He read through the letter a second time.

The Mercator Globes!

Suddenly, all of his dreams seemed real enough to touch. Where they had been pale and blurry, they were now rich with color and drawn with strong lines. He would not be Emperor Karl's youngest, forgotten son, the ruler of an insignificant country. He would become the emperor himself.

He scanned the letter a third time, and smiled when he saw Stan Novak's signature. The spymaster of North Africa would be well rewarded for discovering that the globes were not just the stuff of legend. In his letter, the spymaster apologized for acting without the prince's permission, but the prince heartily approved of the man's decision. How daring, how *right* of Novak to chase after the Gypsy ship! It would not be long before Novak returned to Prague, bearing the Terrestrial Globe.

Then the prince's eyes fell on the date scribbled after Novak's signature. His smile faltered, for the letter had been written two weeks ago. Mail traveled so slowly. It was painful to wonder whether Novak had succeeded.

But of course he had, the prince assured himself. The spymaster had no other option. As for Prince Rodolfo, he knew that now he had many options. With the promise of the Mercator Globes, certain things and people were no longer useful to him. Why should he crave a patched-up clock built by a broken old man? A handful of gears was nothing compared to being able to navigate the world's Rifts, and surely Rodolfo's father would agree. It was no secret that inheriting the title of Hapsburg Emperor was a competition in which his father was the only judge and his brothers were opponents. Yet when Emperor Karl chose his successor, Rodolfo would win.

It was a long walk from his suite to the Thinkers' Wing, but the prince prided himself on facing people whose lives he was about to change. There was honor in that.

Because the prince was fairly crackling with energy, he couldn't help looking at Mikal Kronos with disgust. The frail clockmaker shuffled when the prince entered the room, and a scrap of metal floating in the air abruptly crashed to the man's feet. Mikal Kronos bowed, but the prince knew it was not out of respect. There was anger in the clockmaker's stooped shoulders, and grief, and worry.

"Your Highness," the clockmaker began, "I am making some progress."

"Do you know what my favorite fairy tale was as a child?"

Master Kronos opened his mouth, then closed it, no doubt afraid the question was a trap.

"I had none," the prince continued, "for I never enjoy hearing the same story told twice."

"Forgive me, but I don't know what you mean."

"I shall explain. I do not care about your clock. I do not care about you. I do not need you." Suddenly furious with himself, the prince corrected his words. "I have *never* needed you, or your invention."

As soon as the words were uttered, a peace settled over the

prince. He imagined the Mercator Globes. He caressed them with his mind.

"Your Highness, if you no longer want me to rebuild the clock's heart, then . . ." The question on Mikal Kronos's face was plain: *Then what will become of me?*

"I have other plans for you."

WEEKS DRAGGED BY. Rodolfo thought of the now-empty laboratory in the Thinkers' Wing, and the date on Novak's letter, and wondered if he had not made a terrible mistake. When the prince looked in the mirror, he saw the bluish shadows of sleepless nights—there, right under his eyes. He touched the delicate skin and thought of storms, sea battles, and sunken ships.

Had something gone wrong? Why had he received no news? Where was Novak? Most important, where was the Terrestrial Globe?

The prince smoothed pale powder over his cheekbones, hiding the shadows. He must remain calm.

But that afternoon, at a luncheon twittering with lords and ladies, someone dropped a fork. The metallic sound of it hitting the floor rang through the prince's head like an evil bell. He thought of the clockmaker and his annoying daughter, who was somehow *still* missing. She was just as absent as the Terrestrial Globe.

Rodolfo stood up from the table and left the room.

He stalked to his suite, and ordered everyone to leave him alone. He stood before the enchanted window in his chambers. The lilacs were in bloom. It was far too early in the year for this, and snow still blanketed the ground, but much can be accomplished with magic. The sight of the flowers should have put him in a fine mood. Their purple softness had never failed to soothe him with their beauty.

Instead he made a fist, but he did not punch the window. Even in his frustration, he was aware that punching was something dirty men did in tavern brawls. His fingers curled, he backhanded the windowpane. It did not shatter, for the window was enspelled rock. The prince knew this—and his bloodied knuckles knew it, too.

Why did the thought of the clockmaker's daughter disturb him so?

He remembered when he had interviewed her—here, in this very room. She had been bold for a servant. Her voice had a country twang that set his teeth on edge. But there had been something mysterious about her . . . Rodolfo cursed himself. He should have listened to his instincts. The girl had reminded him of something. He knew now that her face resembled her father's. But it was more than that. He was certain that he had seen her face—*her* face, not just her father's—before.

Suddenly, he understood. Petra Kronos looked like the statue of Life on the clocktower her father had designed. The prince recalled how, a year ago, he had told Master Kronos that he thought the designs for that statue were too plain. But the clockmaker had stood firm, so the prince had allowed it.

He strode across the room and down the hallway, wrenched open the double doors, and called for his carriage.

It was not long before he stood before the Staro Clock in the center of his city. His people stared at the unexpected sight of their prince, but he ignored them. He watched the silver minute hand sweep over the clock's face to join the golden hour hand. When they met, the clock began to toll. The blue doors opened and statues began to file out, but the prince had eyes for only one. There she was: Petra Kronos, the statue of Life.

This was love. Even Rodolfo recognized this, though he knew very little about the subject. Mikal Kronos loved his daugh-

ter. The prince could see it in every carved line of the statue's
face.

His own father was an obstacle. Someone who *simply would not
die*. His mother was an idiot. Rodolfo suffered during every dinner
of every night of every visit to the Austrian court. There, he could
not escape his parents' presence, and the empress was fond of trying to be witty. She never seemed to realize she was telling only
one joke, and it was about herself.

The blue doors shut.

The prince closed his eyes. He was doing something that was
rare for him: reevaluating his position. When he had learned that
a gawky girl had breached every measure of his castle's security to
steal from him, he had wanted nothing more than to tear her to
pieces. He was enraged not merely by the fact that she had taken
precious objects and destroyed others. She had also made him
look weak. He was nineteen, the youngest of Emperor Karl's three
sons, and he could not afford to be seen as a ruler whose castle had
become a playground for a girl and a Gypsy. So Petra Kronos
would have to die—publicly, unpleasantly.

But . . .

The prince pinched the bridge of his nose, his eyes still shut.

The features of the statue were not beautiful, but they haunted
him, and that fact alone made him realize that Petra Kronos had to
be special. Indeed, she must be, if she had been able to deceive
him and destroy the most important piece of her father's clock.
And she had escaped the Gristleki—how had this been possible?
His scouts had hauled back the four blood-soaked bodies. Had *she*
killed the Gristleki? All *four*? And *where was she?*

The prince was forced to conclude that the girl had hidden talents, and he wanted to know what they were. She would be more
interesting to him alive than dead. She could be useful.

Prince Rodolfo opened his eyes, and they blazed with something that those who had watched him build his collection in the Cabinet of Wonders knew well.

It was possession.

He would have the globes. He *would*. And he would have Petra Kronos, too.

17

The Only One Left

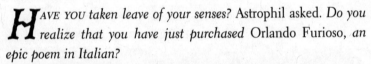

*H*AVE YOU *taken leave of your senses?* Astrophil asked. *Do you realize that you have just purchased* Orlando Furioso, *an epic poem in Italian?*

Did I? Petra replied. *I thought it was a recipe book.*

Petra walked away from the stall. Astrophil risked poking his head out of her hair for a better look at the book she held against her chest.

*But you loathe cooking. And Dee's servants prepare all the food. And you—you—*he spluttered—*you did* not *think it was such a book. You cannot fool me. Even you are not so oblivious as to think that a recipe book could be so finely bound. Why, look at that Moroccan leather. The letters are tooled with gold, and—*

Astrophil, are you drooling?

There was a pause. *No.*

Petra touched her neck and examined her fingers. *Yes, you are.*

Late February is a grim time in London. The sky was as gray as slate, and almost as heavy. But life went on, and Petra had a secret that made her smile and hum.

You are quite cheerful for someone who has just wasted money on a book she will never read, Astrophil said crankily.

Oh, I wouldn't say I wasted money. I'm sure I can find a use for

Orlando Furioso. *I do need something for target practice, after all. How deep do you think my dagger will go into the book?*

Her earlobe vibrated with a metallic spasm.

Astrophil, don't have a seizure! I'm joking! This book is not for me. It's a gift.

Really?

Yes, for Madinia and Margaret.

Oh.

Astrophil was silent the entire way back to the house on Throgmorton Street. Petra could feel him drooping on her ear like a wilted flower. He seemed so depressed that once Petra had locked her bedroom door behind her, she couldn't help telling him the truth. She set the book on the desk. "Astrophil, I have a confession to make."

"I am not interested." He lowered himself to the floor and began to creep away.

"Oh, Astro." She scooped him up. "The book is a gift, but not for Madinia and Margaret. It's for *you*, for your birthday." She set the spider down on top of the red book. "I wanted it to be a surprise, but I can never hide anything from you."

"It is for me?" The spider gazed with awe at the golden title. "For my birthday?" He turned to look at Petra. "You remembered!"

"Have I ever forgotten? Seven years ago, Father"—Petra's smile slipped—"Father gave you to me. I was so happy."

"You screamed," Astrophil corrected. "And at a very high pitch, I might add. I thought you would break the windows."

"I was scared of spiders. That's why Father made you for me—so I would learn not to be afraid."

Astrophil tiptoed across the leather cover and leaned over the edge to peer at the spine. Then he began to jump up and down. "I knew it! I knew it was for me!" He rubbed his forelegs together like a fly. "Open it, Petra! The cover is too heavy for me to lift."

As the spider raced through the pages, Petra was surprised and guilty to find that, for the first time since she had been snatched out of Bohemia, her heart felt light.

The past several weeks had been hard. She had become stronger, healthier. But she'd also grown more desperate. The only thing that kept her from smashing anything valuable in the house and running as far as her legs could take her was the knowledge that Dee would just yank her back like a puppet on strings.

There were two things that gave Petra hope. One of them was her goal: *Outwit Dee. Go home. Find Father.* Margaret had taught her how to play chess, and Petra quickly learned that she could lose almost any piece and still win. So if Petra had to sit through lessons with Dee, she did it. If she was encouraged to take every meal with Madinia and Margaret, she dined in their rooms. And every moment she looked for a way to end this terrible game in which she had been trapped.

The second thing that Petra clung to was Astrophil.

She sat on the window seat's velvet cushions, hugging her knees to her chest and watching the spider read. "I don't know what I'd do without you."

"Something impressively foolish, I imagine," the spider said dryly. But then he glanced up at Petra. He saw that her pleasure in giving him the book had been momentary, and that it was already gone. He climbed off the book and lowered himself to the ground, then picked his way across the carpet, crawled up her leg, and came to rest on the plateau of her bended knee.

"I also miss our home," he said. "I miss Master Kronos. I worry about him, too."

"You do?"

"Of course. Why would that surprise you?"

"You're always so much more . . . normal than I am. You seem the same. I don't feel the same. Sometimes it's as if nothing bothers you."

"I am often bothered," said Astrophil. "It is hard to know, however, what to do with such feelings. I study books partly because I need to know how to hold myself in times like these. Through my reading, I have learned that people can choose to remain silent out of love for others. But there are also moments when a person might share his troubles for precisely the same reason."

Petra held out her forefinger, and the spider wrapped his legs around it.

"Thank you, Astrophil."

Since the day Petra and Dee reached an agreement in the shallow boat on the Thames, she had tried to find out information about Gabriel Thorn. The problem was that there was a limited number of people she could ask. Dee, she knew, would smirk. She could imagine his response. "What, conceding already, Petra?" he would say. "You do understand that we are *competitors*, and that if you ask for my help, it can only mean you are admitting defeat."

So Petra tried talking to Sarah.

"Gabriel Thorn?" The servant gnawed her lip. "Never heard of him. Wait—he's one of the queen's men, isn't he? I think he's visited our house before. Talk to the porter, Jack. He'd've seen Thorn come and go. Now stand up straight, dear heart, and let me measure you for a new set of those unspeakable trousers. Ah! You've put on weight. There's a good girl."

The porter refused to speak to Petra. Jack heard her questions, gave her one disapproving look, and then ignored her.

But Petra was able to glean a little more information from Madinia and Margaret. She saw them several times a day, for the sisters never took meals with their parents ("They have so little time alone," Margaret explained). The twins sought out Petra's presence, so she tried not to throw her fork at Madinia when she criticized Petra's table manners, and she listened to their endless gossip. Petra was sure that the sisters knew something about Gabriel Thorn, and they did.

"Who would want him dead?" Madinia echoed Petra's question. "Everybody! No one liked that nasty toad."

"But he was the West," Petra said. "The queen must have liked him."

"That just shows how much you know!"

"The queen doesn't always give important positions to the most popular people," Margaret explained, "or the strongest or most capable."

How wise of Queen Elizabeth, observed Astrophil, whose English had vastly improved with the help of the stolen grammar book. He was now able to follow conversations easily.

Why is it smart to give power to people who can't use it? Petra asked.

There are other female monarchs in Europe, but none of them actually rules like Queen Elizabeth. She is very old. She has no children to succeed her, and in some ways must be vulnerable . . . she needs advisers, but what if they were to gain great authority?

Petra understood. *They might overthrow her.*

Exactly. It would be easy for a group of truly powerful councillors to decide that their old, heirless female ruler should no longer rule.

"Some of the councillors," Margaret was saying, "like Robert Cecil, deserve their positions. Others are useless, or despised."

Petra remembered how respectful Cecil had been of Dee's opinion, and something occurred to her. "Your father's the true secretary of defense, isn't he? Walsingham's just a figurehead."

"In some ways, yes," Margaret said. "A spymaster can't do his job really well if he's always chasing after knighthoods and titles, like Walsingham."

"He's not bad." Madinia shrugged. "Just puffed up."

"Walsingham has many friends and connections," Margaret continued. "His underlings respect him—though maybe like you respect anyone who puts money in your purse. But Walsingham wants what's best for this country."

"And Gabriel Thorn?" Petra asked.

Madinia looked at Margaret, who replied, "He wanted what was best for himself."

"And your father?"

"What are you implying, Petra?" Margaret asked icily.

Madinia added, "Dad would give his life for England!"

Maybe so, but Petra knew that he would go to any length to do what he believed was right. "Why would Dee be glad that the West is dead?"

"He isn't glad!" Madinia slammed her teacup onto its saucer. "And don't you dare suggest it!"

Margaret didn't say anything, but she bit her lip in a way that Petra recognized. She always did this when Madinia had said too much. Petra didn't want to press the sisters too hard on the topic, though, for fear that they would clam up entirely. Thinking of Cotton's shield and Ariel's strange words, she changed tack: "Do you know anything about Robert Cotton?"

"No," Madinia said. "He's boring, and so are you."

"He's a recluse," said Margaret. "He never comes to court. All he cares about is his library and greenhouse."

"What about—?" Petra began.

"What about going for a walk down Goldsmiths' Row to look at jewelry?" Madinia interrupted. "Just to look."

The twins dodged any more discussion of Gabriel Thorn and the court.

There were two other people Petra could question. One of them was Agatha Dee, but Petra never saw her. If it weren't for the fact that Petra was able to slip from Czech to English with perfect ease, she would have thought that her encounter with Agatha Dee had been a feverish hallucination. Whenever she asked a servant where she could find Agatha, she was told with cold finality, "The mistress doesn't want to be disturbed."

There was one person left: Kit.

She saw him every day. Petra had steadily improved in her ability to fence, and was able to parry and dodge Kit's sword with natural grace. But she rarely managed to strike a blow of her own, or succeed in a counterattack. Sometimes her sword managed to slip past Kit's defenses, but Petra was never good enough to put him in any real danger.

Petra often wished that she was able to bring Astrophil with her into the practice room. But there was no good way for Petra to hide him except under her clothes, and Astrophil had immediately put a stop to that idea.

Yet perhaps it was for the best that the spider was not in the room with Petra and Kit today, because he would have disapproved of how close Petra was to asking the boy for help. *Kit said himself that he is untrustworthy!* Astrophil had scolded her when she suggested that they enlist Kit's aid to find Thorn's murderer. Nevertheless, Petra wanted to take the risk.

When they had finished their last bout, Kit said something unexpected. "The winter ball is this Friday night. Are you going?"

Petra snorted. "No."

Kit was silent. He set his sword very carefully on its rack.

"Why?" Petra asked. "Will it be interesting?"

"Not if you don't come."

She couldn't tell if he was joking.

"I'll be there," he said. "Yes, I know. Silly, isn't it? Walsingham used to drag me to every dance when I worked for him. Throw the entire court together, pour wine down their throats, and what do they do? They say things they shouldn't. Of course, I haven't been officially on the guest list since I was fired, but the guards and I are old friends."

"So you think balls are fun," Petra said skeptically.

"I didn't say that."

"Then why . . . ?"

"The free food." He grinned. "Also, I like to keep my hand in the spying game. I don't get paid for it anymore, but I still enjoy knowing what's going on." He paused. "Petra, can I be frank with you?"

"Yes," she said. "I'd like that."

"That's what I thought. Actually, it's one of your problems in fencing. *You* are too frank. Every move you make is obvious. You're too direct, and you expect everyone else to fight the same way."

She folded her arms. The conversation had quickly moved from being confusing to being irritating, and she said so.

"There!" Kit pointed. "You see? What if you had to pretend that you liked somebody? Could you do it? I don't think so. I hate to talk in clichés, but your face is an open book. And it's been hard for me to see you almost every day, when I have no idea *why* I've been hired to train you, and why you look so"—he took a breath—"so lost."

Petra was silent.

"You don't have to tell me anything," said Kit, "but I think there's something wrong, and I'd like to help."

She hesitated. "What would going to the winter ball have to do with helping me?"

"Petra, you don't belong here. I can tell. You didn't even know who Walsingham is! I've spent more than a month of afternoons with you, and I can say that you are as clueless about England's politics as you are about its history, towns, and countryside."

Petra instantly regretted (again) that she never brought Astrophil to sword practice. He would have been able to fill in the holes of her ignorance.

"You look like no English girl I've ever seen," Kit continued. "You speak my language perfectly, but you're a foreigner. I know what Agatha Dee can do, and I think she's done it to you. Let me show you around Whitehall Palace. I can tell you who's who, and take your mind off whatever is bothering you."

Petra looked away.

"And if you don't come to the ball," Kit persuaded, "I'll end up stuffing myself full of quail eggs, and will be utterly bored."

Petra was weakening.

"Can I bribe you?" asked Kit. "How about this: I promise to teach you a neat little sequence with the sword. I invented it myself. To your opponent, it will look like defensive moves, but they're actually steps of attack."

"You're supposed to teach me things like that anyway."

"Yes, but if I see you in the Watching Chamber in four days' time, I promise to teach it to you nicely."

18

The Winter Ball

PETRA SET DOWN the iron key and reached for a silver bracelet, the second item to be covered in that day's lesson with John Dee. "I'd like to go to the winter ball," she told him.

"You would?" Dee arched one brow.

You would? Astrophil nearly fell off her ear. *Petra, are you feeling ill?*

"What?" she said to both of them. "Do you think I can't dance?"

I know you cannot, Astrophil replied.

Dee folded his hands. "I suppose you believe you can gather some information about Gabriel Thorn from the courtiers. Anybody who would know anything is not going to talk about it to a thirteen-year-old girl. We made an amusing little bargain, my dear, but I don't see how you can keep it. Perhaps you should give it up. Focus on your training."

Petra flung the bracelet across the room.

"Oh, very well," said Dee. "If you insist on being childish, then perhaps you belong in a room full of self-absorbed courtiers. And, as it happens, Madinia and Margaret have been pressuring me for weeks to make you go to the ball."

"They have?" Petra hadn't thought that the sisters cared whether she went or not.

"Yes. But I assumed you would not enjoy it, and I didn't think it was wise to force you to do yet one more thing against your will." He paused, then added, "It is helpful that you wish to attend the ball. Queen Elizabeth is curious to meet you."

"What? *Why?* What did you tell her about me?"

"Everything. She is my queen."

"But you told me to be careful! To keep my identity secret! What about Kit? You told me not to tell *him*."

"He is an entirely different matter than the queen of England," Dee said sharply. "I hired him to train you because he is highly skilled, and roughly your size and age. But he is not to be trusted."

"I don't trust *you*."

"I know that, my dear. Now, fetch that bracelet. Open your mind and answer these questions. Where does it come from? What was it before it was forged? Who used to own it, and how did it come into my possession?"

LAUGHTER ECHOED OVER the twilit Thames as the many boats drew closer to Whitehall Palace. The Dees, however, were silent. Petra studied Agatha Dee. The woman's face was as blank as ever. It was unnatural.

But when they reached the dockhouse, Petra forgot about Agatha Dee as her stomach swarmed with nervousness.

Petra and the Dees slipped into the stream of guests walking down a mirrored hallway, and she caught a glimpse of herself. She looked like a stranger.

She wore an old garnet-colored dress of Margaret's with a high collar that hid the Gristleki scar, and the neckline was square-cut, just enough to expose the small wings of her collarbone. "That's too plain!" Madinia had shrilled. "You'll look frumpy!"

"Good," replied Petra.

Sarah had lengthened the dress. Then she fussed over Petra, combing and trimming, braiding and pinning, twisting and curling. When Petra had asked Madinia if she could borrow some silver hairpins, the girl agreed, and gleefully jabbed them into place. Later, Madinia was too excited about the ball to notice an extra metallic glint in Petra's hair. It was Astrophil, clutched like a flower-shaped pin around a small braid.

Petra followed the Dees into the Watching Chamber, where torches blazed. A long table was heaped with roasted meat and candied fruit. Musicians played their string instruments in a corner, and people danced in the center of the room. The swift, complex dance was dizzying to Petra's eyes.

Ready to join the dancers? Astrophil said wickedly. *I promise not to count the number of times you step on people's feet.* If the spider had seen Petra fencing with Kit, he might not have teased her like this. He would have realized that she moved gracefully when she was confident that she could.

Petra looked at the dancers and shuddered.

"Come." Margaret reached for Petra's hand. "We are going to greet the queen."

Petra walked between the sisters, behind their parents. John Dee ignored Petra, which was more than fine with her.

As they drew closer to Queen Elizabeth, Petra's jaw tightened with determination. She had a question to ask.

A bubble of space surrounded the seated queen. When she spoke with a lord or lady, their conversation was both private and public. It was private, because no one could hear what was being said. It was public, because no one could mistake the expression on the queen's face. Just as John Dee had said to Petra during her first visit to the palace, there was always somebody watching in the Watching Chamber, and tonight they were all watching the queen. Right now, several eyes in the room were turned toward the man kneeling at her feet, and everyone could see the frown on Queen Elizabeth's face as she spoke. The old woman pounded the arm of her throne, her bullet-black eyes wide with anger. The man slunk away.

Then Petra and the Dees were brought before the queen. Petra had thought she would be forced to wait while the adults said whatever dull things they had to say, but Dee waved her forward. "This is the girl in question, Your Majesty."

Petra stepped in front of the throne.

"Come closer," the queen ordered, so Petra did.

Queen Elizabeth's face was sunken, her gaze sharp. Petra could tell that her orange hair was a wig, but the queen wore it like a battle helmet.

"Well, child, did no one teach you how to kneel?"

Petra obeyed. Then she drew her breath to speak.

But Queen Elizabeth spoke first, her hand lifting Petra's chin. "Petra Kronos, our little Bohemian refugee." The queen studied her. "So young, and so ready to break hearts."

Petra asked her question: "Your Majesty, do you have any news of my father?"

The queen's eyes shot to Dee. "No," she said in a final tone.

"But will you—?"

Dee looked appalled.

The queen's grip on Petra's chin tightened. "People so rarely recognize when they have become tiresome. Why is that, do you think?"

"Please, I—"

Stop, said Astrophil.

But she knows something! I can tell!

And I can tell that she will not answer you. Petra, she could gain political favor with Bohemia by turning you over to the prince. You are under Queen Elizabeth's protection. Do not make her regret it. Now, repeat after me . . .

"I am sorry, Your Majesty," Petra mouthed Astrophil's words. "I know my manners are poor. Forgive me. I was startled by your brilliance."

"Oh ho!" The queen chuckled merrily. "A flatterer! Well, go play now, child, and speak your sugared words to someone who believes them." She patted Petra's cheek, and the girl knew their conversation was over.

Without paying attention to where she was going, Petra stalked away. She fumed at Astrophil: *You were laying it on a bit thick, weren't you? "Brilliance"! Hah! I can't believe I let you talk me into doing that.*

It was for your own good.

Who cares about my own good? Petra argued, walking into a shadowy corner of the room. There was only one other person near her, a seated man scribbling on a piece of paper he had spread over his right knee. *Maybe it would be better if the queen sent me back to Prague. Dee wouldn't cross her decision. And at least then I'd be with Father.*

In a jail cell, or worse! The spider trembled in her hair. *Please do not talk like that. We have a plan, remember?*

"Pardon me," said the man next to her. He was the same one she had seen kneeling before the queen. "I don't recall seeing you at court before, and I thought I knew everyone. Who are you?"

"No one special," she muttered.

Though still seated, he bowed from the waist. "A pleasure to make your acquaintance, No One Special. I am a Courtier in Disgrace. Perhaps we are distantly related. I wonder if you can help me. Do you know of a word that rhymes with *entangles*?"

"Um . . . *strangles*?"

"No, no, no! That won't do. Lovers don't strangle each other. At least, not at first. I'm writing a love poem, not a coroner's report. Absolutely no strangling."

What had Ariel said to Astrophil? *Never trust a poet.* Petra considered the man more carefully. It was hard to believe that this man had any connection to Ariel's dire words, but Petra asked, "You're a poet?"

"Sometimes. Especially when I'm in deep trouble. Between you and me, I'm not really writing a love poem. It's more of a flatter-the-queen poem. But it's not going so well . . . I am better at composing humorous verse. Have you ever heard my poem 'To a Lady with an Unruly and Ill-Mannered Dog Who Bit Several Persons of Great Importance'?"

"No."

His face drooped in mock disappointment. "That was my finest hour."

"Why do you have to flatter the queen? Is she mad at you?"

"It breaks my heart to say it"—he gave a comically sad sigh—"but yes."

"Why?"

A look of real discomfort crossed his face. "I don't want to talk about it. Let's just say I disappointed her."

"Well, I don't see how a bunch of words is going to make her like you."

"You are wise beyond your years, my sweet No One Special. But it's my fate to do things I regret, and say words that don't matter."

Petra decided to do what Kit always encouraged in fencing. She made an aggressive move. "Did you know Gabriel Thorn?"

The man's expression darkened. "The West? Of course! He's the reason I'm stuck here in the shadows. And you know this, don't you?" He narrowed his eyes.

She shook her head.

"You do! You *must*. The whole court knows. Why, just the other day that busybody John Dee was asking me about him, wanting to know where I was on the morning of Thorn's death. I'll tell you truly, I'd spit on Thorn's grave and laugh about it, but I wouldn't be the only one, as Dee himself knows very well!" The man stood, crumpling the paper in his fist, and stormed off.

Petra watched him go, wondering if this man was the murderer. After all, he clearly hated Thorn, and had just admitted to having done things he regretted.

Kit would tell her more about the poet. The only problem was that Kit was nowhere to be seen, so Petra drifted over to Madinia and Margaret. They chattered away, used to Petra's silence. Petra was wondering why Kit had been so insistent about her coming to this ball if he wasn't going to bother to show up, when Madinia (for once) fell silent.

"Mmm." Madinia was looking over Petra's shoulder. "I suddenly feel an enormous urge to take fencing lessons . . ."

Petra turned. It was Kit. She told herself there was no reason to feel nervous. But her heart stuttered, and she was sure that if she looked down at the thick cloth of her dress, it would be trembling with her pulse.

Kit was finely, though somewhat shabbily, dressed. His eyes lit up when they found Petra's.

Margaret was good at recognizing a lost cause when she saw one. She took in Madinia's admiring gaze, Kit's eagerness, and Petra's flushed cheeks. Then she said to her twin, "Look at the Essex boys standing over there. Let's see if they'll ask us to dance."

"Ooh, let's!" Madinia pulled her sister in the direction of the two young men.

Left alone, Petra watched Kit approach.

When he reached her, he bowed in the same manner as all the gentlemen in the room were doing when they encountered a lady. Petra should have curtsied in response, but didn't.

"You look very different," Kit said.

"Don't I know it."

Kit was startled.

I think you just sounded arrogant, Astrophil observed.

What? When?

When Kit said you looked different and you said—

I know what I said, and of course I look different! I look like a stuffed doll, or a monkey that's gotten into its mistress's things, or—

Astrophil poked her scalp.

Petra bit back a cry. *What'd you do that for?*

I did that because I am not large enough to grab you by the shoulders and shake you!

Then she realized that Kit was touching her sleeve. "That's samite," he said, rubbing the fabric under his fingers.

"I guess," she said, and knew she sounded rude. But she was just saying whatever words sprang to mind so that she could buy herself time to think about why warm hope gushed through her when she felt Kit's hand on her arm.

His hand fell to his side and his expression changed. She saw the disappointment, and then he just looked cold.

"The Dees keep you well," he said. "Samite is a very expensive fabric." Kit looked across the room, and Petra followed his gaze to see John and Agatha Dee speaking with Queen Elizabeth.

"The dress is a hand-me-down."

"Well, then, it's an *expensive* hand-me-down." He looked at her again, but warily. "Let's show it off." He gestured at the dancers.

"No," Petra said. Then, anxious not to be misunderstood again, she added, "I can't. Not like that. I only know folk dances. What they're doing looks . . ."

One corner of his mouth lifted. "Unnecessarily complicated?"

Petra found herself wanting to keep the half smile on Kit's face, so she said, "Can I tell you a secret?"

"You can, but you'd better not, but I can't *resist* a question like that, so yes. Tell."

Petra, do be careful. Astrophil clutched her braid more tightly.

Petra ignored him. She said to Kit, "You were right about me."

"Of course I was! But, er . . . right about what, exactly?"

"I don't belong here. I feel really out of place."

"Well, that's no crime. Not like murder." His voice was teasing. "I hear that you've been grilling poor Walter Raleigh about Gabriel Thorn."

"Walter Raleigh? The poet?"

"The *bad* poet," Kit corrected. "But he's other things, too."

"How do you know what we talked about? I met him only a half hour ago, and you weren't even here then."

"You noticed."

She blushed. "I want to know how you know," she insisted. "Do you have a magical gift for eavesdropping or something?"

"I am offended." Kit laid a hand on his heart. "Here I am, trained from the time I was a toddler to be a spy, and you mistake intelligence and skill for magic. You want to know how I heard about your tête-à-tête with Raleigh? He told me. You really upset him, Petra. I saw him in the hallway as he was leaving. As I've said before (once? Twice? Hmm, I must stop bragging), I know a lot of things about a lot of people. How did this come to be? I trade secrets. I have built up a system of favors. If I tell Courtier X that Lady So-and-So is cheating on her husband, then Courtier X owes me a secret later on down the road. Sir Walter Raleigh decided to ask me if I knew something about a pretty, prying, strange girl with gray eyes who was bothering him about Gabriel Thorn."

Petra tried not to be distracted by the fact that she had been called "pretty." *Raleigh's word,* she told herself. *Not Kit's.*

"I would have said *silver* eyes, not gray," Kit continued, "but maybe that's just me."

"What did you tell him?"

He shrugged. "Not much. I don't know much."

"But what did you *say?*"

"That you were Dee's distant cousin and I'd been hired to teach you fencing. Nothing more."

Petra relaxed a little, but still demanded, "Tell me about Raleigh."

"Even if that means you owe me?"

Petra, Astrophil warned.

But she was tired of listening to him, and tired of being safe. "Yes," she told Kit.

He looked smug. "What do you want to know?"

"Why is the queen mad at Raleigh, and what does that have to do with Thorn?"

Kit seized her hand. "I'll show you."

"Where are we going?"

"Don't you have a sense of adventure?"

"*Yes.*"

"Then follow me."

Kit led her away from the Watching Chamber and down narrow hallways. Petra hadn't been in this part of the palace, but it looked familiar. Then she realized why: the dimly lit halls reminded her of the underground part of Salamander Castle where all the servants worked. "Are we going to the servants' quarters?"

Kit glanced back at her and gently tightened his hand, which Petra took to mean yes.

He opened a rough wooden door, and they stepped into the

kitchen. It was bustling with activity, but one middle-aged woman wasn't too busy to notice who had just entered her domain. "Kit! Have you come to talk me out of a cut of the queen's finest beef?"

"Why, no, Jessie. But if you're offering . . ."

She ruffled Kit's cropped hair with greasy fingers. "Well, what do you want, you rogue?"

"I'd like to show my friend Raleigh's gift to the queen."

"Oh, that! Go ahead, lad."

"Petra, do you remember what I told you about Drake, who stole gold from Spain?" Kit asked as he brought her into the pantry. "Well, Raleigh's an explorer, too. He's an experienced sea captain, and many people thought that Drake's assignment should have gone to him. But Thorn spoke up at a councillors' meeting and said, 'Why should that brainless Raleigh get the plum job? Drake's your man. Send Raleigh to America instead, Your Majesty. That's the place for dreamers like him.' So Drake went one way, and Raleigh went the other. Drake brought back a boatload of gold and was knighted for it. Raleigh brought back this." Kit opened a bin and pulled out something that looked like a clod of dirt. He placed it in Petra's hand.

"What is it?"

"It's called a potato. You eat it."

Petra looked at Kit incredulously.

"Now you see," he said, "why Queen E isn't so happy with Raleigh, and why he thinks he was cheated out of a different destiny by Gabriel Thorn. You know"—Kit took back the potato—"this thing isn't half bad." He stepped back into the kitchen. He reached behind Jessie for a knife, and turned to the wooden table to chop the vegetable. Petra sat on a stool nearby, watching him and remembering her last experience in a castle kitchen. It seemed so long ago.

Kit swept the white cubes into a skillet, added a pat of butter, and placed the pan on the wood-burning stove. Servants scurried around him as he cooked. They didn't seem to think there was anything out of the ordinary about Kit frying a potato in their kitchen. They all knew him. It was Petra who drew curious glances.

When the cubes had browned, Kit tipped them onto a plate. Then he pulled up a stool and sat next to Petra, the plate balanced on his knees. He and Petra ate with burning, oily fingers.

"Delicious," Petra declared.

"You can't eat gold," Kit agreed. "Raleigh deserves more credit than he gets." When Kit set aside the empty plate, he said, "In the Watching Chamber, you seemed very much against the idea of dancing. Do you really hate it?"

"No. I'm just not good at it. I used to dance with my father sometimes, at festivals in my village." She fell silent.

"Petra, about my system of favors and secrets . . . You don't owe me anything for information about Raleigh, or about anyone else," Kit said, "*if* you dance with me."

"What, here? Now?"

Kit grinned, and Petra realized that she could hear a muffled piping. The servants had disappeared from the kitchen, and Petra guessed they were in a room close by—perhaps in their dining hall, where they had shoved aside the wooden table and benches to clear a space for dancing.

"I won't know the steps," Petra warned.

"Am I not a good teacher?" Kit pretended to pout. Petra rolled her eyes. But it was she who led the way toward the piping music, and when Petra and Kit danced with the servants of Whitehall Palace, she stepped on no one's feet. She easily mastered the steps Kit taught her, and had no trouble keeping the fast, whirling beat of the music.

19

The Court of Wards

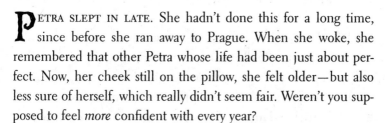

PETRA SLEPT IN LATE. She hadn't done this for a long time, since before she ran away to Prague. When she woke, she remembered that other Petra whose life had been just about perfect. Now, her cheek still on the pillow, she felt older—but also less sure of herself, which really didn't seem fair. Weren't you supposed to feel *more* confident with every year?

She thought about Kit's hand on her sleeve and how lightly she had turned in his arms as they danced. She wondered if he had been as nervous as she, and as thrilled.

Petra scowled. She hated feeling confused. Well, then, she wouldn't. She wouldn't think about Kit at all. She knew what was important: her goal. She clung to its ice-cold clarity: *Outwit Dee. Go home. Find Father.* A boy she liked too much had nothing to do with her plans.

She hung her head over the edge of the bed and looked into the dark shadows underneath. Astrophil was sleeping soundly in a corner where the bed slats met the frame. "Astrophil!"

The spider gasped and fell to the floor.

"I thought spiders were supposed to be graceful," said Petra.

Astrophil scrambled to his feet. "Spiders are supposed to be given a decent rest after staying up late posing as hairpins." He crept over to one of Petra's dangling braids, which he began to climb.

Petra sat up, and the spider jumped to her earlobe. He continued to speak: "What, precisely, was the point of going to the ball? Beyond flirtation and attempting to insult the queen of England?"

Petra didn't like the word *flirtation*, and so she pretended she hadn't heard it. "We now have a suspect: Walter Raleigh."

"Him! He wouldn't hurt a fly."

"Well, neither would you, and you're supposed to eat them. Think about it: Raleigh is a poet, like Ariel said, *and* he had a motive for killing Thorn. We just have to prove that he did it."

"You cannot take what Ariel said to heart. She also mentioned black teeth, a dirty river, and a tree dressed in robes. We both know that she was not actually talking about a river or a tree. So are we supposed to find Thorn's killer by looking in the mouths of poets to see if they have bad dental habits? No. We must remember that although Ariel said many things, we do not know what they mean."

"But Raleigh is our best lead!"

"I agree. However, we should consider other possibilities before focusing on him."

Petra mulled over the events of last night. There was something she was forgetting, something that had been troubling her little by little over her stay at Throgmorton Street. It nibbled at the back of her mind. Suddenly, Petra knew what it was. "Agatha Dee."

"Surely not. Why would you suspect her? You do not know anything about her."

"That's just it. She's a mystery. You know that look Madinia and Margaret always give each other? I bet it's because of their mother, because they want to keep some secret about her hidden from me. You've seen Agatha Dee. There's something wrong with her. Maybe she's not a killer, but whatever she is, it's worth finding out."

• • •

As usual, Agatha Dee was nowhere to be found. This time, however, Petra would not be put off so easily by the servants. "I need to talk with her," she insisted.

The housekeeper turned away. "Mistress Dee sees nobody unless she pleases."

"I'm going to keep asking."

"You're telling, not asking, and it'll do you no good."

"Every day," Petra said, "I'll find you and say the same thing."

The woman's face twisted. "Brat," she muttered at Petra's retreating back.

Kit had the day off, so there would be no fencing lesson. But even though Dee himself had stayed up late, and even though his daughters were probably still sleeping, he had told Petra to meet him at the usual early hour. Which was just like him.

Although . . . Petra had to admit that she didn't hate their meetings. Not exactly. Not like she had thought she would.

"Forget trying to make a penny spin in the air," he had told her during their first lesson in the library, the day after Petra had sensed quicksilver in Thorn's dead body. "Do not even bother with such tricks. Your gift for metal is clearly less powerful than your father's. But that doesn't mean that it is useless. It is simply more subtle. I am sure you can influence metal to some degree. Perhaps you could nudge away an opponent's sword if you focused enough. Perhaps . . . I wonder . . . you might even be able to change the shape of a metal object, so long as you maintained physical contact with it. We will try such things later on, after you have mastered what I consider to be some basic steps in your training. Now, sit still, be quiet, and tell me what you know about the *history* of this knife. If it were a person, what would it say?"

Petra didn't like being still, or being quiet, or being in Dee's presence, but she quickly became fascinated by the stories metal had to tell—the knife, for example, had been used in a tavern brawl three years ago to stab a man.

Dee rarely mentioned her second magical talent, the one she tried so hard to ignore.

Today, when Petra entered Dee's library, he was not seated as usual at his desk. He waited in a leather-backed chair, and gestured for her to sit in the one across from him.

She did, and decided to let him speak first. When he remained silent, she pointedly yawned.

No response from Dee.

Petra yawned again, her mouth opening as far as it could stretch.

"Why are you afraid of mind-magic?" Dee abruptly asked.

Petra's jaw snapped shut.

Dee gazed at her as if he were willing to wait all day for her reply.

Petra could feel how tense Astrophil was, gripping her ear behind the curtain of her loose hair. *I would like to hear your answer, Petra.*

She blurted, "I don't want to know the future."

"Why not?"

"What if . . . I see something horrible, and I can't change it?"

"Many of us see horrible things we cannot change," said Dee. "As the queen's spy, I do nothing but see and hear, and there have been many times when I wished I did neither.

"You could be glad that your gift is not strong. For those who have powerful Second Sight, the magic is worthless. They see machines that run on the liquefied bones of long-dead animals, and endless cities with buildings like tall spears. Then the Second Sight can be almost a curse, since the people who have it are always aware of a future so far removed from our time that it does not even matter."

Petra thought about her mother, who could see into the future. How far had she been able to see, and how much had she known?

"Your gift," Dee continued, "is something far weaker, and far better."

He was speaking delicately to Petra, as if his words were made of glass—or as if she were. She asked, "Why? Why is it better?"

"What makes a horse know that a storm is coming, or a courtier realize the right words to say? We all have it, and it is called intuition. An internal system of warnings and suggestions that we use without being aware of it. You might not be able to predict the future with any clarity. You might not be able to read minds. But your intuition is stronger than that of the average person." He smiled slightly. "If you like, I could throw another knife at your head to prove it."

In spite of herself, Petra smiled back. Dee's words gave her a relief she hadn't even known she needed. So Petra had inherited just a little bit of mind-magic. She thought she could handle that. Yes, she could.

"But, Petra," said Dee, "you should realize that this gift, which Ariel called 'dream-thinking,' can be useful only if you have faith in it. Let me be clearer. You need to set aside your fear and learn to have faith in yourself."

Petra didn't reply to this, because Dee's words were all too easy to say, and all too difficult to do.

Dee folded his long-nailed fingers.

"Is that it?" Petra asked.

"Yes. You may go."

She had her hand on the door when Dee called, "There is one more thing I wish to discuss."

She turned.

His face had changed. It was stony. "I understand that you have been trying to speak with my wife. Do not do that again."

This broke the fragile peace between them.

"Or what?" Petra taunted. "You'll kick me out of your house?"

She left while she still had the last word.

MORE THAN A WEEK PASSED. Petra kept asking to see Agatha Dee, and was always denied. But she loved watching John Dee's mouth grow tighter every day. He knew perfectly well that she was disobeying him, and she knew perfectly well that he wasn't going to do anything to stop her.

As for Kit, her lessons with him were better . . . and they were worse. As Dee shifted his attention to developing Petra's "intuition," as he called it, Petra found that her fencing rapidly improved. Her parries were quick, her thrusts were true, and she had rediscovered the ease with which she was able to bury a dagger in a target many paces away.

But her encounters with Kit were worse, too, because they rarely spoke. During their first lesson after the winter ball, Kit had looked at Petra expectantly. He had started to speak. But Petra's cheeks grew hot, and she cut him off. "Let's get started," she said. He coolly raised his sword. They fought in silence. And that, it seemed, was that.

One late afternoon, Petra went to the top floor of the Dees' house, to a long gallery with paintings and small sculptures. Astrophil had wanted to inspect the art, saying something about "chiaroscuro" and "contrapposto."

"Whatever," Petra interrupted. "Let's just go."

They are very important Italian terms for art, Astrophil lectured as they climbed the staircase.

I don't care about chiaropposto and contrascuro.

You are saying it all wrong! he moaned.

They were still arguing when Petra opened the gallery door and realized that someone was already in the room.

It was Agatha Dee, watching the sun set from one of the large windows. She stood as still as one of the marble statues.

Even though Petra had spent weeks hoping for an opportunity like this, she felt a flare of nervousness. This woman's blank face wasn't just strange. It was creepy.

Petra cleared her throat. "Hello, Mistress Dee."

"Call me Agatha." She watched Petra cross the distance between them. "You have been trying to see me for a long time. I am sorry I have ignored you. I am not a very good hostess. What do you wish to discuss?"

For a moment, Petra couldn't remember, because all she wanted to ask was, *What is wrong with you? What happened to make you be like this?*

Astrophil prompted her: *The death of the West.*

Petra took a deep breath. "What do you know about Gabriel Thorn?"

"Yes," said Agatha. "I suspected this would be your question. I heard about your wager with my husband. That is why I have refused to meet with you."

"I don't understand."

"No. You wouldn't."

Petra studied her. The woman's voice had been expressionless, but Petra thought that the words had been tenderly meant, as if it were a good thing that Petra didn't understand. She remembered Raleigh's suggestion that several people might have been pleased by Gabriel Thorn's death, so she asked, "Who would have wanted Thorn dead?"

"I."

Petra stared.

"I did not poison him," said Agatha, "but I did wish he would die." She turned to study an oil painting of a forest so dark green that it was almost black. "Do you miss your parents, Petra?"

"I—yes. My father," Petra stammered.

"And your mother?"

"She died when I was born. You can't miss something you never had."

Agatha gave her a look. It was empty, but it still made Petra feel as if her skin had been peeled back, exposing something soft and raw. "That sounds like something you say a lot, but I think we both know it is not true. It is very easy to miss something you never had."

Petra remembered Agatha's hands stroking her hair when she was sick, thought of Dita far away in Bohemia, and was silent.

"My parents died of the plague when I was little," Agatha said. "If I had been a poor child, I would have been sent to an orphanage. But my family had been wealthy, though I could not touch my money until I came of age, so I was given to the Court of Wards. You do not know what that is, of course. Perhaps it is not so different from an orphanage after all, except the children are rich and so are the people who adopt them. Gabriel and Letticia Thorn adopted me. The Thorns were childless. They only discovered after the adoption that they never really wanted children anyway. My earliest memories are dull and lonely. But that is not so terrible.

"Gabriel Thorn was a scryer. What could be more convenient than using the child in his own home? His wife did not mind. At first Thorn was careful, but he was an ambitious man. He sought a position of power at court, and wanted to know about secret conversations and political deals. He became impatient, and I became insane.

"When you look at me, you do not think I feel anything, do you? Yet when Letticia Thorn died, I was glad. When her husband was murdered, I felt a cruel joy."

"But . . . you're not scryer-cracked," Petra said uncertainly. "Children broken by scryers stay mad forever."

"I was mad for many years of my life. I was not aware then that I had any magical talent, but I also wasn't aware of the difference between night and day. Legally, I became an adult, yet how could I use my inheritance to buy my freedom when I didn't even know my own name? The Thorns locked me up, and it was easy to hide me from the world, for I had never had any friends.

"Then, when I was twenty, pieces of my memory began to return. Every day I found a part of myself. I realized where I was, and eventually I could see who stood in the room with me. A young man had approached Gabriel Thorn and asked if he could try to cure his scryer-mad daughter. Thorn initially refused, saying he had no idea what he was talking about. But this man, John Dee, was a spy. He knew the truth about me, and about other things besides, so Thorn agreed.

"John healed me, as best as he was able. Even if you can fix something broken, you can rarely make it whole again.

"Some people say I married him out of gratitude. Others say that he fell in love with his success—with the cure, and not with me. Sometimes I am not sure if they are right or wrong. But I never think that this matters, because I know the fact of our love, whatever its source may be."

Petra didn't know what to say.

"You resent my husband. Maybe you have cause. But he is a good man, and wants to do well by you." Agatha paused. "Do you have any more questions for me, Petra?"

"No," she whispered, and fled.

FEBRUARY TURNED INTO MARCH, and March lengthened. Petra continued her lessons, and although she couldn't like Dee any better, Agatha's story made her wonder if she should respect him. She didn't—not yet—but waited to see if she would.

"We've got news for you, Petra," Madinia crowed. Petra was sitting with the twins in the parlor, which was decorated with potted plants.

Oh, no, said Astrophil. *If I have to listen to her describe the spring dress patterns one more time, I might scream. Loud enough for everyone to hear. I mean it, Petra. I will open my tin mouth and tell her that*—

"Robert Cotton is dead!" said Madinia.

"What?" said Petra.

"It's true," said Margaret. "He was found in his library."

"With his head bashed in," her sister added. "And you know what else? He had been *dead for months.*"

"For several weeks, anyway," Margaret corrected.

"His corpse must have been a nasty, pulpy, bloated, purple stink."

My, said Astrophil, *how unpleasant. I am glad I will not decompose when I die.*

"Astrophil!"

"What did you say?" said Margaret.

"Nothing," said Petra. Then she shouted at the spider, *Don't talk like that! You won't die!*

The sisters were still staring at her.

"What?" Petra snapped.

"You said, 'Astro-something,' " said Madinia. "What's that supposed to mean?"

"I . . . used a Czech word. Sorry. I forgot my English."

"The news about Robert Cotton *is* startling." Margaret nodded.

"But we thought you'd like to know," said Madinia. "You were asking questions about him, and I'm always ready to share good gossip."

"Cotton was murdered," Margaret reproved. "That's not exactly *good* gossip."

"Well, it's his own fault if I don't care a jot that he's dead. He never left his library, unless it was to buy books. It's a miracle anyone ever found out he had died, *and* that he didn't have any pets, because I would bet you my new ivory-handled fan that if he *had*, there wouldn't have been anything left of his corpse."

"Madinia, you're disgusting! Could we please stop talking about dead bodies and animals that eat them?"

"Why? You're the one who brought it up!"

Margaret grabbed a book and flung herself into a chair in the corner of the room. Madinia decided she was going to ignore her sister, too, so she snatched a watering can from a nearby end table and huffily began watering the plants.

Petra's mind was racing. Robert Cotton was murdered, too? This must be linked to the death of the West . . . but how?

She wanted to figure this out, but was soon distracted by a fresh burst of conversation between the sisters.

"Madinia"—Margaret turned a page of her book—"those cuckooflowers are fake."

"Fake?" Madinia was pouring a thin arc of water onto pink petals.

"The flowers are made of silk."

"Since when? I've been watering that plant for two years!" The water flowed over the pot and dripped onto the floor. "Oh, *fig!*"

"You shouldn't swear. And that plant has *always* been fake. You can't possibly think Dad would allow real cuckooflowers in the house."

"Why not?" Petra had never heard of the plant before.

"Cuckooflowers can't keep their mouths shut," said Madinia.

"Flowers don't have mouths," said Margaret.

"You know what I mean!"

"You know how flowers have pollen?" Margaret asked Petra, who nodded. "And how humans shed pieces of themselves?"

"Um, no. Do people have detachable toes in England?"

Madinia giggled, but since one of Petra's closest friends had fingers with invisible tips that could extend very far, she wasn't taking anything for granted. As far as Petra knew, the English *did* have detachable toes.

"You do it all the time: you lose eyelashes, a hair falls from your head, you scratch away a patch of dry skin," Margaret explained. "If you do that around a cuckooflower, it will absorb this into its pollen. And the flower will remember you. If this plant was a real cuckooflower, and I ripped off a petal, it might yell 'Margaret!' or 'Madinia!' or 'Petra!' "

"So," said Petra, "a cuckooflower isn't so great to have in a house with a spy who wants to keep his meetings secret."

"Not so much," Madinia said. "I mean, if someone found out that Dad had met with the West on the morning of his death—"

"Madinia!" Margaret's eyes widened in shock.

"Oops." Madinia bit her lip.

"What she means to say"—Margaret turned to Petra—"is that if, *hypothetically*, Dad had met with the West, it would raise some questions. But since he was listening to us play the lute that morning, there's no problem."

No problem? Astrophil murmured. *Did that sound like a lie to you, Petra? Because it certainly did to me.*

Petra agreed. She didn't understand how the deaths of Robert Cotton and Gabriel Thorn were related, but this conversation with Madinia and Margaret made other things fall into place. Petra remembered how Walsingham and Cecil had expected some kind of reaction from Dee on the day they met at Whitehall to inspect Thorn's body. She knew that Thorn had almost destroyed Agatha's mind. Petra recalled Dee's anger when Walsingham referred to his "brain-addled charity cases." Madinia and Margaret must know Agatha's story, or they wouldn't be worried about protecting their father—and maybe they should be worried, if Dee had met with Thorn so soon before his death. Dee could have easily slipped quicksilver into Thorn's wine.

Petra settled back into her chair, and into the comfort of an old habit: believing the worst of John Dee.

20

A Letter for the Prince

ASTROPHIL WAS NOT CONVINCED. "It is not logical," he said once they had returned to Petra's room. "Why would Dee poison the West?"

"Do we have to go over this again?" Petra said, exasperated. "Thorn scryed Agatha until she lost her mind. Dee wanted revenge. Makes sense to me."

"Only because you have always hated John Dee."

"And see how right I was? He's a murderer."

"Thorn scryed Agatha almost two decades ago," Astrophil pointed out. "Why would Dee poison him now when, despite however Dee might have felt, he and Thorn were able to work together for years on the queen's council?"

Petra shrugged. "Dee's patient. Like a snake under a rock. He was probably just waiting for the best moment to strike."

"Then why is it that when Walsingham was convinced that Thorn died of heart failure, Dee revealed that quicksilver had killed him? If Dee had murdered Thorn, he would want everyone to believe the death was natural, just as Francis Walsingham claimed it was."

Petra was silent.

"And then there's Dee's wager with you," Astrophil continued. "Why would he encourage you to discover Thorn's killer if he himself did it?"

Petra had already thought about this. "Dee's arrogant, and has a twisted sense of humor. He's betting I won't be able to figure it out, and he can watch and laugh while I try."

"I hope you are not right, Petra, because if you go to him and say you have won the wager, and that he killed Gabriel Thorn, Dee will not send you on your merry way to Bohemia. Whoever killed one man is not likely to think twice about hurting you to protect his secret. If Dee poisoned Thorn, it would be better for you not to know. And you certainly should not reveal that you suspect him."

Petra promised, "I'll be careful."

"Oh, of course."

"Sarcasm is beneath you, Astro."

The spider sighed and shook his head.

Petra said, "Maybe my idea doesn't make perfect sense. Maybe it's not totally logical that Dee killed Thorn. But Dee says and does weird things. The only thing you can know for sure about Dee is that you can never know anything for sure."

"Well," said Astrophil, "that much is true."

THE SERVANT PLUCKED up his courage. It was not an easy thing to interrupt Prince Rodolfo's dinner, especially if he had chosen to eat alone. "Please, Your Highness." He offered the tray, which bore a letter. "This just arrived. It was delivered with the utmost urgency. It is from your contact in England."

"Ah." The prince accepted the letter and then waved it at the servant, as if fanning away a bad smell.

The servant scuttled out the door. Then the prince took a knife from the dining set and eagerly broke the wax seal.

Your Royal Highness,

I bear exciting news: the Mercator Globes do exist, and I am certain that one of them, the Celestial Globe, is here in London. I regret to say that I have not yet discovered its exact location, but I believe I am close.

Two men stood in my way: Gabriel Thorn and Robert Cotton. They are now gone. Cotton was in possession of the globe. I have a record saying that he purchased it from a North African merchant. Unfortunately, Cotton hid it. Forgive me, Your Highness, but he died before I finished questioning him. I am confident, however, that Cotton must have left some clue to the globe's whereabouts. Cotton loved his books and antiquities, and publicly declared on many occasions that he wished all of his possessions to go to the queen of England after his death. A wish, however, is not quite a legal will, and I do have some time before the state seizes Cotton's house and all the items within it, for the authorities must wait several months in case an heir presents himself. In the meantime, I search for some note Cotton might have made, or some casual word he might have dropped, about where he hid the globe. You know my great ability to uncover secret information.

I have heard that you seek a Bohemian girl, Petra Kronos. It may interest you to know that she is in this very city.

The prince folded the letter.

"I am going to England," he whispered to himself.

21

The Left Hand

PETRA PLAYED WITH the end of her braid, tightly drawn back from her face and neck. Was it possible for one's ears to feel naked? She looked at Kit and longed for the familiar touch of Astrophil's tin legs.

Petra had graduated to using a dagger in her left hand in addition to the sword in her right. During their last several meetings, Kit had grown irritated—he always seemed on the verge of anger lately—that she used her left hand so infrequently. Petra knew she could expect Kit to attack her left side. That would mean bruises for her and frustration for them both.

So she wasn't wholly surprised when Kit began by saying, "Once upon a time there were a limited number of moves in swordplay. The parry-and-riposte. The bind. The coupe. The cruise. The feint. I seem, however, to have developed a new technique, which is the art of giving a warning rap with the flat of the blade when a cut would be in order. I'm not sure what to call this move, but I could name it after you, Petra, since your sloppiness gives me so many opportunities to practice it."

Today there was a mean edge in Kit's voice.

"It's not as easy as it looks," he continued. "I think I've mastered it by now, though I confess I find it boring."

If Astrophil were here, he'd warn Petra that Kit expected her to make a move that was aggressive and backed by wounded pride. So she gave Kit what he was waiting for—in order to deliver something else. She lunged into a continuous attack, which he countered with evident disappointment. But then, having exaggerated her attack, Petra suddenly fell back, twisted her sword under his, and slapped his ribs with her blade.

Kit winced and smiled at the same time.

As they continued, Petra let her mind drift, which is exactly what Kit always told her not to do. She relaxed into a state that was almost like dreaming, and she thought that she could sense where Kit's blade could go. She couldn't *predict* its movements, but she felt herself reacting to his parries and thrusts effortlessly, and perfectly.

Then Kit caught her by surprise. She had come to know his fighting style. It was light and nimble, so Petra wasn't ready for brute strength. His sword hit hers in a blunt push. This move was like arm wrestling—pure force used to shove an opponent's blade away for a deadly thrust.

His sword rasped against hers, sliding closer. Petra held against him, but this couldn't last. Feeling her wrist tremble, Petra decided to push back—with her magic, not her arm. She focused on the line where their blades crossed, and felt power surge through metal. She *shoved* at Kit's sword.

There was a sharp, metallic squeal. The tip of Kit's blade sheared off and dropped to the floor.

Astonished, Petra did nothing to stop her sword as it swung wide, leaving her open for attack. In a split second, she realized several things: Kit's blade was sweeping toward her face, his eyes were wide with horror, and a broken sword is very sharp.

She jerked her left hand up, and her dagger crashed against Kit's blade just before it struck her. Her arm shook from the blow.

Both she and Kit dropped their weapons, and Petra saw someone's blood spatter.

Oh, she realized. It was hers.

"Petra!" Kit's face was white. "Are you all right?" He reached for her left hand, and then she saw the cut across the back of her wrist, where the broken edge of Kit's sword had skimmed over her dagger. "I'm so sorry!"

Now she felt the pain. But it wasn't bad, and the drops of blood were small. "It's just a cut. It's fine."

"No, it's not!" Kit pushed her onto a bench and flung open a chest. He pulled out a cloth bandage and rushed to kneel next to her. Quickly, he bandaged her wrist.

He was almost frantic, which, Petra thought, was kind of funny, considering that fencing is supposed to be all about slicing people up. "Kit, it doesn't hurt that much. I know you didn't mean to do it."

"But I've tried so hard to be *careful!*"

"It was an accident. Don't worry about it." Petra paused. "Why am I consoling *you* when *I'm* the one bleeding?"

He chuckled weakly.

"Something like this was bound to happen sooner or later," she said. "We use real weapons."

"That's just it! We're not *supposed* to be doing that. You're a beginner, and we should be fencing with practice swords made of *wood*. I told Dee. I told him, and he wouldn't listen. He insisted we use metal!"

At this, Petra stood, remembering that this whole situation had come about because she had used magic, and had broken Kit's sword. She walked over to where the metal tip, about three inches long, lay on the floor. She picked it up.

"Nothing like this has happened to me before." Kit inspected his sword. "There must have been a flaw in the blade."

"I suppose so." Petra looked at the piece of metal in her palm. Then, because she didn't know what else to do with it, she put it in her pocket.

"Let's get out of here," Kit said abruptly.

"Where to?"

"Anywhere."

HE WAS SILENT as they walked, which was fine with Petra because she had a lot of things to think about, beginning with this new turn her magical ability had taken. And then there was the fact that Kit had gotten so upset over a little cut. Was it wrong for this to please her?

She stole a glance at Kit—and promptly stepped in a puddle. *So this is spring in London*, she thought, annoyed. *Mud and water.* In Okno, the buds on the trees would be curled into little fists. In London, there were no trees. The sky was pale, the streets dirty.

Petra didn't recognize this part of town. It was west of Cheapside, she knew. The buildings were small, close, and shabby. The people were much the same.

Kit muttered, "I don't get it. What's Dee playing at?"

"What do you mean?"

"For starters, why does he want you to learn fencing?"

"My father . . . gave me a sword. Dee thought I should learn how to use it. And I wanted to."

"Why?"

Petra's voice was low. "I thought I might be good at it."

"You are," he said. "You're a natural. Sometimes I can't believe you haven't been practicing for years." He looked at her. "I think I know another reason why you take our lessons so seriously."

She felt a leap of fear. Could he know about the Gristleki? About how, even after five months in London, she had nightmares, and felt the burning touch of gray skin? She hadn't quite realized—not until this moment—that she was still deeply afraid of them, and that learning how to fence had helped keep that terror under control.

"It's because of your father," Kit continued gently. "I can tell that you miss him. Dee said that he died recently."

"But—"

"I'm an orphan, too. It doesn't bother me. Not really. My parents died from the pox when I was a baby. I don't even remember them. But if I had something of theirs, like your father's sword, I'd want to use it, too."

"Listen." She stopped in her tracks, and Kit halted by her side. "My father is *not* dead."

"But then, why did Dee say . . . ?" He bit his lip. "Forget it. Forget I said anything. I'm terrible when it comes to minding my own business."

Petra decided to make it his business. In a rush, she said, "I'm not English, I'm Bohemian. My father was kidnapped by Prince Rodolfo's monsters. I would have been, too, if Dee hadn't stuck his nose in. He rescued me, if that's what you want to call it, and I'm trapped here. If I try to escape, he'll track me down with the help of his daughters. I guess you know what they can do."

Kit nodded, a little stunned.

"I made a wager with Dee," Petra continued. "If I can solve the mystery of who killed Gabriel Thorn, I can go home, and Dee will give me information about my father."

Slowly, Kit said, "Why would you make a bet about Thorn's death? What does he have to do with you?"

"I'm not sure," she answered, and told him about summoning Ariel, and everything she had said.

"So," Kit replied, "on the basis of the mutterings of an air spirit, you think that Thorn's death has something to do with you, and something to do with Robert Cotton."

Put like that, it sounded very unlikely. But Petra set her jaw and said, "Yes. And I think Dee might have poisoned Thorn."

Kit's eyebrows shot up, so Petra explained. To her relief, Kit didn't attack her idea like Astrophil had. He merely said, "That's interesting." Then he seemed to struggle over a decision. When he spoke, his tone was tentative. "Petra . . . how do you know that your father is really still alive?"

It was as if Kit had struck her. She reeled, and for a moment, not one single thing in the world made sense. Panic flooded through her as she realized something she had never allowed herself to consider fully: Dee had told her that her father was alive, but he was telling anyone who would listen that Petra was an orphan. Dee *was* lying. The question was, to whom?

Kit touched her shoulder, his face full of concern. "Petra?"

She took a shaky breath. "He's alive. He has to be." She had to believe this, or nothing she did in London would have any meaning.

Kit nodded, but still looked worried. "You shouldn't have told me about all of this. Secret-keeping isn't my strong suit."

"You won't tell anyone."

"No," he agreed fervently. "I won't. I promise."

"Besides, we're hundreds of miles from Bohemia. No one here is going to care where I'm from or who I am."

"That's not true."

Kit's eyes were just a bit warmer when he said this. Petra was searching for a way to respond when his head snapped up. He took a look at his surroundings and frowned. "I shouldn't have brought you here."

"Why not?" Petra glanced around. She had seen worse in Prague. "Where's 'here'?"

"I wasn't thinking . . . I was walking home without realizing it. This isn't a nice part of London."

"It's not so bad."

"It's too close to the Liberties."

"Really? Where there are no laws?"

"Yes, and a lot of thieves and other people of poor character."

"Thieves can be fun."

"Petra, you are a strange girl."

"I want to see the Liberties. Let's go," she urged.

He shook his head. "I'm not taking you."

"I'll go by myself, then," she replied, irritated.

"You don't know where you're going."

"I'll wander until I find it. You said we're not far."

"Some other time, please?" he begged. "Haven't I endangered you enough for one day? Anyway, I have an idea, and it will take us to Friday Street, not the Liberties."

"You're trying to distract me."

"And I will succeed. You mentioned the possibility of some connection between Thorn's murder and the decidedly more gruesome death of Robert Cotton."

"Did you know Cotton?"

"No, but I know somebody who might know somebody who might have known him."

"Hmph." Petra narrowed her eyes.

"That was a very doubtful 'hmph.' You don't believe me? You think the connection is too weak to pursue? If you had been trained in espionage, you would know to investigate *all* possibilities."

"Well, I'm not a spy."

"Then it's a good thing I can be one for you. Though, Petra . . . helping you *is* against my best interest."

She paused. "Why?"

"I don't want you to go home," he said simply.

Her pulse jumped, and before she knew what she was doing,

she kissed him. Her lips grazed across his so quickly, so barely, and so awkwardly that when she leaned back she wasn't sure she hadn't just daydreamed this. But then she knew. She knew, because her lips were tingling and she dreaded Kit's reaction almost as much as she feared the Gristleki.

He stood frozen. Then he twisted his thin mouth. Confusion flitted across his face.

Not good, not good, Petra thought in dismay.

He began, "I thought—" Kit didn't say what he had thought, but in the sudden glow of his smile, Petra understood that he cared for her, she had ignored him, he had been hurt, and what mattered now was that he was reaching for her.

This time their kiss was not brief.

22

Mermaid Tavern

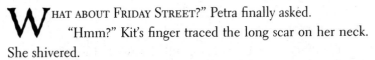

WHAT ABOUT FRIDAY STREET?" Petra finally asked.

"Hmm?" Kit's finger traced the long scar on her neck. She shivered.

"Friday Street," she said. "Thorn. Dee. Cotton. Murder. Remember?"

"No."

"*Kit.*"

"Sorry." He took a step back, and damp spring air rushed between them. He glanced away from Petra. When he looked back, his angular features were composed and alert. "We"—he curled her hand in his—"are going to the Mermaid Tavern."

THERE WAS NOTHING remotely mermaidlike about the tavern, aside from the sign of a fish-tailed woman whose scales were flakes of peeling paint. Inside, the floor smelled of spilled ale. There were no proper tables, only booths with low panels erected between them to give people privacy. Petra watched as two men in adjoining booths slid away the panel dividing them and leaned across the opening to whisper.

Kit scanned the room. "He's not here," he said. "We'll have to wait."

Petra crossed her arms. "I—"

"Yes, I know. You hate waiting. But there's no help for it. Let's sit. He'll turn up. He always does."

"And who are we waiting for, exactly?" Petra asked as they settled into a booth, facing each other across the table.

"A writer."

"A poet?"

"Sometimes."

Of course. Petra groaned. Ariel's warning was proving to be useless, since practically *everybody* in England seemed to write poetry.

Kit rubbed the fencing calluses on his palms. "Petra, why do you think Dee hired *me* to teach you? Aside from my great and obvious skill?"

"You mean your skill at being full of yourself, I suppose."

He grinned.

"It is strange," she admitted. "Dee's given me plenty of reasons for why he hired you. Maybe too many. He didn't have to explain himself to me at all. I'm his prisoner. He could have hired a three-headed cow to teach me fencing and I would have had to accept it. What if he explained his decision because he didn't want me to ask any questions? Like about whether it mattered that you used to work for Walsingham. For Dee's . . . rival." She said the last word carefully, as if testing it.

"Yes," said Kit. "Go on."

But she didn't, because a voice behind her said, "Hello, Kit."

Kit looked up past Petra's head. He nodded in greeting. "Will."

"Lying in wait?"

"For you? Of course," Kit said.

"Then you're buying."

Kit grimaced and stood up to get some ale, giving his seat to the middle-aged man. Will was short and balding, with a mouth like a button. "And who are you?" he asked.

"I'm Petra."

"That's a Bohemian name," Will said, and Petra thought she saw a flash of keen interest in his heavy-lidded eyes. "Have you ever been to the Bohemian seacoast?"

Petra stared. "Bohemia has no seas."

"That's not what I heard."

It was fortunate that Kit arrived just then with a tankard of ale, because Petra might have said something rude. As it was, the look she shot Kit wasn't exactly polite. Her frown said something along the lines of, *And this is the man who's supposed to help us? He's either ignorant or crazy!*

Will drank, his gaze flicking between Petra and Kit. From the slight crinkling in the corners of his eyes, Petra thought there was a smile hidden behind his tankard of ale. But when Will set it down, his face had the same bland expression as before. "Well, Kit," he said, "what do you want to talk about?"

"Books."

"Books?"

Petra half turned to Kit in surprise. Then she remembered what Madinia and Margaret had told her: that Robert Cotton was obsessed with his library. "Right," she said. "Books."

"Will rubs elbows with the nobility," Kit explained to her, "and he knows the booksellers in London well."

"I should," Will said. "I give them enough of my money."

"So he might know if Robert Cotton had a favorite bookshop."

Now there was definitely a smile playing on the man's lips. "The dead Robert Cotton? The one whose brains spilled out of his split skull?"

"The same."

"Try Richard Field, at the Sign of the White Greyhound."

"Thanks, Will. I'm in your debt."

"You certainly are." The man drained his tankard. "But I'll wait to collect on my secret."

Petra and Kit had already risen to leave when Will added, "It's good to see you up to your old tricks again, Kit."

Kit looked uneasy. "Let's go," he said to Petra.

Will watched Petra and Kit walk away. They were tall and lean, keeping the same pace, like a well-matched set of horses. When the door creaked shut behind them, Will ordered another tankard of ale, and asked the barmaid to bring him a pot of ink, a quill, and paper. He had no coins to pay for this, but he wasn't worried. The Mermaid Tavern would let him have them on credit, and he knew he could expect payment soon from a certain individual. Will began to write a letter to him:

> *Dear Master Dee,*
> *Your Bohemian pet came to see me. She's keeping interest-ing company and asking very interesting questions . . .*

WHEN KIT AND PETRA reached the Sign of the White Greyhound, it was nearly dusk. The shop smelled: the sharp scent of ink and leather, and the yeasty odor of paper. It was cramped, and stacked with a dark rainbow of books. Some were as large as Petra's torso, others so small they could fit neatly in the palm of her hand. Muf-fled thumps came from behind a closed door at the other end of the shop.

An elderly man sat at a square-shaped desk. He didn't bother looking up, but continued reading a manuscript.

"Are you Richard Field?" Petra asked.

"Hmm." The man turned a scribbled page.

"Well, are you or aren't you?"

At this, the man glanced at Petra. "What? Sorry. I'm Master Field. May I help you?"

"Did you know Robert Cotton?" Petra asked.

"Certainly. He will be missed."

"He was a friend of yours?"

Field opened his hands and spread them. "He was a good customer."

"Did he ever say anything about Gabriel Thorn?"

"Thorn? The councillor to the queen? No, I think not. Cotton wasn't interested in politics. His passion was for plants and books."

"Did he ever buy anything unusual from you?" asked Kit.

"What difference is it to you whether Cotton bought anything odd or not?"

Petra lifted her chin. "We just want to know."

"Well . . ." said Field. "I can't say that he ever *purchased* anything out of the ordinary, but he did take a special interest in the printing of a certain book."

"Which one?" asked Kit.

"*An Account of My Many Astonishing Voyages*, by Gerard Mercator."

"A travel book?" Petra's brow furrowed. "Was Cotton planning on taking a trip?"

"Oh, no." Field shook his head. "Definitely not. He was a shy man who liked the comfort of home. He had visitors, of course. His home is a large manor, filled with bedrooms that were only used once in a great while, when merchants came to sell him rare books and the occasional pretty object. But Cotton didn't like to leave his house. I'm probably the only person in London he ever came to see on a regular basis."

"You said he took an interest in the *printing* of the book," Petra said. "What did you mean by that?"

Field pointed at the closed door with its thumping sounds. "I'll show you."

Kit and Petra followed him into a large room that was almost as noisy as the Sign of the Compass had once been. Petra felt a wave of homesickness.

Several apprentices stood by large printing presses they were slamming down onto paper. Large, ink-wet sheets were hung to dry like clothes on a line.

A towheaded boy, startled by the sudden appearance of his master, dropped the case he was carrying. Tiny black letters and punctuation marks tumbled all over the floor.

Petra and Kit stopped to help him. Kit poured the blocks he had collected back into the case, but Petra paused for a moment, considering the blackened pieces of metal in her palm.

A memory tugged at her. It was something about the way these letters looked. But the boy shoved his case at her impatiently, so she tilted her hand and let the little blocks trickle over her fingers into it.

"You'll have to sort them all over again," Field sternly told the apprentice, who nodded and returned to his press. Petra watched as the girl who stood next to him picked letters and punctuation marks from her own case, which contained dozens of compartments. The girl set the last few blocks into the frame, padded on ink with a soft leather ball, covered the frame with a sheet of paper, and brought the press down. Petra couldn't see the letters, but she knew they were biting into the paper, and would leave the indentations she could feel whenever she ran a finger over a typed page in one of her father's books.

"Is something wrong?" Kit asked, following Petra's gaze.

Petra shook her head. She was almost *right* about something, and it had to do with those blocks and the way the press closed down on its frame, like a giant mouth snapping together.

She reached into the wooden box at the girl's side and plucked out a few metal blocks. They were all question marks. Maybe it was because she felt like she was being asked a question that she suddenly knew the answer, and understanding dawned upon her. "Black teeth?"

Kit's eyes darted to Petra's, and she saw that he recalled what she had told him of Ariel's mysterious words.

"Why, yes," Field said indulgently. "Black teeth. That's what you've got in your hand. Officially, those metal blocks are called type. But in the printing business, we have a nickname for them: 'black teeth,' because they look a lot like what ends up on the floor after a nasty fistfight, not that I've ever been in one of those. Each block is just the right size of a tiny molar dyed with ink."

Petra squeezed her hand around the blocks. She looked at Field and knew, in that way she was starting to recognize she had, that whatever he said next was going to be important.

"Cotton liked to play with the teeth," Field said. "He was a rich man, and a knight to boot, but he wasn't afraid of getting his hands dirty. You asked me if Cotton ever bought anything unusual. Well, I can't say that he did, but when he learned that I sold copies of Mercator's travels, he did make an unusual request. He asked if he could print the title page for his own copy. Normally, I wouldn't let a customer do such a thing, but Cotton had been coming here for years, and I'd earned plenty by him. I thought, what's the harm? So I let him do it."

"I want your copy of the title page," said Petra.

"How did you know?" Field was startled. "Well, yes, indeed, there *were* two copies made of that page. Cotton hadn't put enough ink on the teeth, so the first sheet came out too light. I set it aside, he made a second one, and I had that page bound into the book that he bought. But this happened months ago, in January. I haven't the foggiest idea where I put that first pressing."

"It's in your desk," Petra said clearly. Her words sounded like an order. "In the third drawer to the bottom on the right-hand side."

Field stared at her, first with amused disbelief, and then wariness. He led them back into the shop. When he opened the drawer Petra had mentioned and saw the paper inside, he looked up in anger.

Magic. That's what this girl had, and she'd wormed her way into his kindness with it. "Take it, then!" He snatched the printed sheet and thrust it at her. What else might this girl know about him? His mind flashed over all the bad things a person might do just by living long enough.

"Thank you," said Petra.

"You'll get no thanks from me! Take your nosy self and your skinny friend out of my shop!"

"But I didn't—I'm not— I'm sorry," Petra stammered. The paper crackled in her left hand.

"Petra." Kit was pulling her toward the door.

When the shop door jangled behind them, Petra opened her right hand and let the black teeth fall into the mud. She looked at her palm. On her skin were three inky question marks.

23

Sutton Hoo

P ETRA'S TROUSER POCKETS were starting to feel full. In her right pocket was Tomik's Glowstone, and in the left, a broken piece of steel and a wad of paper. She pulled out the title page and unfolded it, smoothing it over the desk in her bedroom. Astrophil stepped onto the paper.

"Kit thinks it's an ordinary title page," said Petra. "But this *is* special. I just don't know why. You're the expert on books, Astro. I want to know your opinion."

"Hmm." The spider crawled over the sheet, considering the artwork. Below the title was a map of the world, and below this were the words "Printed and sold in London by R. Field at the Sign of the White Greyhound, 1598."

Finally, Astrophil said, "There is indeed something out of place."

"What is it?"

He walked to the very bottom of the page. "This." He pointed one shiny leg at a letter followed by a number: N6.

"N6?" said Petra. "It can't be a page number."

"Correct. A title page is never numbered, and if it were, it would not make any sense to use *N* or 6 or both."

Petra asked hopefully, "Do you have any idea what N6 means?"

"None whatsoever."

WHEN PETRA opened the library door, Dee was dressed for the outdoors. He held out a cloak.

She whirled it onto her shoulders, glad to escape the library. Lately, her lessons with Dee had been tedious. Sometimes he would make Petra guess which hand he would lift in the air. He could spend a whole hour listening to Petra drone, "Left. Left. Right. Left. This is boring. Can we stop? Oh, *fine*! Right. Right . . ."

Petra tied the cloak. "Where are we going?"

"Sutton Hoo."

Astrophil murmured, *I wonder what we shall find there. Almost everything Ariel said has so far proven to be important. Surely Sutton Hoo will be no exception.*

When they entered the courtyard, Madinia and Margaret were waiting. There was a sack slung over Madinia's arm, and Margaret carried a large wooden box drilled with holes. It was squeaking.

"What's in there?" asked Petra.

"Mice." Margaret passed the box to her father, who tucked it under one arm.

"Mice?" said Petra. "For what?"

"You'll see," said Dee. "Madinia, would you please open the Rift?"

Madinia set the bag down and slapped her hands together as if brushing off dirt. "I *love* doing this."

"How do you open a Rift, exactly?" asked Petra. "Could we go anywhere? Like to Spain?"

"No, I've never been to Spain, and wouldn't want to, either. It's dirty and hot. I can only open a Rift to a place where I've actually been before. But I've visited lots of places." Madinia was preening, flattered by Petra's curiosity. "Though I'd never seen Bohemia before I met you. Dad had to give me tons of instructions for how to open that Rift. You're lucky, though, that you and Dad have got that mental-link thing, otherwise you'd be four-Gray-Men-times-helpless-you-equals-dead.

"Now watch and be amazed." Madinia took a deep breath and thrust her fingers in front of her as if jamming them into a crack. With a twist of her shoulders, Madinia wrenched her hands apart. A line of light split the air, then vanished.

"After you," said Dee to Petra.

She examined the space in front of them. She still saw the flagstones, and the arched gate leading to the street. "Nothing looks any different."

"It is," Margaret assured.

Petra, Astrophil said anxiously, *why don't you let one of them go first?*

But she was already stepping forward.

One second, her foot was on stone. The next, it was on tall grass. One second, Petra heard the clattering of horses in the street. The next, birds were singing.

She was standing on a hilly field. She spun around. Petra was alone.

Astro, where are they? Had they tricked her? Was she stranded here in Sutton Hoo?

Do not panic, said Astrophil, though he sounded a little panicky.

Petra was about to lunge at the spot in the air she thought she had come from, when Dee and his daughters appeared.

Dee observed Petra, and his eyes were (yes, there was no mistaking it) mischievous. "Did you think we had abandoned you?"

"No," she lied.

Madinia opened her sack and pulled out a clean horse blanket, which she shook out over the ground. She sat down, and Margaret joined her, unpacking bread, cheese, cold meat, and green apples.

Her stomach growling, Petra stepped toward the blanket.

Dee blocked her. "Not you."

"But I'm hungry!"

"I am unsympathetic."

"Here." Margaret tossed an apple to Petra.

"Have fun!" Madinia leaned back against the gentle rise of a hill.

"Come, Petra," said Dee.

"You'll like it," said Margaret. "We'd go with you, but we've been here dozens of times."

"It's Dad's hobby," Madinia added.

"But it's just a field!"

"Is it?" Dee quietly asked.

Petra might have chucked her apple at him, but then decided that would be a waste of a good apple. She bit into it, looking around. *I don't see anything interesting,* she told Astrophil. *Only hills.*

The spider peeked through strands of her blowing hair. *True . . . but are they not rather small?*

Petra chewed thoughtfully. *You're right, Astro.* The swells of grass were also spread around them in a regular pattern, as if they had been made deliberately. "Is there something . . . hidden underground?"

"Buried," said Dee.

Petra swallowed. Then she looked at the white flesh of her apple and remembered the orange-colored seed she had found by Thorn's body. She bit again, crunching through to the core. She spat the fruit into her hand.

The seeds were brown.

"Can't you *try* to eat your food properly?" said Madinia.

Petra put the fruit back in her mouth and ate it. She walked to the top of a mound. Dee strode at her side, carrying the box of mice.

"What's buried here?" she asked.

"What do you think?"

And Petra could sense it, beneath her feet. "Metal. Gold. A lot of it."

"Yes, and many other things as well."

"Why did you bring me here?"

Dee paused. "When I asked Ariel for information about you, I got more than I bargained for. I knew—or as good as knew—that you were a chimera. But I was surprised by how much Ariel had to say. There is a great deal even I don't understand. What do the heavens pressed into a ball have to do with you? Or a king of the air-swimmers? Or black teeth?"

Petra fought back a superior grin, remembering the inky blocks. She knew something he didn't.

"But Sutton Hoo . . ." continued Dee. "This is a place I know well. For years I have come here in fair weather to unearth its secret treasures, at the queen's command. Last autumn, I had hired diggers to excavate another one of the mounds, and they uncovered what seemed to be a doorway. But then the order came from the queen to travel without delay to Bohemia as an ambassador to Prince Rodolfo's court. I haven't been back to Sutton Hoo since."

Dee led the way to a mound not far in the distance, one that had been stripped of grass. Petra readily followed, drawn by the desire to understand one more piece of Ariel's puzzle.

They walked to the other side of the excavated mound, where piles of sandy dirt were heaped up by a square door about three feet wide and tall. It was fastened with an ancient iron lock, but it was corroded and green. Dee swept aside his cloak to reveal a leather satchel at his waist. He pulled out a hammer, and swung it at the lock. It broke easily.

"Stand back," he ordered, and heaved at the door, which opened with a splintery moan.

"Now for the mice," Dee said, and lifted the crate's lid to reveal many wire cages, with one mouse in each. He took a length of twine from his satchel and attached it to a cage. The mouse pressed its paws against the bars.

"What are you doing?" Petra asked.

He didn't answer, but lowered the cage into the open doorway. Petra watched it descend until it disappeared in the shadows.

He is testing the air, Astrophil explained. *Whatever is below, it has been there for hundreds of years. Sometimes dangerous gases build up in sealed sites like these. We will need to wait until the foul air has flowed out, and fresh air has filtered in.*

After a few minutes, Dee raised the cage. The mouse was dead. He untied the string and attached it to the next cage. He lowered it, and Petra could hear the mouse squeaking below.

She said, "This is cruel."

"It is necessary."

After four more dead mice, Dee lifted a live one out of the cavern. Then he unpacked a stout rope from the satchel, knotted it around the base of a tree several feet away, and tossed it through the doorway. There was the sound of the rope hitting bottom.

"Wait until you see a light below," said Dee. "Then follow after me." He grasped the rope, and began to climb down.

When she saw the flickering of candle flame, Petra asked Astrophil, *What if Ariel is evil? Dee said she could be dangerous. We've been so focused on trying to understand what her words meant that we didn't think that she might be trying to trap us.*

But there is the light. Dee seems to be just fine.

Yes. Pity about that.

"Petra?" Dee's voice echoed. "You will want to see this."

And she did. Whatever Ariel was, whatever she meant, Petra had to know what was below. She grabbed the rope.

As she lowered herself, she watched the square of sunshine above her shrink. She glanced at the bottom, where Dee's face was distorted by shadows.

When her feet touched wood, Dee drew another candle out of his satchel, lit it with his own flaming wick, and passed it to Petra. Tomik's Glowstone would have worked far better, but she didn't want to reveal it to Dee, so she raised her candle high.

They were surrounded by gold. As Petra looked more closely, she saw curved wooden beams arching above them, and treasure heaped on either side. There were shields decorated with winking garnets, and pins shaped like eagles. She saw scabbards with golden, twisting dragons. There was a great deal of weaponry, but most of it was iron, and had rusted.

Petra looked at the walls and noticed poles sticking out among the gold. She stepped forward to examine one. "Are these . . . oars? Are we in some kind of boat?"

"Yes," said Dee. "The ancient kings of England were buried in ships. Tread carefully, Petra. The wood is hundreds of years old, and fragile. One false move could bring the ship's roof down on us."

But Petra had not walked very far before she gave a strangled cry.

She was face-to-face with a skull.

A ghost! cried Astrophil.

The Gray Men! Petra saw their bony faces. She felt the burning tongue.

Petra tripped and fell. Her candle went out, and she heard something metallic spilling across the floor. She spun around in terror. Dee's candlelit face loomed before her. "I said to be *care-*

ful." He grabbed her elbow and hauled her to her feet. "Do you *want* to be buried alive by rotten timber?"

"I saw—"

"This?" Dee swung his candle, illuminating a skeleton. It stood before them, arms crossed, wearing a golden helmet. Its jaw had fallen off, and lay by the bones of its feet. "It's a skeleton, nothing more. Learn to control your fear, Petra, or it will control you."

But Petra couldn't look away from the jawbone. She saw then that it rested on a pile of coins mixed with scraps of disintegrated cloth. More coins were scattered into the shadows. She realized that she had tripped over the remains of a purse. Her heart still hammering, she bent to pick up a handful of gold coins.

Dee brought his candle close to her palm.

Each coin is unique, Astrophil observed. *Each one bears a different mark, and language.*

"They come from many countries," said Dee. "From hundreds of years ago. Some of the kingdoms that forged these coins no longer exist."

Petra stirred the coins with her finger, and then froze.

In the center of her palm was a disk stamped with a fierce bird. Its wings were flung wide, and it was hatched with lines. She touched the bird. "An air-swimmer?" she muttered. "Is an air-swimmer . . . a bird? Maybe, for Ariel, flying is like swimming through air."

"King of the air-swimmers." Dee nodded. "Changed into gold. Tell me, Petra: what is the history of this coin?"

Her finger still resting on the image of the bird, Petra closed her eyes. Only a few seconds had passed before they flung open in shock.

"What is it?" Dee asked.

"Nothing," she said, but saw that he didn't believe her. "It's . . . each of these coins is from a different country, like you said. They were sent by rulers from all over the world as a sign of friendship to him." She pointed at the skeleton.

That is not the whole story, said Astrophil. *What else did you see? I'll tell you later.*

"Keep the coin," said Dee. "This must be what we came for, and it clearly belongs to you."

Petra slipped it into her right trouser pocket, and heard it clink against the Glowstone.

Petra and Dee scaled the rope. When they were in the sun again, Petra leaned against the hill. She sucked in the spring air, pondering what she had just discovered about the coin.

Dee fastened a new lock on the door, which Petra now knew was a ship hatch. He asked, "How have your lessons with Christopher progressed?"

"What? Uh . . . they've been all right."

"Hmm." He packed his satchel with the coiled rope. "Have you grown fond of him?"

The last thing Petra wanted to say was the truth. *"No."*

"Good. Because I fired him."

He turned away then, toward his daughters picnicking on the grass. For a moment, Petra stood stock-still, her hands balled into fists. Then she strode after him, because she had no choice but to follow.

Petra was ruthlessly glad that she had hidden what she had learned about the coin from Dee, who was not only her competitor in the race to solve Thorn's murder. Dee was also someone who seemed determined to thwart Petra's every chance at happiness, however slender or slight.

The gold coin is Romany, she told Astrophil. *It was minted during the reign of Danior of the Kalderash, about eight hundred years ago.*

She reached into her pocket, touched the coin nestled against the crystal, and wished that her friends were with her now.

24

Arrival at Deptford

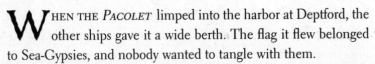

WHEN THE *PACOLET* limped into the harbor at Deptford, the other ships gave it a wide berth. The flag it flew belonged to Sea-Gypsies, and nobody wanted to tangle with them.

The *Pacolet* docked, and the sailors on ships close by watched curiously as the Gypsy crew lowered a small boat. When it hit the water, everyone could see that there were four people seated at the oars. And—how odd—one of them was blond. His hair was stiff and long and filthy, but there was no mistaking its color as it fluttered in the late April breeze.

Murmurs were exchanged. Everyone knew that Gypsies didn't like outsiders. But—the English sailors took one look at the dark-skinned crew thronged along the deck—they also didn't like people nosing into their business.

The whispers died, and Treb, Andras, Neel, and Tomik rowed up the Thames toward London.

TREB TAPPED ASH from his pipe into the water. "The *Pacolet's* taken a beating."

"That last storm . . ." muttered Andras as he pulled on the oars.

Tomik never saw anything to rival the tempest. But over the past few months, he had sailed through many storms where the green sea washed over the deck and the ship was surrounded by glittering hills of water.

"The rest of the crew can patch up the *Pacolet* in Deptford and guard the Terrestrial Globe while we search for its twin," Andras continued. "We're not far from London Bridge."

Soon they were slipping under the bridge along with dozens of other small boats, and pulling into a wharf that reeked of fish. Tomik swung his legs over the side of the boat. Oyster shells cracked under his feet as he stood quickly, and swayed.

"Steady, Tom," said Neel, though he was wobbling, too.

"It'll pass," Andras told Tomik. "Your legs aren't used to being on land."

"Where do we go now?" asked Tomik.

"Why"—Treb grinned—"to the Liberties, of course."

As Tomik and Neel walked side by side, they were day and night, sun and moon. Looking at them stroll into the lawless part of London, you might not think they were friends, but you would still sense that to raise your hand against one of them would mean facing both.

"Get two rooms at the Sign of the Spoked Wheel," Treb told them. "Andras and I are going to scout around and see what happens when we say the English word *cotton*."

"Someone'll try to sell you a dress?" Neel smirked. "You'd look awfully pretty in one."

"Make sure you take a bath before we get back, little cousin, because you *and* your jokes stink." With that, Treb and Andras turned away, walking toward a knot of villainous-looking people prowling on a street corner.

The Liberties were slummy and rough. Tomik had never seen so many fights in such a short space of time. Before he and Neel reached the inn, Tomik had counted two broken noses. There was also an incident where a whip-thin girl pulled a knife on a grown man and began pummeling his head with the hilt. That might have been funny—if there hadn't been so much blood.

When they entered the Sign of the Spoked Wheel, Tomik had begun to doubt that they would find anything so civilized as a bath. But the inn was clean and even cozy.

"Two rooms for me and mine." Neel spoke to the innkeeper in Romany. "And a hot bath. Name's Neel."

"Tribe?"

"Lovari. Got two more men coming, though, and they're Maraki."

"And who's this?" The innkeeper jerked a thumb at Tomik. "Your pigeon?"

"Nah," said Neel.

The man reassessed Tomik. "Not your courtesy-man, then?"

Tomik had had enough. In clear Romany, he said, "Will you say something resembling sense, or do I have to make you?" Months with the Maraki had taught him that if there's anything people like better than kindness, it's a bit of backbone.

The man held up his palms. "Sorry, lads. No offense meant. My wife will see to your rooms. Have a seat while you wait."

"What's a pigeon?" Tomik asked Neel as they took a table by the window. "And don't tell me it's a bird."

"A pigeon's someone caught in a trap set by—oh, me, for example. Like, say I was to tell you I knew that this tavern's got a card game going between a lot of sloppy drunks and that you could make a killing. But really I just want to make you put in enough money for my cardsharp pals—who are faking their drunkenness—to take it all off you. You're not a courtesy-man, either. Though . . ." Neel examined Tomik thoughtfully. "You could be, come to that."

"A courtesy-man."

"Yeah. Someone who plays the gentleman. The one who people will trust. If you cleaned up and threw some rich clothes on
you, we could pull off a nice scam. We'd head into the market,
find someone with a fat-looking purse, and I'd play the scary
Gypsy. You'd sail in and pretend to save the day. Then you'd pick
their pockets. Except you don't speak English. And you don't know
the first thing about thieving."

"And we have better things to do."

"Like play some cards to see who'll get to use the bath first?"

To his horror, and even though he cheated, Neel lost.

FRESHLY SCRUBBED, Tomik waited downstairs, eating a spicy stew
and grateful to have a dinner that wasn't dried. Neel skipped down
the stairs and sat down with him, dragging his fingers through his
wet, knotted hair. "We've got some plotting to do," Neel said. "First
thing, we check the weavers' halls and the cloth sellers of London.
We'll see who deals in cotton, and ask after the globe and Petra."

"Forget the globe."

"You know, we wouldn't be in this uncertain situation if it
weren't for you. At the scrying, you were supposed to question me
about Petra *after* the Maraki got their turn with the globe. It was
supposed to be a two-birds, one-stone kind of thing. Instead, you
had to confuse everything. It's not my fault if we don't know what
we're after. We'll follow the leads we've got."

"What about talking to that English ambassador who visited
Salamander Castle? Maybe he's back in London. Wouldn't John
Dee help us? He helped Petra in Prague, after all."

"I kind of got the impression that he *used* her," said Neel.
"Sketchy fellow. I'd trust him like I'd trust a viper not to bite me.
Plus, he's a spy for the queen of England. It's never a good idea to
catch the attention of governmental types, especially not when

you're looking for someone the Bohemian prince wants well and truly dead. Best to stay away from Dee. Let's tramp a bit about London and see what that shows us."

"London's a big place, but I have an idea about how to find Petra." Tomik slipped the Glowstone out of his pocket and placed it on the table. He explained.

Neel inspected the crystal, holding it up to the light. "Don't you know Petra's twitchy about spies? She hates 'em."

Tomik was silent.

"And you gave her a gift that tracks her every move. Very spy-like. She's not gonna appreciate that."

"I don't care."

"Oh, you do, Tom. You do."

25

Shoe Lane

NEEL AND TOMIK were discouraged. They had visited the shops of drapers and dressmakers, weavers and embroiderers, but Neel had a hard time getting anyone to answer his questions. The shopkeepers narrowed their eyes at him as if he were a scheming thief—which he was. He should have done exactly what Treb and Andras were doing. They had hired a respectable, white Englishman to investigate the cloth shops for them.

Tomik was worse than no help. His regular, European features might have softened people up, but he didn't understand English. Plus, he spent every second staring hopefully at his Glowstone like a moonstruck fool, waiting for it to glimmer with light.

"The Glowstone's dark," Tomik muttered as they walked down a narrow lane.

"Stop it."

"But the scrying . . . you said Petra was in London, and there's no light at all in the Glowstone."

"Tom, who knows what I meant at the scrying?"

"Maybe Petra's never been to *this* part of London. We need to keep looking."

"No, you need to *stop*." Neel seized Tomik's wrist, and the other boy curled his fingers protectively around the crystal. "Don't you get it? There's nothing here to make your crystal shine, and if you don't put it back in your pocket I'm going to crush it under my heel into a thousand shards."

The hand that held the Glowstone became a fist.

"Try it," Neel taunted. "See where hitting me gets you, 'cause neither of us thinks that'll make Petra alive and here."

"What am I supposed to do, then?"

"Put that blasted thing away. We're going back to the inn."

Tomik thrust the Glowstone into his pocket, but it was Neel who felt defeated.

"It would not be difficult for me to spy on John Dee," offered Astrophil. "I could creep into his library, see with whom he meets, and overhear his conversations."

"No," said Petra.

"I am not afraid. I do not think I could possibly be more frightened than when I slipped into the prince's Cabinet of Wonders. Oh, how my legs trembled!"

"Dee is cleverer than the prince. He could catch you."

"Petra, I am no use to anyone hiding under a dusty bed. I am proposing a sensible idea, one that we should have considered a long time ago. Do you not wish to know what Dee says when he thinks a conversation is private?"

"No."

"Petra, listen—"

"I can't!" Her voice broke. "You have to stay safe, and with me. I can't risk losing you, too."

Astrophil was silent. Then he said, "Very well. We will stay together. But we must do something. We cannot simply wait for Kit to help us."

"That's not the plan."

"Then what is?"

"Today we go to Whitehall Palace. Tomorrow, Robert Cotton's home."

ONE THING PETRA had learned from her time at Salamander Castle was that it is easier to be sneaky when you're a servant, because wealthy people have a lifetime's experience of pretending that the hired help don't exist. After stealing a plain dress from the clothesline in Dee's garden, and a sack of turnips from his kitchen, Petra was well equipped to escape the attention of anyone who mattered at the palace.

She avoided the grand dockhouse she remembered from her previous visit. Instead, she asked the oarsman to take her to the servants' wharf, where deliveries were made. From there, it was easy to mingle with the palace servants, who all thought that she worked in a different quarter of the palace than theirs.

It wasn't long before Petra found the kitchens, and Jessie.

"Hello," said Petra, "I'm—"

"Oh, I remember you. You're Kit's friend. What's this?" Jessie pointed at Petra's sack.

"Turnips. Do you want them?"

"If you'll help me chop." Jessie passed Petra a knife. "I'm guessing that, since you don't look like a lady today, you don't mind not acting like one."

As they cut the vegetables, Petra asked, "Do you remember the morning Gabriel Thorn died?"

"Didn't Kit tell you?"

"Tell me what?"

"What I told him. The same thing I said to the queen's councillors—Walsingham and Dee—when they questioned me. What curious eyes you have, girl! Well, I don't mind repeating to you what I said. You can't keep a secret here." She waved a rough, red hand at the kitchen. "We're a pack of gossips."

No wonder Kit knows the kitchen staff so well, Astrophil commented.

"The guards who walk the hallway by the library say that Thorn never met anyone that morning," Jessie began, "and as far as I know or care, he didn't. But I was the one who popped upstairs to see if Thorn needed anything. And from the smell of him, he'd already had plenty of wine, and it being early in the morning, too! He was muttering to himself. Total nonsense, as far as I could tell, but I would have thought that even if Thorn didn't meet anybody that day, he *meant* to, because he was saying, 'Cotton's got the globe. I have to tell him. Why isn't he here already?' "

"Cotton? A globe? Tell who? Tell Cotton, or tell somebody else? Who's 'he'?"

"How am I to know?"

Ask about Raleigh and Dee, Astrophil suggested.

"Could Thorn have been talking about seeing Walter Raleigh?" Petra asked.

"Raleigh?" Jessie grinned. "He was in the palace, all right, but he went nowhere near the library that morning."

"How do you know?"

"Why, because he's a rake."

"A rake?"

"A flirt. He was making pretty with Eleanor over there, and if you doubt that, her blush will tell you the truth."

Petra glanced over at the young woman standing within earshot, stuffing a game hen, her cheeks on fire. "I see. Well, do you think Thorn wanted to meet with John Dee?"

"Maybe. They're both on the queen's council, and see each other often. I hear they don't much care for each other, though."

Ask about Walsingham, said Astrophil.

Him? Petra remembered the self-important man, with his pointed beard and hair oil that smelled like dead flowers. *Why?*

On that day you went to this palace for the first time, Walsingham was very convinced that Thorn died of heart failure. A murderer would, of course, want everyone to think that the victim died of natural causes.

"What about Francis Walsingham?" Petra asked Jessie.

"Well, I suppose that whatever's true for Dee is true for him, right? It's just as likely that Thorn would have met with one as with the other. And Walsingham's got more power, politically speaking, than Dee. Walsingham's the South, and he sure lets us know it when we have to prepare a special dish for him!"

"Thanks, Jessie." Petra handed her the knife.

"You'll always get a straight answer from me. And I'll tell you something else: you and Kit are two peas in a pod. Here you are, echoing the very same questions he asked."

Astrophil said, *What I would like to know is this: why has he not shared this information with you, Petra, if he really wishes to help?*

"Jessie . . . have you seen Kit lately?"

Jessie paused before replying, and Petra instantly regretted her question, because it made her sound like someone who had been kissed and forgotten—and this, it seemed, was exactly the case.

Sympathetically, the woman said, "No, dear."

Petra left the kitchen, left the palace, left the grounds, and left the servants' wharf, but as the hired boat rowed toward the center of London, Petra couldn't leave behind the dull weight of rejection and disappointment. And by the time her boat docked cityside, anger had kindled within her. Kit owed her some answers.

Petra walked through west London, searching for Shoe Lane. This was where she and Kit had stopped, and he had said his home was nearby, and he had confessed that he didn't want her to leave England.

Was this why he hadn't told her about his conversation with

Jessie? Was Kit only pretending to help Petra? Maybe he was really just trying to keep her in London.

Petra sped up her pace. When she reached Shoe Lane, she began to stop strangers, asking after Kit. She turned from street to street, but with no success.

She kicked at a pile of trash.

Where was he?

"Том." Neel nudged him.

Tomik was staring straight ahead as they walked toward the Liberties.

"*Hey*," Neel persisted.

"I'm not talking to you. If you don't want to try to find Petra, that's your—"

Neel grabbed Tomik's shoulder and dragged him to a halt. "Look!" He pointed at Tomik's pocket.

It was glowing. Tomik snatched the crystal from his pocket.

Neel and Tomik had almost reached the Liberties when they veered west with eager feet. They began to run, the Glowstone shining a deeper and brighter blue in Tomik's palm.

Neel gasped, and Tomik wrenched his gaze away from the crystal.

There, standing not ten feet from them, was a tall girl. Her dark, glossy hair was loose, her chin a little square. She was scowling in a way they knew very well.

Tomik's shout was triumphant. "Petra!"

26

In the Liberties

S HE TURNED at the sound of her name. Her silver eyes lit up like stars. Then she hurtled across the distance between them and leaped into Tomik's arms. He caught her and spun in a circle.

"Put me down!" She laughed, not meaning what she said.

And that was a good thing, because Tomik didn't let go of her until Neel cleared his throat.

A tin leg poked out of Petra's hair and swept it aside. "Tomik! Neel!" Astrophil, perched as usual on her ear, waved another leg. "How extraordinary to find you here! Is it really you?"

Petra went to Neel. He stood, uncertain and still. She slipped her hand into his. It had changed since the time they had sworn a blood oath to each other. It had grown hard, like an animal's paw. Neel shifted his fingers to turn her palm up toward the sky and pressed his thumb against her fencing calluses.

Slyly, he said, "All right, Petali. What have you been up to?"

Petra smiled, and her face held a joy that bursts to life only when an impossible dream has come true.

She bubbled with questions as her friends led her through the Liberties. This part of town, which had once intrigued Petra, suddenly became uninteresting in the face of the miracle that had made Tomik and Neel appear before her.

"How did you get here?" she asked.

"By ship," said Tomik.

"But how do you and Neel even know each other?"

Neel warily glanced at Tomik.

"Um," Tomik began, "when you disappeared from Okno, I tried to find you and . . . got lost. I ran into Neel, and . . . we didn't know who the other was at first. But then we figured it out, and . . . became friends."

"Exactly," said Neel.

"How did you find us?" Petra asked.

"And how did you know that we were in London?" Astrophil added.

Tomik jammed a closed fist deep into his pocket.

Neel answered, "Just luck, I guess."

"Luck?" said Astrophil.

"I don't believe you," Petra stated.

"Well, it's a bit more complicated than luck," Neel admitted. "We went to a scryer, and—"

"You *scryed*?"

"No need to count the ways in which I'm not the wisest fellow ever born. I've heard it all before. But the scrying *did* give us a clue to where you were. During the scrying, Tomik asked about you."

"Neel said, 'London,' " Tomik added. "And then he mentioned something else that we don't understand. He said an English word: *cotton*."

"Wait," said Petra. "You don't mean *Robert* Cotton, do you?"

THEY SAT IN Neel and Tomik's room at the Sign of the Spoked Wheel. Crowded around a small table by a smaller window, the friends talked for hours. They didn't discuss everything that had happened to them since they last saw each other, but they came close.

Then Petra said, "Tell me more about the Celestial Globe."

"The globe doesn't matter," Tomik curtly replied. "We found you. We'll sail away as soon as we tell Treb and Andras."

"Right." Neel rolled his eyes. "Treb's going to be oh so pleased with that idea."

"Petra cannot leave London," said Astrophil, and then explained.

"You can't be serious," said Tomik, when the spider had finished telling them about Dee's hold on Petra.

Neel groaned. "Pet, you've got to break that mental link with Dee."

"I'd love to. Just tell me *how*."

Neel spread his hands helplessly. "I'm not a mind-magician. But we're talking about something that's a lot like scrying. So my guess is that you should get him to look at something shiny long enough, then control his attention, and . . . well, I don't know what you do next."

"You and John Dee handle metal on a regular basis," Astrophil reminded Petra. "It would not be hard to make him focus on a shiny object."

Though Petra didn't think Dee would be easily deceived, she nodded. "I can try."

"Now," said Astrophil, "let us discuss the globe."

"Why?" Tomik tilted his chair back, folding his arms across his chest. "What's the point? Before, we didn't know whether Neel was talking about the Celestial Globe or Petra when he scryed. Now we do. The globe's not here. Petra is."

Astrophil jumped to the window and began to pace along the sill. "At the scrying, you asked Neel about Petra. Treb asked him about the globe. Neel gave the same response to you both. Perhaps the globe *and* Petra are in London."

They all turned to Neel.

"What're you looking at me for?" he asked. "*I* don't know."

"Say the Celestial Globe is here," Tomik said. "So what? It's got nothing to do with Petra."

"No?" said Astrophil. "Then why did Ariel mention 'the heavens pressed into a ball'? That description sounds a great deal like the Celestial Globe. If the word *terrestrial* refers to the earth, then *celestial* refers to the sky — the heavens."

Petra studied Tomik. "You're worried, aren't you?" she told him. "Not because you think that the globe isn't here, or that it has nothing to do with me, but because it *is* and it *does*, and you think it's dangerous."

Tomik brought his chair down with a thud. "All I know is that the two globes combined would give someone too much power."

"Enough to die for? Enough to *kill* someone for?" Petra dug Robert Cotton's title page out of her pocket and spread it on the table. "Look at this: *An Account of My Many Astonishing Voyages*, by Gerard Mercator. Neel, you said that Mercator made the globes. This title page is a copy of a book that belonged to Cotton. What if he had the globe, and was murdered because somebody wanted it for himself?"

"That is an excellent deduction," said Astrophil. "It is a pity, however, that you are solving the wrong murder. What about your wager with John Dee? What about Thorn?"

"The deaths are connected."

"How?"

Petra wasn't sure, but she knew she was right. "Well . . . they were murdered around the same time."

"Yet they were killed in very different ways," Astrophil said. "Thorn was poisoned. Cotton was beaten with a blunt object. This does not suggest the work of the same person."

Then Petra remembered. "Jessie."

"Pardon?"

"Jessie! She said that Thorn was talking to himself in the Whitehall Palace library. He said, 'Cotton's got the globe. I have to tell him. Why isn't he here already?' It's so obvious! Cotton had the Celestial Globe, and Thorn found out. He arranged a meeting to tell someone about it. The guards claim that no one was in the library except Thorn, but let's say our murderer is well connected—he could have bribed the guards to keep quiet. Or maybe he's magically talented enough, like Dee, to slip in and out of the library with no one noticing."

"You don't need magic to do that," Neel reminded her.

"The murderer meets with Thorn, hears about the globe, and gives him wine mixed with quicksilver. Thorn's a drunk. It's morning, but he's already had some wine, and wants more. He takes the poisoned cup."

"But who carries poison around with them?" Tomik asked skeptically.

"I don't know," Petra replied, frustrated. "Dee might."

"Perhaps," said Astrophil. "However, please try to be objective, Petra. Continue with your explanation of what you think happened."

There wasn't much more to say. "After the murderer killed Thorn so that nobody else would know about the globe, he went to Cotton's house. Cotton gets his head bashed in. The globe is taken—or, at least, the murderer tries to take it."

"Let me get this straight," said Tomik. "If we figure out who killed Thorn, Dee won't try to stop Petra from leaving England, and he will give her information about Master Kronos."

"That is what he promised," said Astrophil.

"And this murder mystery is definitely connected with the Celestial Globe," Tomik continued.

"Seems like," said Neel.

"Then let's make a list of everything Ariel said, everything it could mean, and all of our suspects."

"An excellent suggestion," said Astrophil. He loved lists.

Neel rubbed his temples. He hated lists.

"So who could have killed Thorn?" asked Tomik.

Petra counted them on her fingers. "John Dee, Francis Walsingham, and Walter Raleigh."

"What about Dee's wife?" Neel asked. "She's got plenty of reason to kill Thorn."

"She said she didn't do it," Petra replied. Then she realized how silly that sounded.

Neel scoffed. "You're too trusting by half."

"According to Jessie, Thorn planned to meet a man," Astrophil pointed out. "Thorn was wondering when *he* would arrive."

"Just because this Jessie person said so? You're putting an awful lot of faith in the word of somebody remembering something she eavesdropped. Put Agatha Dee down on the list," Neel insisted, so Tomik did. He and Petra hunched over the table, and Astrophil walked across the list, imperiously ordering them to add a detail here and there. Neel stretched out on one of the two pallets on the floor. He didn't know how to read or write, and saw no reason to learn.

"You could at least pay attention," the spider lectured Neel.

"I am." He crossed his arms behind his head. "And I'll prove it. In my humble opinion, you're all thinking about something in the wrong way."

"Would you care to elaborate?" said Astrophil.

"Ariel said 'murder,' 'betrayal,' and 'assassin,' and you're clumping the three together as if they were the same thing. Well, I guess Thorn and Cotton were betrayed, 'cause someone snuffed 'em. And sure, you could say they were assassinated. But when Dee conjured that air spirit—and believe me, Pet, that was a crazy thing to do. Don't you know Ariel could have ripped your spine out of your throat?—it was asked about *Petra*." He faced her. "Dee's eager to train you. But in what? *Swordplay?* Predicting his moves? That ain't normal. Those are exactly the sort of tricks you've got to learn to kill someone on the sly. What if Ariel wasn't talking about Thorn or Cotton? What if the word *assassin* means *you?*"

27

The Queen's Council

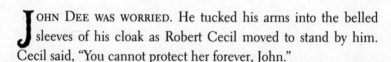

JOHN DEE WAS WORRIED. He tucked his arms into the belled sleeves of his cloak as Robert Cecil moved to stand by him. Cecil said, "You cannot protect her forever, John."

"That is for the queen to decide."

Cecil nodded as best as his crooked back would allow. When the doors to the queen's reception chamber were opened, Dee and the rest of her councillors filed in.

Seated next to the queen was Prince Rodolfo, who looked up in surprise. When he spoke, his English was perfect. "Your Majesty, surely you do not need your council. My request is such a little matter."

"Your Highness, my councillors merely honor you with their presence," Queen Elizabeth replied.

"Of course." The prince fidgeted in the uncomfortable (if grand) chair next to the queen. "I believe that, somewhere in your great realm, there is a girl—"

"I daresay there are thousands of girls in England. What of it?"

"This particular girl is *mine*. She is Bohemian, which makes her *my* subject. Her name is Petra Kronos, and I ask that she be given to me."

"*If* she happens to be in my country."

"She is."

"Are you suggesting that I *do not know* whether she is or is not?" The queen's tone was dangerous.

"Certainly you must know," answered the prince.

"Then you accuse me of hiding her from you?"

The prince looked flustered. "No. But if she is here, I demand that she be turned over to me."

"*Demand?*" The queen turned to her councillors, catching Dee's eye. "Am I to be ordered about by a stripling boy? You"—the queen pointed a knobby finger at the prince, and it did not shake—"what are you, Prince Rodolfo? A third son. A ruler of a forgettable country. Do you truly believe Emperor Karl will choose *you* to succeed him? Go, you political nothing, and return to make demands of me when there is some possibility that I will listen."

The prince stood, white with anger. "Then I shall find her myself." He stalked out of the chamber.

When he was gone, Queen Elizabeth pursed her lips. "The performance is over," she told her council. "You may leave."

They stood.

"Dee," she called. "Stay."

He approached the throne. The last councillor to leave, Walsingham, threw a glance at them before the doors shut behind him.

"Well?" she asked.

"I am pleased and grateful, of course," said Dee.

"But?"

He murmured, "You did not need to offend the prince."

"Indeed. However, to do so amused me a great deal. Now, do you have any news of the Celestial Globe?"

"Soon, Your Majesty. Soon."

• • •

THAT AFTERNOON, Petra seemed different. Perhaps it was Dee's imagination, but she appeared to glow . . . with happiness? Yes, he thought so. He allowed himself to hope that she had grown used to life at Throgmorton Street. After all, this was now her home.

Before he could begin their lesson, she asked, "What kind of person would always carry quicksilver?"

Dee was not easily startled, but he was now. He considered. It was best to tell her the truth. She could learn the answer from another source . . . Dee regretted ever having hired Christopher. That had been a bad idea. But where Petra Kronos was concerned, Dee so often made mistakes.

She was waiting, her eyes narrowed.

Dee reached into a pocket and drew out a small vial. He shook it and the silvery liquid inside. "Anyone who spies for the queen carries this, in case of capture and torture. A spy would rather drink quicksilver than tell Her Majesty's secrets. But, my dear, before you accuse me of Thorn's murder, I would like you to take notice that my vial is still full."

"That doesn't matter. You could have filled it up again."

"True," he acknowledged. He decided to let her make the next move.

Again, she did something unexpected. She approached him and, with a humility that really didn't suit her, said, "I think there's something strange about the coin we found at Sutton Hoo. Would you look at it, please?" She held it out to him.

He took it. He should have thought twice about how friendly she suddenly seemed, but he inspected the golden coin because he was curious. Because he was also thorough, he took his time.

A peace settled over him, like that feeling just before sleep.

His head snapped up. He saw Petra staring at him with great intensity, and even though Dee knew that this would be yet one more mistake, he laughed.

He tossed the coin, and she snatched it out of the air, looking infuriated.

"Clever girl." Dee wagged a finger. "Where did you learn that? Not from just anywhere, I imagine. But even if you discovered the *fact* of tricking me into looking at an object that gleams, how would you know the *process* of breaking the mental link? Very few people could teach you that. Or are you improvising? You are, aren't you?" He added, "How proud you make me."

That did it. She spun on her heel and slammed the library door on her way out.

A visitor entered Prince Rodolfo's residence in London. He joined the prince for dinner, which was delicious and prepared with imaginative flair.

Prince Rodolfo patted his lips with a napkin. "So you still have not found the Celestial Globe, in spite of having killed Gabriel Thorn and Robert Cotton."

"I will, Your Highness. I just need more time. It must be somewhere in Cotton's manor. Please—"

"Stop. It hurts my ears when you whine. If you have made no progress on the globe, which is the least you could do for the enormous sum of money I have given you, then let us discuss Petra Kronos. We know where she is, but she has to be taken without giving Queen Elizabeth any cause to take offense."

"Of course, Your Highness," said Francis Walsingham. "I have a plan."

28

Help

"WHERE ARE YOU going, Petra?"

"Just take a look at her, Meggie. She's dressed in those wretched trousers and she's got a glint in her eye. Her clothes are dark, like she's planning some nighttime stealthiness. She is *so* up to something."

"Madinia, be quiet! Let her answer."

"Why? It's obvious. See that?" Madinia pointed at Petra's face. "That's new."

"*What* is?"

"Her expression. She looks *hopeful*. She's figured out a way to leave London without us having to chase after her through a Rift. Do you think she'll outsmart Dad? I'd like to see that."

"Me, too," said Margaret.

"You would?" Petra let her hand fall from the garden door. She turned to the sisters. "But I asked you to bring me back to Bohemia, and you refused."

"Well, yes." Margaret shifted uncomfortably. "Dad had warned that you would ask. He told us not to listen, and we agreed. He's our father, after all."

"Plus, once we got to know you, we wanted you to stay," Madinia added.

This surprised Petra. "Why?"

"We like you," said Margaret. "You're smart. And brave. You went down into the grave at Sutton Hoo. I'd never do that."

"Of course, you are also a little cranky," said Madinia.

"Which is understandable"—Margaret elbowed her twin—"given the circumstances."

"But you're strong," Madinia continued. "If I were in your shoes, I'd be a whiny, weepy puddle of a person, and you're not."

"Maybe we could help you go home," Margaret offered, "without actually disobeying our father."

"He only told us not to create a Rift to Bohemia for you. But we could be useful in other ways, *if* you let us in on the plan that you clearly have."

Petra studied them. Their faces shone with affection and . . . yes, admiration. How could that be? Petra had done so little to earn it, she felt. She had always thought of the girls as obstacles, but now she remembered Margaret's acts of kindness, Madinia's energy, and their readiness to treat her like a sister. *They seem genuine*, Petra said to Astrophil.

But he was a spider who knew his priorities, and at the top of his list was Petra. *Seeming to tell the truth and actually doing it are two very different things. You cannot trust them. The sun is setting. It is time to meet Tomik and Neel. Stay silent, and leave this house.*

"I'm sorry," Petra told the sisters, and stepped into the garden, knowing without looking back that Madinia would be crestfallen, and that Margaret would have been expecting Petra's response all along.

She didn't get very far down the street before she heard a set of running footsteps behind her.

"Wait!" someone called. It was Kit.

Hurt snaked through Petra. It stung, bit, and gnawed. A week had gone by since Dee had dismissed him, and Kit hadn't even bothered to visit. He had ignored her. Well, she could do that, too. She kept walking.

"Petra, please." He stood in front of her.

She sidestepped him, but not before she saw that he was dressed much like she. His clothes were black, and he was armed with a short sword that looked good for using in close quarters, like the narrow hallway of a house. Petra carried a sword as well, even if no one could see it.

Kit blocked her path again, and Petra's temper flared. She placed a hand on her father's invisible rapier, which she wore for the first time in months. But she did not draw the sword—because she did not want to reveal its existence, because she thought that any swordfight with Kit would result in her quick defeat, and mostly because she was not sure she really wanted to start a duel.

"I spoke with Jessie," Petra accused. "I know what she told you, and you kept it from me!"

"Yes, I should be proud of that. I'm making leaps and bounds in my ability to keep certain things secret." His tone was joking, but nervous. "Please don't walk away, Petra. Listen to me. I didn't want to tell you what Jessie said without understanding first what it *meant*. What good would a fragment of information do you? I did some investigating. Remember that title page of the travel book by Gerard Mercator? It turns out that Thorn had discovered that Robert Cotton owned something called the Celestial Globe, which was made by Mercator—"

"I know all about that," Petra cut him off. "It turns out that a fragment of information does me lots of good. So if you don't have anything worthwhile to say, get out of my way."

He took a step closer. "I'm sorry, Petra, and I've missed you every day for the last week. Why do you think I'm here now, not twenty feet from Dee's house? Dee forbade me to see you. He could destroy me easily. You know that. He'd sweep the pieces of what's left of my miserable career under a dusty rug, and he took care to remind me of that when he said I'd no longer be needed at Throgmorton Street. You've seen what part of town I live in. Do you think I can afford to disobey John Dee? How would I eat if I could no longer earn what little I do by teaching swordplay?

"I'm not rich, and I'm not even wise, because even though I knew I should, I couldn't stay away from you for long. I had to tell you everything I had learned. I arrived just after you left Dee's house, and found Madinia and Margaret in the garden. They told me which direction you had taken." He looked at her searchingly, then dared to continue. "Do you still have that title page? With you?"

Hesitantly, Petra nodded.

"Good," said Kit. "I was wrong to think it wasn't important, but then, I've been wrong about many things. Though never about you."

"Why did you change your mind about the title page?"

"Because we're going to sneak into the home of Robert Cotton." Kit's eyes burned with excitement. "That title page might be connected to the globe, and the globe might be connected to the murders. Little is certain, but the one thing I know absolutely is that we have to explore every possibility of getting to the bottom of Thorn's death. I want you to win your wager with Dee. I want you to be free, Petra."

His fingers lifted to touch her cheek.

"NO." TOMIK SHOOK HIS HEAD.

"No way," agreed Neel. "He ain't tagging along. We don't know him. Also—and I'm just mentioning this by way of pointing out how little you've told us about this fellow, Pet—we were under the impression that Kit was a *she*. What kind of girly name is Kit? Makes me think of kittens. And I can't stand kittens, what with their needle claws and mewing—"

"What Neel's saying is: we don't trust him," Tomik interjected.

"You stole my purse, and I trusted you," Petra told Neel.

He spread his arms wide. "That's different!"

"I don't see how," she replied. "Kit says someone has set up guards on Cotton's land, but he knows them. He can get us inside."

Kit stood in Neel and Tomik's room at the Spoked Wheel, looking bewildered as the three friends argued in Czech. "What's going on?" he asked Petra in his own tongue.

"You're coming with us to Cotton's house," she told him.

"If he gets to go, so do we!" came an indignant cry from behind the closed door. It flung open, and there stood Madinia, with Margaret right behind her.

"Who are *they*?" Tomik was exasperated.

"Who is *he*?" Madinia gazed at him hungrily. "Is he speaking Czech, Petra? Will you teach me?"

"What are you doing here?" Petra asked them.

"We followed you," Margaret said, stating the obvious.

"If you haven't forgotten, we have certain magical talents," Madinia added, "that would be great for breaking into houses, as it sounds like you're planning on doing. We've been to Cotton's home before, with our parents, for some draggingly dull dinner, but Meggie and I snuck upstairs to the bedrooms, and I swear the curtains are out of fashion by about a *hundred years*, which should be against the law—"

Margaret interrupted, "Madinia's trying to say that we're going to help you, Petra, whether you like it or not."

29

The Greenhouse

TOMIK CROUCHED under the whispering trees of Robert Cotton's estate. "Why do I let Petra talk me into things I know are stupid?"

Neel thought it best not to answer that question.

Half an hour earlier, as the six of them rowed up the moonlit river toward the grand manors stretched along the Thames, Petra had suggested they split into three groups and enter Cotton's house at as many points. "We'll have to spread out. Maybe we'll be able to find the globe for Neel, but we've no idea how or where, and we don't know what kind of clues we might find about the deaths of Thorn and Cotton."

"Our father didn't do it," interrupted Margaret. "I don't care what you think."

Petra continued as if she hadn't heard. "So we need to cover as much ground as possible. Each group will explore a different area of the mansion."

Neel had quickly agreed, adding that a dimwit would know that there's no use trying to snoop around in a group of six. "Even two-by-two might be too noisy," he said, leveling a meaningful look at Madinia.

Tomik pulled at the oars of the *Pacolet*'s launch, which they had taken from its dock at Oyster Wharf. He was willing to go along with Petra's plan as long as he was her partner.

But she had had other ideas. "We'll pair off like this: Madinia and Margaret, Tomik and Neel, Kit and me."

Tomik immediately objected.

"It makes sense," Petra argued. "We don't even all speak the same language! And this way, each pair has somebody who can break into the house: Madinia can open a Rift, Neel can pick a lock, and Kit can talk his way past any guards."

" 'It makes sense,' " Tomik mimicked Petra now as he and Neel moved over the wet grass. "Just like running off to Prague without me last year made sense." Tomik stepped into a particularly soft patch of earth and glared at the mud on his shoe. "Ugh."

"Hey, Tom," said Neel. "Know what I like about mud? It's *quiet*."

Tomik gave him a sour look but didn't say anything after that—not when they followed the trees' shadows to the back of the looming house, not when Neel slipped his ghost fingers into the lock of the servants' door, and not when they finally stepped inside the cavernous home of Sir Robert Cotton.

"WELL, THAT WAS EASY," said Madinia when she and her sister entered one of the many bedchambers on the second floor. Most of the rooms had never been used, except by book collectors and scholars who had visited Cotton over the years—and a Moroccan merchant who had purchased a particularly lovely globe for next to nothing in a Sallay market. But Madinia and Margaret didn't know this, and they didn't know that Cotton had gladly paid a small fortune for the globe. When the merchant took leave of Cotton's hospitality, both men thought that they had cheated the other.

"Aren't you going to close that?" Madinia pointed at the Rift.

"No." Margaret swallowed nervously. "We'd better leave it open. Just in case."

• • •

KIT AND PETRA walked right up to the front door, which faced the river.

"It's unlocked." Kit opened the door. "That's lucky."

"I thought you said there would be guards."

"It seems I was misinformed."

"Kit . . . why don't you know who hired the guards?"

He blinked at her in confusion. "But there aren't any."

"But you said there *were*, and that you would probably know them and they would let you in, just like the guards always do at Whitehall Palace for balls. How is it possible that you would know the guards but not know who *hired* them?"

"Spies don't always get the whole story. We take the information we can get."

Petra looked over the threshold into the empty, dark house and suddenly wondered if her plan to split into pairs was a really bad one.

"Petra, the moonlight's clear enough for me to see the suspicion on your face. Have some faith in me, because if you don't, I'm not sure who else will. I swear that I would never let any harm come to you." Kit stepped into the house and drew her toward him.

Let's leave, Petra, Astrophil said. *We shall turn around, and try to find the others.*

"Kit, I—"

"Is this any time to argue? Your friends are probably already inside the manor. They're expecting you to do your part. After all, they came here because of you."

When he said that, the decision was easy. Petra slipped inside.

"TREB AND ANDRAS aren't going to thank you for not telling them about this," Tomik muttered. Moonlight glowed through the windows, illuminating huge laundry tubs.

"I want to surprise them with that starry globe. Treb said some things to me once in the *Pacolet* pantry that he's going to regret."

"Just don't forget why we're here. Our first priority is to help Petra win her wager. The globe comes second."

"No," said a new voice from a dark corner. "It comes first, just like I do." Prince Rodolfo stepped into the moonlight, and guards filed into the laundry room.

Tomik had never seen his country's prince, and did not recognize him, but no one needed to tell Tomik that the appearance of this young, elegantly dressed man meant trouble. He drew his glass knife.

Neel muttered, "I don't think that's going to help."

"Is this the Gypsy?" A bright smile broke across the prince's face. "Forgive me, I did not see you at first. Your skin is so *brown*— not a pleasant color at all—that you blended right into the shadows. But now I know you are here. Yes, the smell is really unmistakable. The stink is even familiar to me, since so many of your kind are currently rotting in my dungeons. Now, you *must* be Petra Kronos's Gypsy. The one who so impolitely rifled through my Cabinet of Wonders. I am very glad to find you here."

Tomik stepped in front of Neel.

The prince tilted his head, evaluating Tomik's glass blade. "That is a pretty toy." He flicked a finger and a guard raised his heavy sword. It chopped through the air and struck Tomik's knife.

The glass shattered. Blood dripped from Tomik's hand.

"But it was nothing special," the prince told Tomik consolingly, "and—really—so fragile."

MADINIA AND MARGARET'S skirts rustled as they took the wide oak stairs to the ground floor and turned down a long hallway. They had seen nothing of interest during their exploration of Cotton's manor. Nothing, that is, until Madinia peeked around a corner and gasped.

"What is it?" Margaret whispered anxiously.

Madinia turned to her. "There are men," she hissed. "One of them is dressed in clothes fit for a king. There are at least ten others with him, they're armed to the teeth, and they've got Tomik and Neel."

"What?"

"I just saw them marching past. Tomik's and Neel's hands are bound. Tomik's bleeding."

Margaret thought of Petra, who always seemed so fearless. What would she do? "We have to help them," Margaret said.

"Are you crazy?" Madinia tugged at her twin's hand, leading her back the way they had come. "We've got to get out of here!"

Their soft-soled shoes padded over the rugs as they raced for the bedroom stairs and the Rift.

"THIS WAY," Kit told Petra. "The library's here, on the ground floor, but we have to go through the greenhouse first."

How does he know that? Petra asked Astrophil, glad for his sharp grip on her ear. She lagged behind Kit as they passed through a dining room. Ghostly cloths covered the tables and chairs. *I remember . . . when I sat in the carriage with Dee and Walsingham on the way to the river, Walsingham was rude to me. Dee told him he shouldn't underestimate youth, and added, "What about Christopher Rhymer?" Walsingham said, "Kit has his uses." Has, Astro, not* had. *As if Kit still works for Walsingham. What if Kit's story about being fired by Walsingham was all a lie?*

"Come on, Petra!" Kit didn't bother to hush his voice. He stood in front of a glass wall that looked like a jeweled box, and opened a brass-handled door. "Don't be a coward! There's nothing but plants inside. They won't eat you."

Astrophil, who had bad memories of a certain Venus flytrap, shuddered under Petra's hair. *I think we should leave. Ariel told me to save my lady, and that is you, Petra. "Never trust a poet," she said. What does a poet do, if not rhyme? And is not Kit's full name Christopher Rhymer?*

Petra had a sick, sinking feeling. Her instincts told her that Astrophil was right, and that she should listen to him, but she didn't want to. Her uncertainty warred against the tenderness she had held for Kit for months now.

Petra had to know who Kit really was. She walked into the greenhouse.

Panes of glass were fitted together into a peaked roof high over their heads. Petra could see the full moon. The air was hot, stifling, and humid.

"Cotton loved plants." Kit fingered an African violet. "He was obsessed with botany, and all because his last name was the same as that of a shrub. That's self-centered, if you ask me. Do *I* go around rhyming every other word? Now, *these* are delicious. I love them." He turned to a low, twisted tree and plucked a fruit. "Have one, Petra." He tossed it to her.

The fruit blurred as it spun through the air. Petra caught it. She knew, even before she opened her hand, that she held a small apple, and she didn't need to cut it open to discover the color of its seeds. But as Kit picked another fruit and began eating, Petra pulled her dagger from her boot and sliced the apple in half.

Its flesh was rosy, and its seeds were orange.

That's not proof, she argued with herself. But she gripped the dagger and braced herself to use it. She turned away from Kit, and began searching among the plants.

"What are you looking for?" he asked. "Does it have something to do with the globe? Or that title page? Tell me, Petra."

But she ignored him, pushing aside enormous flaps of green

leaves. She snagged her foot against a root, but did not fall. Ivy tangled around her arm. And all the while Kit followed at her heels, talking, talking, talking.

Her throat burned. Finally, she shouted, *"Shut up!"*

He did, because they were facing a small plant with pink petals. It was a cuckooflower.

Petra's eyes raged at Kit as she ripped off the first petal.

"Robert Cotton!" named the plant.

Petra tore another flower.

"Francis Walsingham!"

And again.

"Christopher Rhymer!"

30

Damage

*B*EHIND YOU! Astrophil warned.

But Kit's dagger was already at Petra's throat. With his other hand, he reached for her wrist and pinched a nerve against the bone until she cried out and dropped her knife. He kicked it across the floor.

"I swore no hurt would come to you," Kit breathed, "and I don't want to break my promise, but let's admit that my word might not be worth much right now. Take that title page out of your pocket. Master Walsingham thinks that you know something that we don't. Prove it to me. We're going to the library, and you will find the Celestial Globe."

Petra swallowed against the blade. She bowed her head, then reached into her pocket, pulled out the wadded paper, and pressed it into Kit's free hand.

"Thank you," he said, and relaxed the knife.

Then Petra jerked her head back, slamming it into Kit's face. She heard a cracking sound. Kit staggered and swore. Petra ducked down, away from the knife. She sprinted across the greenhouse, scraped past thorny rosebushes, and snatched up her fallen dagger. Good. She had put some distance between herself and Kit. Now she wheeled around to confront him.

His nose was broken, and he was spitting blood, but he had drawn his sword, which was broader and heavier than Petra's. Kit held a weapon in each hand now—his sword in his right hand, and his dagger in his left, just as Petra had practiced for months.

But he had been doing this for *years*. "Petra, you're fierce, and that's one of the things I like about you, but there's a difference between stubborn and *stupid*. What can you hope to do with that dagger? I'll tell you, because I know better than anybody: nothing. Even on your best day, you couldn't do anything against my two blades except prolong the inevitable. *Slightly* prolong it. Drop the knife. This isn't a game or a lesson, and my sword is not blunt."

Petra shifted the dagger to her left hand, and drew the invisible rapier with her right.

Kit recognized the harsh song of a sword being pulled from its scabbard. "What's this?" he murmured, watching Petra crouch into a position he had taught her, one that could just as easily attack or defend. Her right hand was empty, but it acted as if it were not.

With four quick strides, Kit was in front of her. He made the first move, feinting toward her right hip. She didn't take the bait. When his feint turned into a true thrust, she twisted her right wrist. Kit heard and felt (even if he did not *see*) her parry the blow.

And that was precisely what he wanted. He stepped forward and pressed his blade against the air, which couldn't be just air. Kit raked his sword upward, testing the length of whatever Petra held in her right hand. When his blade reached the tip of her sword— and she had one, oh, she did—he swiftly fell back, on guard for an invisible attack.

"That," he declared, "is *cheating*."

"CAN'T YOU DO SOMETHING?" Tomik hissed at Neel in Romany as the prince's men dragged them through Cotton's dining room. Prince Rodolfo led the way.

"Like what, exactly?"

"Like use those ghost fingers you're always bragging about."

"In case you haven't noticed, my hands are tied."

"Stretch your fingertips, I know you can. Untie my hands if you're too scared to untie your own."

Neel gave him a disdainful glance. "Fat lot of good that'll do. There are eleven more of them than us. I'll take my chances when I have one."

"Hey, what're they talking about?" a Czech guard said to the man walking at his side.

"Can't tell. They're talking Gypsy, I'll bet. They sound just like the dogs they are."

"*Woof,*" said a third guard.

"*Arooo,*" howled another.

"Crawl for us, doggie." One of them shoved Neel in the back, and he fell to his knees.

"And you"—a guard yanked Tomik by his hair—"aren't you Bohemian? Why are you babbling dog-speak? What's wrong with Czech? Go on, then, bark and crawl like your brown friend."

"Silence!" ordered the prince. He was staring straight ahead. Suddenly, everyone could hear metal ringing against metal: the unmistakable sounds of a swordfight. He turned to the guards. "You can play with the prisoners later. Haul the Gypsy to his feet. Draw your weapons. Step quickly, and *quietly*, or I'll have your tongues torn out to teach you how."

KIT PRESSED HIS ADVANTAGE, lunging forward. Petra blocked him with the dagger. He pulled back a fraction of an inch, just enough to throw her off balance. Then he beat against her dagger with a savage twist of his blade. Pain jolted up Petra's arm. For the second time, she lost her knife. It clattered against the floor.

What happens if your dagger is knocked away? Petra remembered her father's words to her in the Okno forest. *There's room enough for your left hand as well as your right on this hilt. That will give your blows more force.*

Petra joined her hands on the rapier's hilt. She dodged Kit's steel and thrust toward his shoulder, putting her weight behind it.

He ducked, and she propelled forward, stumbling until she regained her feet. "No, Petra," he instructed. "Thrusts are supposed to be precise. A two-handed grip is only really useful for side-cuts. Like *this*, and *this*." His blows were deliberately easy for Petra to block. He could have been mocking her, or he could have forgotten that they weren't in Dee's practice room, and that he wasn't her friend or anything else but a traitor.

"You're toying with me," she accused.

"I won't if you don't want me to."

She feinted, and feinted again, but he didn't move. "I can't see your blade," he said, "but I can see your face. It tells me what you will do, and you can't hide the movement of your hands. An invisible sword is a neat trick. But it's only a trick. Its best advantage is surprise, and you've already lost that."

Determined to fool him this time, Petra started to swing her sword as if to deliver a coupe, a cut toward the head. But then she lunged past Kit's side. Her blade whistled through the air, slashing toward his back.

He spun around and caught the blow with his crossed sword and dagger. Using both blades, he shoved her away. "A sidecut to the back. Deadly, and dishonorable. Well done. *Almost.*"

He hammered at her hands. *Do you feel the swirls of steel arcing over the hilt?* she recalled her father saying. *That's to protect your fingers, in case someone tries to make you drop the sword by hacking at them.* Petra's arms ached, but she held against the raining steel, her fingers curled safely under the hilt's curves. She jumped back, out of Kit's reach.

Kit paused, and all the humor in his bloodied face vanished. "Let's stop this," he begged. "Can't you see that all I want to do is disarm you? I *care* for you, Petra."

Betrayal burned in her heart like acid. She took a step back, but didn't lower her sword.

Kit thrust.

She stepped back.

And again.

Stand your ground! Astrophil ordered. *He is* herding *you! There is a row of palm trees behind you, and if you keep backing up, you will be trapped!*

Petra listened to him, and was still listening when Kit's sword slipped under her guard and stabbed deep into her left shoulder.

He pulled the sword out. Pain exploded through her. This was no little cut. Blood gushed from the wound, and in a heartbeat her shirt was sticky and wet. Petra looked down and saw thin red rivers trickling between her fingers. She gasped, not realizing until then that she had been holding her breath. This made the pain worse — jagged and bright.

She faltered back. She leaned against a palm tree and stared up at its green fronds.

"Yield," Kit pleaded.

Astrophil's legs stroked her earlobe. *Perhaps you should*, he said sorrowfully.

"It's just a globe," Kit said. "A round, painted ball. Don't you know where it is?"

"No," she whispered.

"Well, can't you help me find it? If I give it to Master Walsingham, I'll be wealthy and secure for life. Why go back to Bohemia, when you could stay in London with me?"

Everything was confused. Why should she care about the globe? It had something to do with Cotton, Thorn, and Dee. But she didn't understand how it all fit together. She *did*, once, but that was before her mind was ruled by agony.

She looked at her sword as if it might give her an answer. As usual, she saw nothing.

But she heard her father's voice: *This sword is meant to do damage, Petra, and I mean for you to do damage against anyone who tries to hurt you. Anyone.*

Petra raised her eyes to Kit's face. She wasn't afraid. Why should she be afraid? She knew what fear was: it was cold and gray and cruel. It was scaled skin and human eyes. It stank of death.

Kit was just a boy.

Petra sucked in her breath. She stood up, and circled away from the trees. Kit's body tracked hers, shifting as she did.

Allow me to explain what you are, Dee had told her, *for truly there are few of your kind in this world.*

A chimera. Wasn't Petra a rare thing? Powerful, even?

She remembered Dee's lessons, the hours she had spent guessing which hand he might raise. She looked at Kit. *Left*, she decided.

His sword darted to the left.

She blocked it.

She advanced, her eyes half-shut. She didn't need to see. She could *feel* Kit's blows coming. She knew his feints for the naked lies they were, and countered his every move.

His sword slashed and lunged. She danced away. She flowed like water, and leaned to kick against his dagger. Her mind reached for Kit's blade against her boot. *Fall*, she told the dagger, and it did.

Petra slid, swept, bowed, and leaped. She didn't even bother noticing the mounting anxiety in Kit's eyes. Not until her rapier snaked around his sword. Her mind felt the blades as if they were knotted strands of silk. Petra tugged, and Kit dropped his sword.

"*You* yield," she said, and pointed the rapier at his throat.

31

Tyrants

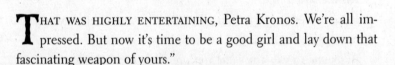

"THAT WAS HIGHLY ENTERTAINING, Petra Kronos. We're all impressed. But now it's time to be a good girl and lay down that fascinating weapon of yours."

Petra snapped her eyes away from Kit's. There, standing several feet ahead in the frame of an open door that surely led to Cotton's library, was Francis Walsingham, a torch blazing in his hand. He continued, "Kit belongs to me, you see, and I'll be irritated if you hurt him. Your little friends won't like it either. Will they, Your Highness?"

"Not unless they enjoy being dead," said someone behind Petra. She knew that voice all too well.

She whirled around to see Prince Rodolfo watching her from the other end of the greenhouse, by the glass door she and Kit had passed through minutes before. The prince's smile was as smooth as marble, and just as cold. A dozen guards ranged behind him. Several held torches. The others clutched Tomik and Neel.

"I wonder," said the prince, "for which one will you weep most? I doubt I am the only person curious to know. Shall we find out? No? Then come to me, Petra Kronos."

Numbly, Petra lifted the sword away from Kit, and crossed to stand before the prince. She glanced once at the faces of her friends, but that was worse than looking at the prince.

"Give me your sword," he commanded, "for we all know you have one, invisible though it may be."

"That's a bad idea—" Tomik shouted at Petra. A guard back-handed him across the mouth.

Neel, who thought it was a *worse* idea to say anything at all, watched Petra's hands shift. She offered up the invisible rapier. Like a blind man, the prince delicately patted the air until his fingers closed around the hilt.

"Now *this* is a work of art," the prince told Tomik. "It is worth a thousand times more than your pathetic knife, and I believe I know who made it."

"Where is my father?" Petra whispered. "Is he all right?"

"Mikal Kronos is perfectly well. He is better than ever, in fact. You have my noble word. You can see him for yourself after you return with me to Bohemia. Along the way, you can introduce me to your friends—the Gypsy, in particular. Why, I do not even know their names!"

Petra pressed a hand against her throbbing wound. "You'll kill me. You'll kill them."

"I am not going to kill you, Petra. I am going to *keep* you. You will make a fine addition to my collection. As for the two boys, I might kill them, or I might not. That depends on you. Will you do me a small service? Walsingham was a little too impatient when questioning Robert Cotton about the location of the Celestial Globe. It seems Walsingham murdered him earlier than he intended, and the secret of the globe's location died with Cotton. But thanks to information passed along by—what is his name? Kit?—we believe that Cotton hid the globe in his library. Why else would he print a copy of Mercator's title page? Clearly, in Cotton's mind, books and the globe went together. All you have to do, Petra, is find the globe and give it to me."

"But I don't know where it is."

"Yet you are extraordinary, are you not? You continually do the impossible. Do it once more. If you find the globe, everyone returns to Bohemia safe and sound. I regret to say that you cannot go *home*, Petra, but there is nothing left for you there anyway. Salamander Castle will be your new home, and you will be treated with honor. You will intrigue the court, and that will entertain me.

"Of course, if you cannot discover the globe's location, this will mean that you are not as unusual as I thought. And if you are not, what good are you to me? Why should I care for the lives of your friends, or for your own?" Then he added in a velvety voice, "Surely, Petra, there is no harm in *trying* to please me? Let us step into the library with Walsingham. Find the globe. Show us your worth."

Petra didn't think she had a choice, and neither did Astrophil. "I'll try."

"Excellent!" Then the prince turned to a guard. "Bind her wound," he ordered. The guard tore off Petra's left sleeve and gripped her bare arm. He used the bloody rag of her sleeve as a bandage, wrapping it around Petra's shoulder so tightly that she whimpered. But the guard knew what he was doing, and the blood stopped flowing.

Tomik and Neel watched anxiously as the prince and half of his guards followed Petra. She approached Kit, who was now standing by Walsingham's side. Kit's broken nose was already swollen.

"Give me the title page," she ordered.

He handed it to her. "Petra, I didn't know Prince Rodolfo wanted to take you back to Bohemia! I thought—"

"We do not care what you think," the prince informed him. "You are a buzzing fly. You will stay right here, and you will stay silent, or someone will swat you."

"I think the girl already has." Walsingham chuck[...] prince, several guards, and Petra entered Cotton's libr[...] ham said to her, "I shouldn't have rubbed his face in[...] should I? Poor Kit. Well, I'll see to it he gets some kind[...] for his troubles. He's been very useful to me. When I poisoned Gabriel Thorn with a dose of quicksilver, Kit was there to help me dispose of the tainted wineglass. He distracted some palace guards and bribed others, so no one important ever knew I visited Thorn in the Whitehall library just before he died. Kit even questioned the servants to make certain they didn't suspect me. And then John Dee was foolish enough to *hire* him to teach you. What a stroke of fortune for me! I swear, John used to be the councillor everyone feared, but he's been slipping lately. A few years ago, John would have known Kit still worked for me, whatever people might say."

Walsingham set his torch in a wall sconce, and the library flickered before them. Windowless and vast, the room smelled like animal skins, paper, and age. It was shaped in a hexagon, and each of the six sides held ten long shelves that were lined with books. Some volumes were new, and gleamed with gold letters. Others had split spines. At the very top of each set of shelves was a statue. They stood like guardians over the library.

Those statues . . . murmured Astrophil. *I would like a closer look at them.*

Petra took Walsingham's torch and illuminated the stone faces one by one. Each face had different features, but they all seemed to sneer at her.

They are tyrants, Astrophil said finally. *Rulers from ancient history who were known for their cruelty. The first one on the left is Phalaris, who enjoyed roasting people alive.*

And the others? asked Petra. *Who were they?*

Astrophil named them as they turned around the room: *Caligula, Nero, Dionysius, Domitian,* and *Tarquin the Proud.*

"I know where the globe is," Petra announced.

"But you haven't even looked at the title page," said Walsingham.

"I don't need to." Petra remembered the only thing that was important about the title page: that mysterious notation, N6.

"You see?" The prince was ecstatic. "Extraordinary! I said that you were, Petra Kronos, and I am never wrong. Now give me the Celestial Globe."

Petra hesitated. What would happen to her, her father, and her friends after she obeyed the prince's command?

There were too many uncertainties, and Petra had never liked feeling uncertain.

But what could she do? The prince had his guards, Walsingham, her sword, and her friends. She needed something he didn't have . . . a weapon, or an ally, or both.

She slid a hand inside her pocket, and felt the gold Romany coin and the Glowstone.

Petra, what are you doing?

Shh, Astro.

She wrapped her fingers around the coin, and traced the outline of the bird stamped on it. *King of the air-swimmers*, she remembered Ariel saying. Then Petra thought of something else: how Dee had used stardust, feathers, and incense to summon Ariel. Dee had said that the air spirit didn't need them to find him. *I use these objects to help me concentrate*, he had said. *They are helpful only because I consider them to be allied with the air.*

Ariel had said that Petra was a dream-thinker. Very well, then, Petra would dream-think. She remembered the sparrow that had flown to the Sign of the Compass on that fateful morning months ago. She imagined the wind in its feathers. She pretended that she was the bird, swimming in the air, diving and breathing and floating. Petra gripped the golden bird coin, and called upon Ariel.

Then Ariel came, and Petra couldn't believe what she had done.

32

The Wind

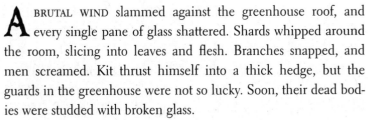

A BRUTAL WIND slammed against the greenhouse roof, and every single pane of glass shattered. Shards whipped around the room, slicing into leaves and flesh. Branches snapped, and men screamed. Kit thrust himself into a thick hedge, but the guards in the greenhouse were not so lucky. Soon, their dead bodies were studded with broken glass.

Tomik knocked Neel to the ground. Afterward, he couldn't say how he did it, but Tomik begged the glass not to touch them, and the glass obeyed.

Then there was a sudden silence, and all Tomik and Neel could hear was the tinkling of glass. The air was very still.

But it was only the eye of the storm.

The wind began to twist in the center of flowers and greenery, spinning. Then it barreled into the library, snaked around Petra, and dragged her back into the greenhouse, flinging her onto a pile of broken plants and glass.

She struggled to her feet. "Ariel? I need your help. Will you—?"

"*You dare?*" the wind howled. "*Are you a juggler? Am I a toy? Idiot dream-thinker! You think I am a floor-washer, a dust-sweeper!*"

"No! I don't think you're my servant! I hoped . . ." Petra searched for the right words. Hadn't Ariel been kind to her? She had kept the secret of Astrophil from Dee. She had smiled at Petra. "I thought . . . I thought you liked me."

"Perhapsss," Ariel hissed. "But I am the wind, and the wind changesss."

The air began to condense in front of Petra. It was foggy.

"But why did you tell me about all those things?" shouted Petra. "Why did you tell me about the coin if you didn't want me to call on you? What were all your predictions for, if not this?"

"Maybe ssso, sssilver-sssinger. Maybe I did want thisss, all along." The fog was taking shape. Then its claws reached for Petra, and her heart leaped into her throat.

Ariel had changed into a skeletal Gristleki. "Maybe," it said, "I offer a word-gift, a whisssper heard far away. A sssecret."

Petra scrambled back. "I don't want it."

The monster brandished its scaly arm. "Do you know why we are ssskin-ssscrapersss?" The Gray Man opened its empty black mouth. "Becaussse we have no teeth, and we like your fear-blood. We ssscrape your fear-blood out and we sssuck . . ."

"Enough!" John Dee strode into the greenhouse. His daughters followed, and rushed to help Neel and Tomik.

The Gristleki snarled. "You did not call me, deep-sssearcher, ssso you do not command. Thossse are the rulesss."

Dee looked at Petra. He placed a hand on her unhurt shoulder, and for once she did not flinch away, because his face held something new: comfort. "Everything will be all right," he promised, and she could not remember the last time someone had said this to her.

Dee turned back to Ariel. "I offer you something better than rules. I offer you freedom. I saved your life, and for years you have served me. Leave Petra alone, and I will consider your debt paid."

The Gray Man vanished, and in its place was a moth. It fluttered, undecided. "A trick! Tricksy deep-searcher! Cunning fox-man! I am worth more than a girl!"

"I do not think so," said Dee. "Not this girl. But if you wish to do more to pay your debt, then take the men who hide inside the library. Bring them here to me, bound and harmless. Forgive Petra. Do all this and I will never call upon you again."

"Never, never, never!" The words were wild, ringing bells.

"Never," Dee vowed.

Prince Rodolfo, Francis Walsingham, and six guards hurtled through the library door, paper whirling behind them. Their arms were tied with ropes of air, so tightly that their skin was purple. The prisoners all stared at Dee with wide eyes, but it was Walsingham who was most afraid.

The moth nipped Petra's cheek, and she couldn't tell if she had been kissed or bitten. Then Ariel flew out through the frame of the shattered greenhouse roof.

Petra was safe. Her enemies were bound and lying at her feet. But that was when Petra realized that Astrophil was missing. He had been ripped from her ear by the wind. She could not feel him. She could not see him. He was gone.

33

The Vatra

"ASTROPHIL!" Petra sobbed. She spun around, grating glass under her feet, flinging aside broken branches. She had believed she knew what fear was, but she didn't, not really, because it was this: it consumed Petra, making her forget who she was. It hollowed out everything inside her, and left a trembling shell who could only search, and *search*, desperate to find a spider who was made of tin, but was as loving as any human, and wiser than most. Astrophil was her protector, and Petra was his, but she could not find him. He was so *small*.

Astrophil!

Petra, you are making a fuss over nothing. I am right here.

She caught her breath. She looked up, and saw a twinkling dot lower itself from the iron frame of the roof.

Astrophil dropped into her open palm. "Oh!" Petra whispered. "I thought I had lost you."

"I am a spider," he reminded her in an offended tone. "Spiders make webs. When they find themselves tumbling through the air, it is a simple matter to shoot a web and climb to safety. Really, Petra. This is common knowledge."

. . .

THAT WAS HOW John Dee (and everyone else in the greenhouse who did not already know) discovered the existence of Astrophil. This fact would have consequences in the future, but for now Petra couldn't worry about it, because so many things happened after that night in Robert Cotton's manor.

Walsingham and Kit were arrested and thrown into Tyburn prison. The six Czech guards who survived Ariel's storm were sent back to Bohemia with the prince. He was not accused of any actual crime. Relations between England and the Hapsburg Empire were already strained, and Queen Elizabeth didn't think it wise to worsen the situation by arresting Emperor Karl's youngest son.

John Dee spent an hour alone with Prince Rodolfo before the Bohemian was escorted by armed Englishmen onto his ship. Few people knew what Dee and the prince discussed, and those who did would not tell.

Tomik had a split lip and a hand full of glass shards, but it was Neel who looked more shaken than Petra had ever seen him. "An air spirit! Pet, don't you *ever* do that again!"

Madinia and Margaret excitedly related their side of what happened in Cotton's manor—how they had escaped through the Rift and rushed to find their father, and how he was such a hero. Once this would have infuriated Petra, but now she had to admit that the sisters had a point. Dee *had* saved Petra, twice.

PETRA WINCED as she sat in the hard leather chair across from John Dee. It hurt to move. Dr. Harvey had said there would be no lasting damage to her shoulder. "There will be a scar, of course," he added apologetically.

Petra wasn't too troubled. She was used to scars by now. She had plenty of them.

"I expect that you'll regain full use of your arm," the doctor had continued. "You are very lucky that the sword missed any tendons."

Missed? Petra wasn't so sure. Kit's blade usually went where he wanted it to go.

"What about Kit?" Petra asked Dee as they sat in his library. Astrophil was crawling over Dee's collection of books, making admiring noises. Petra would never understand the spider's fascination. After the past several months, she was *sick* of libraries. "What will happen to Kit and Walsingham?"

"There will be a trial. They will be found guilty, and executed."

"*Executed?* Kit, too? *He* didn't kill anyone."

"He helped Walsingham cover up his murders and give sensitive information to a foreign ruler. That is treason, and punishable by death. Christopher is an adult. He is responsible for his crimes."

"But he doesn't deserve to die!"

Astrophil said nothing, but in his heart he disagreed. He only had to take one look at Petra's bandage to remember how much danger Kit had put her in.

The spider shot a web to Petra's good shoulder and swung through the air to perch there. He told Dee, "You knew that Kit still worked for Francis Walsingham. I cannot believe otherwise. You warned Petra many times that Kit was not to be trusted. You fired him because he and Petra"—the spider looked at her—"got too close."

Petra glared back, yet didn't deny it.

Dee looked uncomfortable, too, but for a different reason. "Yes," he admitted, "I knew that Kit was still Walsingham's spy."

"Then why—?" Petra remembered the sunny afternoon when Dee had lowered cages of mice to their deaths. "I was a mouse. Like the ones you used at Sutton Hoo. You thought that Walsingham was . . . I don't know. Rotten. Not worthy of being the South, or the secretary of defense. Maybe, when you were in Bohemia, you found out that the prince was bribing Walsingham. So you used me, like a mouse in the cage, and lowered me down to Kit as if you were *testing the air*, to see whether Kit would run to Walsingham with information about me, and whether Walsingham would tell the prince."

"Yes." Dee held her gaze. "It was a mistake."

"That was a dangerous ploy!" Astrophil's voice blazed with anger.

"Did you ever think that maybe I didn't *want* to be a dead mouse?" Petra asked Dee.

"Please, my dear, don't be so melodramatic. Here you are, alive and squeaking. And, as your gallant spider has already pointed out, I warned you not to share your secrets with Christopher Rhymer. If you didn't listen to me, how is that my fault?"

"So that whole business about me learning to fence was just some complicated trap for Kit and Walsingham," she said. "You never cared whether I learned how to use a sword or not."

"Oh, I don't know. Christopher *is* an excellent swordsman, one who has studied the art since the time he could toddle. And you beat him after only six months of training. Now you have a skill that can protect you, and make others wary. Was I mistaken to see that you gained that skill? Or would you have preferred to stay the way you were, a helpless little mouse?"

"Were you training Petra to be an assassin?" Astrophil asked directly.

"An assassin?" Dee leaned back and templed his fingers. "Where would you get that idea?"

"From Ariel," said Petra.

"Hmm. Wasn't Ariel talking about Gabriel Thorn?"

"You didn't answer Astrophil's question," Petra persisted. "All you're doing is asking questions of your own."

"Well, I really don't know what to say." Dee spread his hands helplessly. "I'm at a loss for words."

"Ha!"

"You, Petra Kronos, an assassin," Dee mused. He looked coy. "That *is* an interesting thought. Now, assassins usually work for somebody. For whom would you work? Me? I don't *think* I want anyone murdered. Or is there someone *you* wish to kill?" Dee chuckled. "Aside from me, of course."

He's like an eel, Petra thought, *slipping away from Astro's question again and again.* She was frustrated, but she had known Dee long enough to realize that if he didn't want to say something, he wouldn't. "I don't want you dead," she told him.

"I am glad to hear it."

"I want you to make good on our wager."

"Ah, that. If I recall, the deal was that you were supposed to discover the identity of Thorn's murderer *before* I did."

She gaped at him.

Dee explained, "The West came to Throgmorton Street the morning of his death. I was not pleased. You know what he did to my wife. But scrying is not illegal, and time had taken its revenge on Thorn for me, turning him into a drunken failure. When he said he had news that concerned the benefit of England, I had to listen. He was—whether I liked it or not—a queen's councillor. Thorn was excited, and told me he had learned of something called the Celestial Globe, which was part of a set designed by Gerard Mercator to navigate through Rifts all over the world. I was intrigued, but I was also more impatient than I should have been. I didn't want to speak with him more than I had to. Thorn never told me *who* possessed this globe. But what was I to think when Francis Walsingham came to visit me that afternoon with news of Thorn's death? You remember that day, Petra. You remember how confident Walsingham was that Thorn had died of heart failure. You remember the true cause of Thorn's death: quicksilver, a spy's poison. I had already suspected Walsingham of selling information to Prince Rodolfo. Now I believed him capable of murder."

"Suspicion is nothing," Astrophil said. "Petra gave you *proof*."

Petra added, "It's thanks to me that Walsingham's in prison."

"It's thanks to me that you weren't ripped apart by Ariel."

Petra leaned forward, and her shoulder screamed in protest. "I know you can use our mental link to track me down wherever I go, and haul me back to Throgmorton Street. But how would you like to do that every day? Or three times a day? You won't have time to sit in this dark lair of yours and think about who *else* you might want to treat like a mouse in a cage. I'll make you run after me until your hair turns white, your teeth fall out, and you're so tired you'll just let me *go*."

"I see that you are determined to go back to Bohemia."

"Oh, do you *think* so?"

He stood. "Very well. As we agreed, I will have some information concerning your father to share with you when you leave."

"I want it now."

"Ah, how tragic it is not to get what we want. I'm sorry, my dear, but you will have to wait just a little while longer. Tomorrow night, Madinia will open a Rift to Bohemia. Before then, we'll have a chat concerning your father. In the meantime, I hope you will reconsider your decision to leave. Now, Petra, I have a question for *you*: where is the Celestial Globe?"

Innocently, she said, "I don't know."

"The prince seemed to think that you did."

"I was faking it. What was I supposed to do? Say that I had no clue where the globe was, and watch him lop my friends' heads off?"

Petra and Astrophil left Dee's library, and never returned.

• • •

"I'VE GOT A PRESENT for you, little cousin," Neel sang.

"*Little—?*" Treb narrowed his eyes. "You quit flirting with that English lass and come right over here so I can show you who's *little.*"

"That's not flirting, that's thanking." Neel stood, leaving Tomik and Petra at the tavern table. He joined Treb and Andras by the entrance of the Spoked Wheel. "And that's no English girl. That's Petra. You know, the ghost? The one you said was sure to be dead?"

Treb glanced again. "She *does* look lively to me." The girl's hair was almost as dark as a Roma's. Her left shoulder was stiff with a thick bandage, and there was a kind of toughness to the line of her jaw.

"Don't you want to know why I'm thanking her?" Neel launched into his story. ". . . so Cotton had this code for where he hid the globe," he finished. "N6. Petra figured it had to mean the tyrants, the statues in the library. There was only one tyrant whose name began with N—Nero—so all I had to do was sweep off the books on the sixth shelf below Nero. There was a false panel, and behind that was your present."

"The *Celestial Globe*?" shouted Andras. "You found it?"

"Petra found it. I just fetched it. Petra got roughed up last time we were at Cotton's place, so Tom and I went back there by ourselves. A right easy theft that was. Well, not the *last* time, since that nasty Prince Rodolfo showed up and an air spirit nearly slashed us all into bloody food for crows—"

"Where's the globe?" Treb gripped his cousin.

"Can't remember. Seems I might've left it on your bed, but when a fellow's as important as me, he tends to forget nitpicky details . . ."

Treb and Andras leaped for the stairs, and Neel followed.

Tomik, who had been translating the Romany conversation for Petra, helped her stand, and they walked upstairs together.

A round, black velvet-covered object was sitting on Treb's bed. He snatched away the cloth, and there was a hushed silence.

"It's beautiful," said Andras.

Impulsively, Treb kissed Petra on the cheek. "Oh, you *treasure*."

She smiled, a little puzzled.

"It helps if you thank someone in a language they understand," Neel told Treb.

Treb rested a hand on his shoulder. "I've got no words to give you for what you've done, cousin. But you'll never be 'little' to me."

TREB FOUND a few things to say once he had drunk three tankards of ale. "To the cleverest, most down-and-dirty cutpurse in the four tribes!" He raised his glass. "To Neel of the Lovari!"

The inn cheered.

"To Tom of the Maraki—"

"What?" Tomik looked up in surprise.

"—a noble lad, a true friend, and a fine sailor!"

Tomik flushed. "He's not going to be so nice when he's got a headache tomorrow morning."

"I hope they toast to me," said Astrophil. He didn't speak Romany, but he could still figure out what was going on.

"To Petra Kronos—"

But Petra turned to Neel, fed up with all this cheering she couldn't understand anyway. "Do you have it?" she asked.

"Yep." He handed her the invisible rapier, and she slipped it into the scabbard at her waist. "Wasn't too easy to find in all that mess of glass and plants and paper, though."

"It would have been easier if there had been some blood on the blade," Tomik said darkly. "Kit's blood."

"I wasn't going to *kill* Kit," said Petra.

"You could've cut him up a bit," Neel observed.

Treb joined them. He set down his tankard, ale sloshing over the side. "Why're you all making such grim faces? Are you saying your farewells?"

"Farewells?" Petra looked at Neel.

"We set sail tomorrow," he said.

"Oh." Her voice sank. "Where are you going?"

Neel and Treb exchanged a glance. Then the captain shrugged and said, "Tell them."

Neel explained, "The Roma . . . well, our home is where we make it, see? By wagon or boat or horse or foot, we travel where we like. We've got no country. Except, uh . . . we actually do. It's called the Vatra, and it's our homeland, where our queen rules. It's far away, though, and that's one reason why we wanted the globes so bad. When the Bohemian prince began chucking our people into prison, we knew we needed to find a way for Roma to get to the Vatra *fast*. The Roma have never been well liked, but things are getting ugly, and not just in Bohemia."

"Now that we've got the globes, our duty is to present them to the Roma queen," said Treb. "I hope we can figure out how to make them work, though, or we'll be taking the long route to the Vatra."

"Where is it?" asked Astrophil.

"India," said Neel.

India. That was half a world away. Slowly, Petra said, "Then we won't be seeing each other again . . . not for a long while."

There was a pause. Neel spoke first. "How're you getting back to Bohemia?"

"A Rift," said Petra. She looked at her friends and realized that she had hoped they would stay together, even if that didn't make much sense, even if she didn't know what the future held for her, or how she would rescue her father. She had hoped . . .

"What about you?" Neel asked Tomik. "Are you heading home? Or do you want to sail? I've never been to the Vatra before. Must be something to see. Want to?"

Tomik didn't hesitate. "I'm going with Petra."

"Yeah. I thought you might."

"Oh, don't look so mournful." Treb belched. "Even the spider's ready to start bawling his eyes out. The world's not as big as it seems, and time passes quicker than you'd think. If a slave can become a friend, and a ghost can come back from the dead, I'm sure you four won't be apart for long."

"When will you leave tomorrow?" asked Petra.

"When we wake up." Neel looked at Treb, who had slumped on the table. "Probably late."

"We'll be there to say goodbye. But I have to do something first."

"What's that?" asked Tomik.

"I'm going to see Kit Rhymer."

34

Secrets

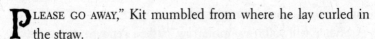

PLEASE GO AWAY," Kit mumbled from where he lay curled in the straw.

"I *am* going away." Petra stepped close to the bars. "I'm leaving London, and I'm never coming back."

"And I am going to die."

"Oh, Kit. Why did you do it?"

He covered his bruised face. "Why does anyone do anything?" He dropped his hands, and his stare was hollow-eyed. "I wanted something better than I had. More money. Walsingham's gratitude —which, before all this, used to go a long way. And I wanted you, too."

"You *deceived* me."

"Yes," he said miserably. "I know what kind of heart you have— open and closed, at the same time. You'd believe the best of a stranger, and abandon a queen's ball to eat a fried potato in the kitchens. But you're hard. Dee saved your life, and you hate him for the way he did it. People are bad, or they are good, and there's no in between with you. So was I supposed to tell you the truth? Hope that you wouldn't mind I was spying for the man who kidnapped your father? I didn't say a word about you to Walsingham . . . not until Dee fired me. I tried not to be tempted, I really did. But Walsingham paid for *information*—not by the hour, or by the day. I was barely able to keep my tiny room in a crummy part of town. Soon I couldn't even buy bread. I thought . . . that I could have everything. That Walsingham would give me gold for the Celestial Globe, that the prince would be so pleased he'd forget all about you, and you'd have no choice but to stay in London."

"That's the worst plan I've ever heard," Petra said disdainfully.

Something flickered in his eyes. Then he spoke in her favorite voice, the one that was serious *and* jesting, but held no hint of mockery. "I face the executioner's ax, Petra, yet no blow could hurt me like those words."

She slipped a hand in her left trouser pocket and carefully curled her fingers around the tip of Kit's broken sword. Its jagged edge pricked against her palm. If Astrophil were here, he would object to what she was about to do. "You owe me something."

He looked at her.

"A promise," she said. "One that you'll *keep* this time." She lifted her free hand and traced the lock's keyhole. "Do you think that you could be . . . better?"

"What do you mean, 'better'? Do you mean, could I promise not to betray my country, conspire to cover up murder, and stab someone I care about?"

"Yes."

His laugh was mirthless. "That's an easy oath to make, considering I'll only have to keep it for another few weeks."

"Just promise me." Petra took her hand out of her pocket, and reached through the bars.

He stood, and walked to meet her. "Christopher Rhymer hereby swears to Petra Kronos that he'll be a good boy." He gave her the shadow of a smile. "I promise to mend my ways and lead a better, if very short, life." He took her hand.

She held it. He widened his eyes in astonishment.

When Petra walked away from the cell, her pocket was empty. The piece of metal was gone.

Kit watched her retreating back until she vanished down the hall. Then his eyes fell to his upturned palm. He blinked, still unbelieving.

In his hand was a small steel key.

PETRA COULD SEE the boats rocking in Oyster Wharf. She was hurrying down the lane to meet Tomik and Neel when she heard someone call her name.

She turned around, and Madinia flew into her arms, giving her a fierce hug.

"I told you this is where we'd find her," Margaret said to her parents.

Confused, Petra asked, "What are you doing here?"

"My daughters told me that your friends are setting sail today," Dee explained. "We've come to bid you farewell."

"Farewell? But I'm not leaving right now. I'm going to Bohemia tonight, through a Rift, with Tomik." Petra looked at Dee with sudden suspicion. "You said I could go! And what about the information you promised me?"

"Madinia can still open a Rift for you. But I think that, after you have heard my news, you will choose another path. I hope you will stay here"—he spoke over her noise of protest—"but if you do not, you will need to be with your friends. I wanted to give you that chance before the ship sets sail."

Petra glanced nervously at the dock several yards away. Treb was lying in the launch, smoking. Andras was loading the boat. Tomik and Neel stood on the wharf, talking.

The May wind was warm and strong, yet Petra shivered. Dread

sat like a chunk of ice in her stomach. A moment ago, she had demanded that Dee tell her what he knew about her father. Now she wasn't so sure she wanted to hear. *But the prince said Father was fine,* she thought desperately. *That he was better than ever.*

The sun shone on Agatha Dee's white hair. "I wish I could teach you how to live happily ever after, Petra," she said, "but that is something you will have to learn on your own."

Petra scanned the woman's face for some hint at what she meant, but Agatha Dee's face was as empty as always.

"Here." Madinia thrust a wrapped oblong object at Petra. "It's my ivory-handled fan. I adore it, but I wanted to give it to you, so that *you* could make everyone jealous!"

Petra accepted the fan, though she had no idea what she would do with it.

Margaret handed her a thick bundle of cloth. "This is the samite dress you wore at the ball. Maybe . . . maybe you think it's a poor gift, since I can't wear the dress anymore anyway, but I hope it will make you think of us."

Petra thanked her for the dress, though she didn't know what she would do with that, either.

"The silver hairpins are in the bundle, too," Madinia said, "in case Astrophil wants to pretend he's one of them again." She peeked through Petra's hair. "Hello? Astrophil? Are you there?"

"Yes, Madinia," said the spider wearily.

Petra embraced the sisters.

"But maybe this isn't goodbye." Margaret smiled. "We'll be waiting for you at Throgmorton Street."

Then the twins and their mother walked back up the lane, disappearing amid the fruit stalls and clopping horses.

Only John Dee remained.

Petra's heart beat quickly. When Madinia and Margaret had

been there, it had been easy to forget, if only for a moment, that Dee had information to give her, and that she didn't want it anymore, because she was increasingly sure it was bad news.

Dee's face was that of a doctor ready to set a bone, or amputate a limb.

"Petra," he spoke gently, "my sources say that soon after your father was brought to the dungeons of Salamander Castle, the prince ordered him to rebuild the clock's heart. But once Prince Rodolfo learned of the Mercator Globes, he became obsessed with finding them, and decided he no longer needed your father. Mikal Kronos was given to Fiala Broshek for experimentation. He was transformed into a Gristleki."

"That's a lie!" But doubt tugged at Petra, and behind doubt loomed despair, bitter and frightening.

"It is true. I am sorry."

Better than ever, the prince had said. Of course. The prince *would* think that being transformed into a monster was better, because he was one. And Ariel. Ariel must have known. She had changed into a Gray Man in front of Petra's eyes. Had she been ready to tell Petra about her father? *I offer a word-gift, a whisssper heard far away,* Ariel had said. *A sssecret.*

Despair gripped Petra by the throat. She began to weep.

"Do you understand now why I wanted to keep this from you as long as I could?" said Dee. "I have spent my life trying to know as much as possible. But the most important thing I discovered is that certain kinds of knowledge can be painful. More than that: they can break the spirit. Stay with my family, Petra. We will protect you. We could make you happy."

"Never!" she sobbed.

"Then what will you choose? To return to Bohemia, where you will be hunted?"

Before this moment, all the possibilities of rescuing her father had seemed difficult beyond measure. Now, any plans she had disintegrated in the face of the thought that her father no longer *was* her father, but a monster. What could she do? Where should she go?

"I have cousins. I can live with them. Dita, Josef, David—"

"But if they shelter you, how long will it be before the prince discovers this? Would you really put them in danger? Here the prince cannot touch you without insulting Queen Elizabeth. That has been made clear to him. But Bohemia is *his* country, and when you are on its soil he can do what he likes to you and anyone who helps you."

Petra looked at the wharf, and it blurred through her tears.

"Go with your friends, then," Dee urged. "Sail far away. You do not need to tell me where you are traveling. But don't return to Bohemia. Not until you are strong enough, and skilled enough, to protect yourself. Here"—he pressed a sealed envelope into her hand—"this is a gift."

"I don't want it!" She began to shred the paper.

He stopped her hands. "I know you don't want to listen to what I have to say. Not now, maybe not ever. But someday you will be grateful for that letter."

She squeezed the paper in her fist. But she wanted to tear something, *anything*. Something must break.

Her eyes were silver pools, shining with tears and misery. When they turned to Dee, he could not look away.

And that was when he felt something slice through his heart, reach into his mind, and *wrench* at a tiny knot. Dee gasped.

Petra had severed the mental link between them. *I am free*, she told herself, and stumbled down to the wharf.

•   •   •

As THEY ROWED toward Deptford, Astrophil tried to console Petra. "I think John Dee was being entirely too grim. I did not wish to say so on the wharf, because it would have been bad manners for me to interrupt." In fact, Astrophil had been too shocked to speak. "What if the Gristleki operation is not permanent? Perhaps it can be reversed."

"You think so?" Petra swiped at her tears.

"Yeah," Neel said eagerly, "and the Vatra's just the place to find out about that. I know you Bohemians have some piddly school for studying magic, but that's nothing compared to what the Roma've got."

"You have an academy of magic?" Tomik pulled a little faster on the oars.

"Something like that. Also, a Kalderash rules the Roma these days, and if there's one thing the Kalderash tribe is good at, it's being all mysterious and knowing things they shouldn't. Can't stand 'em, personally. Give me the Maraki or Ursari any day, if I can't have the Lovari. But my point is that the Vatra will be packed with magical experts who might know a cure for your da, Petra. Or they can think one up."

"Would they do that for me?" she asked.

"They'd better," Treb growled, "or I'll *make* 'em."

Hope trickled into her heart, and when the launch pulled alongside the *Pacolet*, Petra was ready to come aboard—though she didn't like sitting alone in the launch and being hauled upward with rope and pulleys. She watched Neel, Tomik, and the others climb up the Jacob's ladder. *Soon*—she touched her sore shoulder—*I'll be able to do that, too.*

As the Maraki pulled the boat higher, Petra uncrumpled Dee's letter. The seal had been crushed, and waxy dust fell on her lap. There were only a few lines of writing.

My dear Petra,

You once asked me what Prince Rodolfo's magical talent is. I refused to tell you. Now I would like you to know: he has none.

Call upon me if you need me.

John Dee

Petra folded the letter, and stepped aboard the ship.

THE *PACOLET* sailed down the Thames, and then ventured out into the sea. When England was just a fuzzy green line behind them, Treb summoned his crew. Everyone crowded into his cabin. They jostled, each wanting the best view of the globes resting on the table. They had seen the Terrestrial Globe before, of course, but they had heard that its twin was stunning. They were not disappointed. When Treb pulled away the black velvet cloth, several sailors gasped.

The Celestial Globe was almost entirely black. While the Terrestrial Globe was made of wood and paper, its twin was marble. And a strange kind of marble it was, too, one with shades of midnight blue. Points of light were scattered across its large surface. As Petra looked more closely, she saw that they were holes bored into the stone. Thin, inlaid lines of gold swirled around these stars, showing a swan, a man wrestling a snake, a ram with wavy horns, a lyre made from a tortoiseshell, and many other designs. They were the constellations.

Treb spun the Terrestrial Globe on its axis, stopped it with a finger, and pointed at a red spark off the coast of England. "Here's a Loophole."

"Where does it go to?" someone asked.

"Not sure," Treb replied, frustrated.

"Well, you'd better make sure," said Nicolas. "We could end up anywhere. I don't think the *Pacolet* would sail too well on top of a mountain."

"That Celestial Globe is pretty," said Nadia, "but how does it work?"

"I thought it would *do* something," said a disappointed sailor.

Many voices began to join in the conversation.

"What if we have to sail to the Vatra the usual way?"

"That could take a year!"

"Maybe we should cut into the globes. See if there's anything inside."

"Are you a fool? Because that idea sure makes you sound like one."

"Get out of here, all of you." Treb passed a hand over his eyes. "I swear on all the hairy bears, my head *hurts*."

"Been drinking, Treb?"

"Couldn't you celebrate *after* you figured out whether the globe was worth the trouble?"

"I said, *Get out!*" Treb slammed his fist down on the table.

Muttering, the crew began to leave.

"Tom," Treb called.

Tomik, who had been quietly translating the conversation for Petra and Astrophil, looked up.

"Stay," said Treb. "And you all, too." He pointed at Petra, Astrophil, and Neel.

"Well?" Treb flourished a hand at the globes. "You're a sensible lot. What do you think?"

"It is perfectly clear." Astrophil shrugged. "We should wait until nightfall."

"And why is that?"

"How else will we see the stars?"

• • •

IT WAS A CLOUDLESS NIGHT. Petra stood with her friends at the stern of the ship, and watched Treb and Andras walk toward them, each cradling a globe in his arms.

"It's heavy." Andras set the marble globe on top of the table they had brought on deck.

"Actually, so is this one." Treb lowered the Terrestrial Globe. "I never thought about it before, but this thing doesn't weigh like it's made of paper and wood."

"I bet there *is* something inside 'em," said Neel.

"Maybe you're right," said Petra. "Why else would they glow like that?" In the darkness, each globe twinkled with points of light—red for the Loopholes, white for the stars. "It's like they've got candles inside."

Tomik laid a palm on the black marble. "There is a crystal!" he said excitedly. "I can sense it. It's a sphere, nestled inside the globe."

"What're these?" Neel touched the three brass rings that encircled the Terrestrial Globe and gave them a spin.

"They're called armillaries," said Treb. "They're used to help chart a course."

Petra traced one brass circle. What was its history? She caught a glimpse of Gerard Mercator, long dead. He was a man who loved the world, but not the people in it. Petra looked at her friends. When she thought of her father, an aching sadness welled up within her. But Astrophil's legs clung to her right shoulder, she saw Neel's lopsided grin, and she felt the heat of Tomik standing next to her. Petra was not alone.

Thoughtfully, she pulled on two of the rings until they crossed over the red spark that marked the Loophole they sought.

There was a whir, and the third ring moved on its own.

"What did you do, Pet?"

"Look at that!"

On the Terrestrial Globe's surface, the red light off England's coast flared, and so did another light, exactly where the third ring crossed with another.

"The West African coast!" said Treb, peering at the second red flare. "That's perfect. That'll bring us a lot closer to India."

"How do we find the English Loophole?" asked Andras.

"It's somewhere close by." Treb pointed at the darkness ahead.

"But we're talking about a *Loophole*," said Tomik. "You have to enter at exactly the right spot."

"Align the Celestial Globe with the stars in the sky," Astrophil advised. "Turn the globe until the constellations on the top match the ones over our heads."

Neel spun the Celestial Globe.

There was a hum, and a shiver, and everyone stepped back as each globe split in half. Like eggs, they hatched. Inside the globes were bright crystal balls—one red, one white. The two spheres rose into the air and floated over the *Pacolet*, soaring over the waves. Then they came to a halt, hovering fifty yards off the starboard bow.

"It seems," Astrophil observed, "that we should aim for the space between the two spheres."

Treb began shouting orders at the crew, and the *Pacolet* turned. The ship sailed closer to the shining spheres.

"You ready?" Neel turned to Petra. He offered a hand.

She took it, and reached for Tomik's as well. "Yes."

One moment, the *Pacolet* was gliding over the dark sea. The next, it was gone.

Author's Note

THE TITLE ABOVE is very misleading. It should say "Astrophil's Note," for the author has asked me to write this section. She flattered me, saying that I was a wise spider and could beautifully explain the relationship between her story and history. She is correct.

There was indeed a man named Gerard Mercator, and he crafted terrestrial and celestial globes. One was used to chart the earth; the other, the stars. A stunning set is owned by Harvard University. The globes are housed in the basement of Lamont Library, and no one ever goes to see them, but they really should.

Many of the characters in this novel had real historical lives, including Queen Elizabeth, Walter Raleigh, Madinia and Margaret Dee (although John Dee had several other children our author decided to ignore), Robert Cotton, and Francis Walsingham. Each of these people had colorful experiences impossible to describe here in any detail, but the following trivia might interest you. As Kit claimed, Francis Drake turned pirate and stole gold from a Spanish galleon called the *Cacafuego*. And yes, Robert Cotton did have a glorious collection of rare books. As for Francis Walsingham, he was responsible for creating a network of spies who worked for England. He spent almost every penny he had on the project, and died poor. Kit Rhymer was never a real person, but he was inspired by an actual man named Christopher "Kit" Marlowe, a playwright and spy. Marlowe died in a knife fight, though some people believe he was murdered for the secrets he knew.

Whitehall Palace has long since burned to the ground, but during Queen Elizabeth's day it had a shield gallery overlooking the Thames, much like the one in *The Celestial Globe*. A description of the palace can be found in James Shapiro's *A Year in the Life of William Shakespeare: 1599*.

In the early medieval period, several ships were buried in the ground of Sutton Hoo, in the shape of large mounds. They were probably meant to honor the dead people who lay inside the ships, for they were piled high with treasure. Many of these artifacts can be seen today in the British Museum, though, sadly, not all of them, for grave robbers had been stealing from the mounds long before they were excavated by a serious archaeological team. In fact, we know that someone at the end of the sixteenth century dug into several mounds. According to Angela Care Evans's *The Sutton Hoo Ship Burial*, that someone could have been John Dee, whom Queen Elizabeth might have asked to search for treasure in that part of England. There is, however, no firm evidence of this.

It is nonsense to imagine that people would have been able to walk around inside one of these ships like Dee and Petra do. The soil in Sutton Hoo is sandy and acidic, and would have eaten away all the wood by the sixteenth century. The author claims that her portrayal of Dee and Petra exploring a Sutton Hoo ship is "poetic license," which she says means the right of a writer to change the truth in the name of what would make a better story. I think it merely means the author's excuse to do whatever she pleases.

I could explain many more historical facts that have influenced *The Celestial Globe*, but I would hate to spoil the pleasure you would take in researching them all by yourself! I wish you happy hunting among the bookshelves of some lovely library, and remain, as ever, your

Astrophil
Spider and Scholar

Acknowledgments

A S I LOOK BACK over the writing of *The Celestial Globe*, I'm very aware of how much help I had, not least when it came to research. My friend Mark Hanna, expert on early modern piracy, pointed me in the direction of several books about the subject. I thank the Williams-Mystic Sea Program in general and Jim Carleton and Glenn Gordinier in particular. Glenn was unfailingly generous with his advice, and I'd like to clarify that any errors in my representation of ships and sailing in the Renaissance are solely due to my ignorance or willfulness. Thanks to Vic Chica, Paulo Gonçalves, and Gordon MacMullan for information about docking tall ships on the Thames. I'm grateful to Tess Bogart and the New York Yacht Club for letting me poke around in the club's library, and to David Verchere for getting me access to it. David's enthusiasm for sailing was infectious, and his readiness to answer questions I had about it is very much appreciated.

Andrew (AJ) Romig team-taught with me at Harvard University and I appreciate that he and our students shared my enthusiasm about Sutton Hoo. Dan Wolfe helped me on the fencing front. Tanya Pollard advised me on poison. My mother-in-law, Christiane Philippon, accompanied me to the Musée des Arts Décoratifs and taught me what the explanatory placards didn't. Sarah Wall-

Randell discussed the qualities of cotton with me. David Frankland's covers for the Kronos Chronicles continually impress and delight me.

I owe a debt to those friends willing to read parts of *The Celestial Globe* when it was in its first draft, or to talk about ideas: Esther Duflo, Dave Elfving, Doireann Fitzgerald, Dominic Leggett, Becky Rosenthal, Larry Switzky, Steve Zoegall, and, especially, Donna Freitas. My husband, Thomas Philippon, endured many long discussions about *Celestial*, and has made me coffee in the mornings far more frequently than I have for him. I cherish him for that and more.

Thanks, as ever, to superheroes Hilary Costa, Meredith Kaffel, Marcy Posner, Lindsay Winget, and Charlotte Sheedy for fabulous literary agentry.

I'm grateful to everyone at FSG, especially Jay Colvin, Jill Davis, Jennifer Doerr, Michael Eisenberg, Margaret Ferguson, Jeanne McDermott, Lisa Graff, Katie Halata, Liz Kerins, and Beth Potter. My editor, Janine O'Malley, is nonpareil — just like those chocolates, but sweeter and infinitely better for my health.

Aimee Rupsis, my sister, inspired a scene in this novel — she knows which one! I'm so glad to have a sister, and two brothers, Andy and Jonathon Rutkoski. They're the best presents my parents have given me.

GO FISH

MARIE RUTKOSKI

What did you want to be when you grew up?

In kindergarten, I wanted to be an ice skater, a nurse, or a writer when I grew up. I didn't know how to skate, but it looked like a lot of fun. As for being a nurse, that's what all the other girls were writing down on their sheets of construction paper, so I figured I'd better do the same (looking back, I'm astonished by how easily I was influenced by peer pressure and what was expected of girls versus boys). Being a writer, though, was the one choice that felt truly right, truly mine.

When did you realize you wanted to be a writer?

I don't remember. It seems like the desire was always there, just like I always had ten fingers and ten toes.

The first time that I received some sign that maybe I could be a good writer was when I won a Young Authors competition in first grade for an illustrated story called "Midnight Cat," about a black cat that always goes outside at midnight. One night, however, she stays indoors. Midnight Cat's worried owner rushes her to the vet, certain that something is desperately wrong. It turns out, though, that she's just pregnant, and gives birth to three kittens. The "joyful" owner names them

Fuzzy, Corduroy, and Unicorn. "From that day on," I wrote, "everyone was happy!"

What's your first childhood memory?

The clearest, earliest memory I have is of me running into the backyard, which was heaped high with snow. My mother yelled for me to come back inside, saying, "You're going to catch pneumonia!" I remember turning the word "pneumonia" over in my mind, thinking that it sounded funny, and wondering what it meant. I do not remember if I went back inside.

What's your most embarrassing childhood memory?

When I was in second grade, I had a huge crush on a boy named Todd. I wondered how I could make him like me, and it crossed my mind that I needed to find something we had in common. Then, eureka! I remembered that he wore a retainer, which I thought was really cute. Although I didn't have a retainer or braces, at the time I really wanted one or the other. So I made one out of an unbent paper clip and wore it to school. I marched up to Todd, pointed to my mouth, and said, sigh, that my parents had made me get a retainer. Wasn't life tough and didn't he feel my pain? He did, and we became friends. But after a while I began to feel guilty—here I was, living a lie, showing up to school each day with a paper clip in my mouth. One afternoon, I confessed the truth. Todd, feeling betrayed, said he was never going to speak to me again. And he never did.

What's your favorite childhood memory?

Night fishing with my father. My mother reading me bedtime stories.

What was your worst subject in school?
Math! (or Handwriting)

What was your best subject in school?
English!

What was your first job?
When I was sixteen, I worked in a record store with my best friend, Becky, and several twentysomething hipsters who were too cool for school. I worshipped every single one of them (but tried not to show it). They introduced me to bootleg recordings, obscure EPs, and random punk bands that sang about sushi. More importantly, they taught me that there was life outside of high school.

I've stayed in close touch with Becky, and recently have reconnected with some of my other co-workers. One of them is a defense lawyer, another a schoolteacher, and another a furniture designer who lives in New York City. Just last weekend, we met up and chatted while our kids played in the park. It was awesome.

How did you celebrate publishing your first book?
I think I had a fancy dinner with my husband. I'm not sure. It was such a giddy moment for me that my memory's a blur.

Where do you write your books?
Wherever I can. All I ask is either a room with a door that shuts, or to be lost in a crowd of reasonably quiet people.

Which of your characters is most like you?
Astrophil. He's the part of me that gets really excited whenever I go to a rare books room. Once, when I was in Dublin, I went to Marsh's Library to do some research. It had been closed for renovation for several months, and the dear, el-

derly ladies who ran the place greeted me with such joy. I was their very first "reader" since the library had reopened. All afternoon, I sat with sixteenth-century books spread out in front of me, and the librarians would offer me tea and shush the tourists who came in to look around (Marsh's Library is very pretty). "You must be quiet," they told the visitors. "We have a *reader*."

Astrophil would have understood how much I loved those librarians, and how that afternoon is one of my very favorite memories.

When you finish a book, who reads it first?

When I lived in Boston, my housemate Esther did. Usually she's insanely busy saving the world through economics projects in developing countries, but she made time for my books, which I appreciate.

Now that I live in New York, I swap drafts with many children's and YA writers, but my first reader is always Donna Freitas, author of *The Possibilities of Sainthood*. We get bossy and opinionated with each other when we discuss our books, but it's tough love.

Are you a morning person or a night owl?

Now that my baby is sleeping through the night, I am (thank God) a 6:30 A.M. person (though I don't write until I have caffeine in my system).

What's your idea of the best meal ever?

My wedding dinner.

What do you value most in your friends?

What I admire most in my parents: their good hearts.

What makes you laugh out loud?

My son, Eliot, who, as I write this, is almost one year old. He'll laugh at something, I'll laugh because his laugh is so cute, and then he'll laugh because I'm laughing . . . This can go on for a long time.

He made a grab for my pasta the other night, so I pulled a string of spaghetti off my fork and handed it to him. He wiggled it and stretched it and nibbled on it and finally stared, dumbfounded, at the noodle in his hands. WOW, his expression seemed to say, SPAGHETTI. And I had to laugh. A baby is such a special creature, and it's a delight to watch mine explore the world. How often do you get to see a string of spaghetti blow someone's mind?

What's your favorite song?

"Time" by Tom Waits, "A Case of You" by Joni Mitchell, "Pale Green Things" by The Mountain Goats, "Hyperballad" by Bjork, and "I Still Haven't Found What I'm Looking For" by U2.

Who is your favorite fictional character?

I am very fond of Charlotte A. Cavatica (from E.B. White's *Charlotte's Web*). I cry every time I read the last lines of that book: "It's not often someome comes along who is a true friend and a good writer. Charlotte was both."

What are you most afraid of?

Many, many things, most of them perfectly rational. But I do have one fear that has no explanation, and I've had it since I was little. If I'm outside in the dark, I can see the moon overhead, it's cold, there is a wind, and I'm only ten feet or so from my house, I feel something clutch my heart. And I have to run inside. It's a little silly, but there it is.

What time of the year do you like best?
A Manhattan spring, a French summer, a New England fall, or a Midwestern winter.

What is your favorite TV show?
The Wire is the best thing television has produced, as far as I'm concerned. Every episode is excellent. But when I want to curl up on the sofa with a bowl of ice cream and do some comfort TV watching, I'll reach for my *Buffy the Vampire Slayer* DVDs. Or *Battlestar Galactica*.

If you were stranded on a desert island, who would you want for company?
Why, my family, of course.

If you could travel in time, where would you go?
I'd like to have a chat with Shakespeare. I have a lot of questions, and I want answers!

But I don't want to *live* in Renaissance England. I just want to go, hang out for a day, and come right back. People didn't live for very long in the sixteenth century, and the food was bad. If I stayed there for more than a day I'd probably catch a cold and die.

What's the best advice you have ever received about writing?
In *Bird by Bird*, Anne Lamott quotes Thurber: "You might as well fall flat on your face as lean over too far backwards." I make mistakes as a writer, but I'd rather make them by trying too hard than by being too afraid to make a fool out of myself.

What would you do if you ever stopped writing?
I have no idea. If I ever stop wrtiting, I will have changed so drastically from who I am now that I wouldn't recognize myself, and therefore there is no way to predict anything this Not-Me Me would do.

What do you like best about yourself?
I like that I am never bored. Pretty interesting things go on inside my head, so I'm happy to just sit around and think. Sometimes this means that I'm not paying attention to the world around me, though.

What is your worst habit?
I never get straight to the point.
  Except, of course, with this answer.

What do you wish you could do better?
Um, everything.

What would your readers be most surprised to learn about you?
I once rappelled 1,000 feet down into a gorge and then climbed back up. I will never, ever do anything like that again.

Thrones are at stake. Spies are afoot.
Murder is common. Worst of all, Petra's
father has been turned into a Gray Man.

Keep reading for a sneak peak of
the stunning conclusion to
THE KRONOS CHRONICLES

Danior of the Kalderash

I ONA, queen of the Roma, adjusted a silk scarf around her swollen neck. The entire Vatran court knew she was dying, of course, but that didn't mean they needed to be reminded of it.

"Let me help," murmured a lady-in-waiting. She tied the scarf into a clever knot, hiding the ugly lump on the queen's throat, and said, "Arun is waiting in the hall."

Iona nodded, indicating that her advisor could enter. She didn't like to speak unless she had to do so.

Arun, who knew that the queen's silent ways didn't mean that she was a patient person, was brief. "The *Pacolet* will arrive soon with the Mercator Globes. The crew was spotted in Ethiopia, restocking their supplies."

The queen cleared her throat. Her voice was a hideous whisper: "There is someone on board I need to see."

"Of course. The *Pacolet's* captain will be brought to you directly."

Iona shook her head. When she spoke again, it felt as if a crab was lodged in her throat, attacking her with vicious claws. "No. He is not the one I mean."

PETRA JIGGLED the fishing line. There were so many impossible things she wanted to do—find a cure for her father, be with her family again—that it didn't seem fair that she couldn't even catch a measly fish. *Come on*, she ordered the iron hook sunk deep in the sunny water. *Catch a fish. Catch a fish.*

But she was not her father, who could tap a nail into a plank of wood just by thinking about it. Petra had a gift for metal, but it was weak. If she wanted to influence the hook magically, she'd have to be able to touch it.

"Bet you didn't bait it right," said Neel.

"Did you try using some of those dead little squids?" asked Tomik. "Or even meat. That works for catching yellowtail."

"Nah," Neel said. "That's for nabbing sharks."

Petra yanked on the line. It went taut. "I've got something!"

"You didn't use meat, did you, Pet?" Neel widened his eyes. "'Cause I don't want a shark."

"Don't be a baby," said Tomik.

"Baby? Just 'cause I don't fancy dragging up a gnashing, thrashing, biting—"

"Um, *help*?" said Petra.

Neel and Tomik rushed to her side, and the three of them hauled on the line. It was with relief and a little disappointment that they discovered that Petra had not caught a shark. It was a heavy net, dripping with seaweed and crusted with barnacles. A few shrimp wriggled from it and fell to the deck.

"Look." Petra reached into the net, pulled forth a corked bottle, and shook it. Something rattled. "What do you think is inside?"

Neel snatched the bottle from her and tossed it overboard.

"What'd you do that for?" she protested.

"We're in the Arabian Sea," he said. "Look to the east, and you'll find India. But Persia's in the west, and folk there are always trapping nasty spirits in bottles and tossing them into the waves. You already managed to summon an air spirit back in England, and that was a mite too scary. You want to unleash a bottled-up fire spirit, too? Fine. But not around me."

Tomik rolled his eyes. "Don't tell me you believe those silly Persian fairy tales."

"Tales have got to have some truth," Neel said, "else why would people tell 'em?"

"What about the Vatra?" asked Petra. "Are there Romany stories about that?"

"Of course," said Neel with such a satisfied smile that Petra suspected he had only tossed the bottle in the sea to make her ask that very question. "Long ago, there were only three Roma tribes: the Lovari, Maraki, and Ursari. The Lovari danced and sang. The Maraki built swift ships and roved the waves. The Ursari had an uncanny way with animals: horses and hares, camels and cats, dogs and—"

"Elephants?" This was starting to sound familiar to Petra.

"Them too," said Neel. "And there happened to be an Ursari named Danior, who was as keen-eyed and handsome as a hawk. He—"

"I know this story," Petra interrupted. On the first day she had met him, Neel had told her about Danior, who had the same magical talent as he.

"Well, don't you know everything," said Neel. "Guess I'd better not breathe another word."

But the story was new to Tomik, who pressed Neel to continue.

Petra listened as Danior was cast out by the Ursari and left to die in the desert. A cruel desert king sliced off every one of Danior's fingers and, even as the blood dried, Danior discovered that his dead fingers had become magic ghosts. They were longer, stronger, and quicker than any human fingers could be. Danior rode his loyal elephant into the king's city with vengeance on his mind.

Neel said, "Danior hatched a plan, and had something to do before he could take revenge on the king. He strode into a merchant's shop and offered to swap his one valuable possession, a jewel that shone like a star on his right ear."

"You never told me that," said Petra. "About the jewel."

"What's the fun in telling the same tale twice?" Neel replied. "Every story's got to change, or it dies." He frowned. "Interruptions aren't great for its health, either."

Petra stayed silent as Neel resumed his story. "Danior wanted a large wagon like a house on wheels. The merchant asked to inspect the jewel, so Danior suggested that the merchant's pretty daughter take it out of his ear. 'I can't rightly do it myself,' he said with a grin. The girl passed the earring to her da, who agreed to Danior's trade as soon as he clapped eyes on the jewel.

"That night, Danior used his ghost fingers to pick every lock in the wicked king's palace. He stole ten of the king's children and led them to the wagon he had hitched to his elephant. But Danior had a surprise waiting for him. For who was in the wagon but the merchant's daughter, with the jewel in her hand? A touch of Danior's ear and she was mad for him, and swore to go where he would go.

"With his new wife and children, Danior founded the fourth Roma tribe, the Kalderash. You might guess that a kidnapper wouldn't be kind or wise, but Danior was a good father, husband, and leader. He had the idea of binding all the Roma tribes together by creating a homeland. With the help of the other tribe leaders, he built the Vatra and became its first king."

"In London, you told us that the Romany queen is a

Kalderash," said Tomik. "Why do the other tribes let the Kalderash rule all the time?"

"They don't," said Treb, who had appeared behind them. He picked up one of the shrimp squirming on the deck and popped it into his mouth, tail and all. "We rotate."

"The leader of each tribe gets to rule for four years," explained Neel. "Queen Iona's got about two years left."

"Unless she dies first," Treb said, chewing. "Which is likely, from what I've heard."

"Her husband's dead and she's got no kids," said Neel. "She refuses to name an heir, so if she croaks now there'll be no Kalderash to take over, and the next tribe will get two years plus the usual four."

"Which tribe is next in line?" asked Tomik.

"The Maraki," said Treb.

There was a glint in the captain's eye that made Petra gasp. "Not *you*?"

"King Treb!" Neel snickered. "Oh, I can't breathe, that's too funny."

"I'd make a fine king," Treb growled.

"Treb's older brother will take over," said Neel, still giggling.

"It's no laughing matter. The Maraki have been waiting years for this, and we've got plans."

"It's a shame, though." Neel caught Treb's furious glance. "Not that the Maraki will rule, but that no one knows who'll speak for the Kalderash after Queen Iona keels over."

"True," said Treb. "She *is* a direct descendent of Danior, and the line's been unbroken for hundreds of years."

"And you"—Neel wagged his finger at Tomik—"who's so sure there are no facts in fairy tales, just wait until you meet the queen."

"Which won't happen," said Treb. "Not one of you is important enough to rate an audience with the queen. I, on the other hand—"

Neel ignored his cousin. "I've never met the grand lady myself, but word has it that she wears Danior's earring. The very same one of the legend. They call it the Jewel of the Kalderash."

"How close are we to the Vatra?" Petra suddenly asked, staring straight off the ship's prow.

The others turned, and saw the green, scribbled outline of an island.

"Why, very close," said Treb. "Very close, indeed."

The Queen's Command

THE SETTING sun looked like a juicy orange, dripping color onto the mountainous island as the *Pacolet* sailed toward the Vatra. The shelves of limestone just beneath the waves created a natural defense around the island, and caused unfriendly ships to crash and sink miles off the Vatra's shores. The *Pacolet*'s captain, however, knew the secret dance to reach the island safely. The ship swerved left, bore right, and swooped around the cove.

"What if there is no place in the Vatra for me?" Astrophil murmured to Petra.

"What do you mean?" She gently lifted the spider from her ear so that she could face him as he stood on her raised palm. "You will always belong wherever I am."

"Yes, but…what will be my role? When Prince Rodolfo stole your father's eyes and you decided to retrieve them, my purpose was to keep you as safe as possible. When we were trapped in John Dee's London house, I helped you analyze an air spirit's cryptic prophecies. How can I aid you here? I cannot even do research for Master Kronos's cure." He added woefully, "The Roma do not like books. They will have no libraries."

"They use writing for special occasions," Petra pointed out. Dangling from a leather cord around her neck was a miniature iron horseshoe that Neel had had engraved in Romany. "Some of them can read and write, and maybe they do have books. They just don't trust the written word. The Roma believe that it makes things seem permanent, when they're not."

"I know," said the spider, but still looked glum.

"Astro, I'll always want your advice, whether there are books or not."

"Really? Even though you are now an adult? Perhaps you do not need me anymore."

Sternly, she said, "That is the only absolutely brainless thing you've ever said."

"Ah. Well. Very good." He relaxed on her palm, leaning his shiny back legs against her curled fingers.

They heard the rattle and splash of the ship's anchors being dropped, and knew it was time to disembark with the crew, who began boarding small boats strapped to the *Pacolet*'s sides. Petra and Astrophil climbed into a launch with Tomik, Neel, Treb, and the globes, and watched the island grow larger as they rowed to shore. Through the twilight, Petra saw a palace etched into the island's mountain. The cliffs were encrusted with manmade walls and terraces.

"Queen Iona is going to praise me to the pearly skies," Treb said gleefully, patting the two chests that each contained a globe.

"Us," said Neel. "Us to the skies."

The launch's hull scraped against the shore, and the passengers leaped into the shallow water. Dark, warm waves lapped against Petra's calves as she helped push and then drag the launch onto the beach.

"Of course, Neel. *Us*." Treb beckoned for another sailor to help him lift the trunks out of the bottom of the boat. They were heavy, for the globes were not made of merely wood and paper. Each globe had a large, glass sphere hidden at its center. "Our gift's going to let the Roma wander the world wide with a speed like we've never known, now that the globes can show us how to get through the Loopholes," he said, referring to hidden gaps in space that allowed someone to travel instantaneously between two places, even if they were thousands of miles apart. "The globes will go to the queen, but whatever she decides to do with them won't be worth more than a fish bone, since the Maraki will soon inherit the throne, and then the game changes."

Petra glanced at Tomik. He didn't care about Roma politics or the globes, she could tell. His smile was like a lit candle behind a screen that showed his thoughts clearly: he was thrilled to be here, for his own sake as well as Petra's. In the Vatra he might be able to study his magical ability to manipulate glass, an opportunity he would never have in Bohemia. Their country boasted a marvelous university for the practice of magical arts, but only students from high society were admitted to the Academy.

The crew plodded up the beach, some carrying the two chests, and others holding Tomik's colored lanterns high so that they could see the path that led to the foot of the cliffs, and the winding stairs that would lead them through the stone city and up to the palace.

After what felt like an eternity of steep steps, sweat oozed down Petra's back and her feet ached. She was grateful when the rough stone stairs became smooth marble trimmed with coral tiles. She heard the sailors behind her lowering the two chests to the ground, and looked up to see the pillars of the Romany palace.

Someone was waiting for them: a man who stood like a thirsty flower, his body slender and his shoulders slightly stooped. He was framed by the palace entryway, which had no doors. Torches blazed inside the hall, transforming the entrance into a rectangle of red-gold light.

"I am Arun," the man said. "Queen Iona's chief advisor. You

must be the *Pacolet*'s sailors." His gaze flicked over them, pausing at Neel and then resting uncertainly on Petra and Tomik. "The Vatra has heard that two *gadje* sail with you. Bohemian, are they not? Prisoners, passengers, or crew?"

"Well, Tom's a bit of the first and last," said Treb. "For a while, we planned on selling him in Morocco, but then he became too valuable to part with. As for Petra..." he studied her. "She's a passenger," he concluded, but Petra had seen his features soften for a second, and suspected that he didn't want to hurt her by telling the truth: she was a refugee.

Arun pointed to Astrophil, who clung to Petra's shoulder. "And what, precisely, is that?"

"I am a spider," Astrophil gravely replied.

Arun lifted one brow. "If you say so." He turned again to Treb. "You are the *Pacolet*'s captain, I assume?"

"Well spotted," said Treb. "Guess you couldn't miss my air of authority. I'm a natural leader, like my brother. You know him, I'm sure: Tarn of the Maraki, heir to the Roma crown."

An emotion flashed across Arun's face, too quick for Petra to identify. "Tarn happens to be here in the Vatra, and—" Arun spoke over Treb's noise of delighted surprise—"we are also well aware of the gifts you bring for your people."

"That's right," Treb said proudly. "I suppose the queen would like to feast her eyes on the Mercator Globes."

"All in good time. She has more important matters to attend to first. There is someone among you she needs to see right away. A youth. Perhaps you've left him on the ship, or down by the shore, but I think he's here with you now."

"Him? What? Who?" Treb spluttered. "What could be more important than the Mercator Globes?"

"Indraneel of the Lovari," Arun said.